iGeneration

E. SANDOVAL

PUBLISHED BY:
E. Sandoval

* * * * *

CONTENTS

The Second Coming of Christ

"Culture has gone into an economic and political phase where nothing is sacred, and consequently society is disintegrating. The ancient childish view of the universe we're stuck with is useless today. It's up to poets and artists to show eternity shining through the forms of the world we live in."

— Chloe Pentangeli, Selected Talks on The First Cycle

Mind numbing...

That's what it was to Jaster. He was a complete scatterbrain, practically drowned by the new flood of data — numb-shocked by the endless repetition of images he was supposed to look over, day after day after day, and he rarely followed any of the rules he himself created. Every night he wrestled the sheets in a cold sweat, dreaming of abandonment on a wide oil-stained white sand beach, alone for hundreds of miles, a threatening black forest looming behind ill-omened Native American totem poles, the dark trees moving like trance dancing demons in the ocean breeze.

Every morning he jolted awake with his alarm and a shot of fear-adrenaline, pulling his hair exasperated as a dark cloud of depression descended on the glimmer of dawn with the thought of work, picturing the merciless gleaming double glass doors at the entrance of the office in gray morning, the fake smile over browning teeth on the fifty-something hag receptionist with a limp mousy bad perm, blood-red lipstick drawn shakily on a cream cheese face, and his beige cluttered cubicle.

The Second Coming of Christ

He kept his MySpace page up all day, right next to his work, and his Yahoo Mail too, and emailed, instant messaged, texted, and chatted with his friends all day long while he honestly tried his best to do his job, and failed. Not everyone can easily swallow the new deluge of knowledge and stay effective. The "knowluge". He was on Concerta, a time-release anti-ADD medication he'd been on all his adult life, but it didn't seem to help.

Chloe's team looked at over 20,000 aerial photographs a week taken from a company airplane that flew the coast daily with a high-definition rapid-exposure digital camera, and using graphics software, they delineated the area of coastline affected by the oil spill. Chloe's visual acumen was off the scale. It was ideal for theoretical physics where she could visualize problems like Einstein did, and it came in handy for analyzing aerial photographs too.

The shoreline was divided into segments by a team that uploaded the data onto the server, and for every segment Jaster delineated the area supposed to represent the part affected by the oil spill, defined by several rules which he made up, that everyone else was supposed to follow, later delineating the same area in every subsequent identical photo.

The plane flew over the same stretch of coastline repeatedly in order to show the effect of the oil spill over time. It was glacial to Jaster. Clicking through photo after photo of the same stretch over and over again and again made his blood fizz like seltzer water, making his big head feel like it was going to pop. He didn't have the patience, or the resolve, or the discipline, or the strength to simply sit with it, and he never wanted this job in the first place. He had no idea what he really wanted. And it all became like noise, like nails scraping a chalkboard, like a disgruntled DJ trying to find "Robot Girl" (more in a minute), like a hundred dirty homeless people screaming simultaneously, rushing at him, the dissonance of their yells creating a warbling stinky wall of sound. "Jaster the Disaster" Chloe called him — in her mind.

A bunch of segments hadn't been considered at first and now needed to be delineated, but Jaster couldn't muster the wherewithal to do it, so he pushed it off on Justin who quickly assigned it to Chloe. Jaster's dad, an ex-hippie, was a Senior Partner in the environmental consulting firm, and he gave Jaster the job of "Associate Director" straight out of college with his bachelor's degree. Nothing like nepotism. There were PhDs working under Jaster.

His dad was a helicopter parent, always hovering over him (who in the world would name their son Jaster?), never letting him face a risk on his own, guiding him through what he thought was "the right school curriculum", coddling him, hiring tutors, yelling at his counselors and academic advisors, getting him summer internships, calling him three times a day to make sure everything was okay. He'd tried the children's drugs — Ritalin, Adderall and Vyvanse, molecularly the same as cocaine, amphetamine and dexamphetamine. 350 million kids worldwide are medicated with these "legal" drugs for ADD and ADHD (which aren't even really diseases), all becoming future illegal drug abusers.

He'd tried hypnosis, which didn't work at all. And now, as a last resort, his dad actually hired a private meditation instructor and a private yoga teacher, because Jaster could never consistently show up to classes. The next thing the parents of iGeneration are going to try to buy wholesale for their ugly duckling children is the focus and clarity of eastern spirituality, praying they'll finally turn into swans. But even that didn't seem to be doing Jaster much good. His dad lectured him to behave more like the boss, be more authoritative, which meant he had to actually socialize with the employees, and he became increasingly forthcoming with Chloe whenever he ran into her at "the water cooler".

...I don't want to grow up. He said. Corrupt corporations — "the new sovereigns" — are running everything and destroying the environment. Wall Street is raping us. The Market Makers control it. Even if the world has a complete economic melt down they'll never lose money. The President helps his wealthy friends get wealthier by cutting their taxes and bailing them out whenever they blow billions on the stock market while he ignores the needs of average people for education, jobs, pensions. Elections are rigged. The government taps our phones. They torture foreign prisoners. Yeah, the media looks free, but it's secretly controlled by one person and his family in cahoots with the government, and politicians use it to scare people into supporting policies against our better interests. The biggest trick the government ever pulled on the American people is convincing us to be more concerned with the plight of the rich than our own well-being. It's like the idea of Heaven: poor people want to believe there's always hope for them to be rich even though no more than 1% of America has ever been wealthy. There's a world banking conspiracy to keep us enslaved to debt. The

Government creates recessions to make young people sign up for the military to fight and die for the interests of the top 1% and they lie about why we go to war. Have we ever found any WMDs except in our own arsenal? They fill our prisons with one racial group and nobody says or does anything. And most people think this is the greatest nation on earth. Meanwhile, there are at least twenty countries with better standards of living, better healthcare, better education, better environmental policies, real free press, real human rights. Hippies tried to change everything but I don't feel like they failed — I feel like they betrayed us! They quit trying! Everybody's parents are divorced, religion is bankrupt, almost every college graduate owes hundreds of thousands. By the time my sister graduates from med school, she'll owe nearly half a million dollars. My dad only paid a thousand dollars a year to get his degree. How could the cost of education increase over a hundred times in less than three decades? $400 cups of coffee? And back then there were even Free U's! We grow up watching porn; girls have seen hardcore sex before they even kiss a boy; at your high school did guys used to sit around the edge of their parents' bed at parties while all the girls took ecstasy, knelt in front of them and, you know? Now everyone's bipolar, or ADD, or obese, or has got STDs, or doesn't give a shit. ...All I really want is to do something good for the world so at least I can feel good about myself... Jaster said. That, or party... Why not party? Nothing's really going to change. There's no future. Might as well party. Fuck it.

iGeneration... It's no mystery "random" is the most commonly used word in the English language today. The "inumbdation" of new information has reached such a frenzy that without some kind of grounding practice, like sitting on a cushion in zazen, we lose all sense of continuity. The slogan for one music video station is "Silence Sucks". People go to one website with a link to another; click on a link to a third, and another, and before long they don't remember where they started. Relationships aren't seen as real. Say whatever makes it last regardless how you really feel as long as you get what you want — that, or end it. The templates for people trying to connect are "The Bachelor" and "The Bachelorette". You can send them home whenever. They're disposable, like everything else. There's no such thing as closure. Jaster fell in love with some girl online he'd never even met, and when she didn't want to chat anymore "her sister" emailed she was dead. Who knows if it's true? Catphishing. People feel like it's "kewl" to just click off. And it all creates a compulsion to constantly move on faster and faster and faster.

So many hipster intellectuals like to argue that life really is random. It's become cliché for some DJs to play "random" tracks — The Sex Pistols, Beethoven, African drumming, Infected Mushroom, Duke Ellington, The Neon Trees, K.C. and The Sunshine Band, Ravi Shankar — without any rhythm or flow, seemingly to prove the point with flippant relativism that "it's all the same"… while everybody vacates the dance floor. They're trying to show life isn't the robotic logical progression they've been taught in school, but their expression is more like dead static in comparison, and almost anyone can hear the pleading whine in their voices if you listen. It's a cry for help, and even they don't believe what they're saying or doing is true. They would probably ask, What *is* real or true?

But it's *because* there is no continuity that there *is* continuity... Chloe first explained it to me. Every sound starts from silence and ends there. Pretty simple. Discontinuity. But silence itself and the particularities of that sound produce another. And — to put it in DJ terms — it's possible to find an echo of one track of a particular mode and time in a track of a different style and era. Not every moment of life is a random train wreck.

And yet, understanding that Time is a fiction and we're like flames that blaze from the same fire, arisen from nothing, consuming the material world forever in the present, to dissolve inevitably back into the primordial expanse, is what connects beings of higher intelligence beyond beliefs.

Nevertheless, those hipsters all still wake up as more or less the same person from one day to the next — because it's not random — with more or less the same depression they still have to deal with, day after day, and swallow more or less of their pills. It could change, but 30 billion dollars were spent on antidepressants in the US alone last year, more than any other country on the planet. Why is everybody so depressed and confused in the nation envied by every other on earth? Maybe there's a connection between all the greed and self-interest and the freefall in mental and physical health? It's baffling how everyone else still thinks this is the land of opportunity, even the Chinese. And now scientists are discovering anti-depressants cause birth defects. Congratulations.

Jaster even told Chloe the first time in his life he ever felt completely happy was the first time he took Molly, and for a while it became a religion for him, doing it every time he went out, making out with random girls at parties. He never had sex with them because he couldn't get it up when he was high, and usually ended the night playing a video game while she slept in bed next to him. Even so, he finally realized he was depending on it and quit. But then he was only unhappy again. Eighty percent of all the opiates produced in the world are consumed in the United States. What are we trying so hard to numb ourselves from?

The thing is, Jaster could screw up endlessly and never get fired, and by now he simply expected everyone in the office to take care of him, like all the bloated corporations and arrogant Wall Street firms he whined about, with bonuses of over $20 million a year for new hires (Seriously!), that expect to get bailed out by the government and ultimately us unfortunate taxpayers if they fail. Chloe understood he was overwhelmed and felt sorry for him one morning as he filled his mug at the coffee maker and she made a cup of tea, and noticed he wasn't wearing one shoe. His foot was wrapped in white gauze slightly bloodstained, and dirty because he'd been walking around in it. It looked like there was a sixth toe growing on his foot. Was he mutating?

She asked him, Jaster, are you okay? She really wanted to know. He looked like a disaster — hair messed up, pasty unshaven face, untucked shirt buttoned up the wrong way, dirty pants unzipped.

He responded creakily, It's really great to have a bump and a piece of chocolate for breakfast... And stared at her indignantly, as if he expected her to whip him up an omelet on the spot...

Wow. She thought. There are at least ten restaurants within walking distance where he could buy breakfast.

Can I do something for you? She asked.

He suddenly looked like he was about to cry, I don't know, Chloe… I don't know what's real or fake anymore. I mean, all through school they told us "don't trust your instincts", "be rational", "think what you'll gain"… They always gave that example of the kid and the psychologist in a room with a camera where he offered her a cookie and said, You can have this one now, but if you wait till I come back I'll give you another one, then you'll have two cookies. They told us the kid who ate the one cookie was the bad kid, and the one who waited till he got a second cookie was the good kid… But I was always the bad kid, and I don't know anybody who was the good kid. Everybody I know spends their money as fast as they make it, and the media keeps saying how our generation is so sought after by employers but almost all my friends can barely hold a job; I'd be homeless if it weren't for my dad. It's all a lie.

She chose her words carefully…

…How you feel isn't a lie. She replied. How you feel is real. Trust that. Your experience is truer than anything anybody tells you to believe. Trust your gut. We're all more intelligent than "the powers that be" want us to think. Be intuitive. But other people can help you if you ask. Change starts with three words: I need help.

I don't know what to ask for help with.

…You've got to figure that out first. She said finally, and walked from the kitchen on the second floor back to her desk.

She had to go outside, through the glass front doors down a flight of concrete stairs to the ground floor to get to the cavernous room where everybody working on the oil spill sat at row after row of computers with double flat screens on their desks.

She found it ironic that in an environmental consulting firm run by ex-hippies, the culture was more cutthroat than in any of the more conventional corporate situations she'd been in, as if they were trying to be "more backstabbing than backstabbing" to break any notion of a stereotype. Turnover was high, people getting fired and hired all the time, executives complaining constantly about all the bullshit they had to endure to work there — occasionally she heard the faint sounds of them screaming at each other upstairs. Yet despite all the defiantly dead-eyed posturing of the upper echelons, it was still a fun place to work for Chloe.

Chloe wasn't looking for a dream job. That's one of those interview questions you're supposed to answer cleverly: "What would your ideal work situation be?" When the interviewer first asked Chloe she paused briefly because it sounded like a strange question to even put. She remembered meeting a girl on her last trip out to California, a software engineer who purred in sugary lilting tones that the people she worked with were all into the same things she was, and they all went cycling every weekend, and that she was really hired by the flush dot-com just because they liked her — she literally had nothing to do but show up and hang out everyday.

Chloe told the interviewer, I really don't think that way. Everything's impermanent. The work you get today could be gone by tomorrow. I do my best in whatever situation.

She didn't know if that's why they didn't give her the job, but she went to a temp agency a few days later and they placed her at Nimbus right away. Her dream job just fell in her lap. Chloe was confident that whatever she needed would always come to her as long as she was true.

It didn't start out as her dream job though. At first they had her doing data entry, entering handwritten survey results into a database. Nimbus had hundreds of people on the sands of Alaska interviewing beachgoers, asking if they were affected by the oil spill. Imagine how wildly inconsistent those results were. But because she wasn't jacked on caffeine and nervous, trying to prove something all the time, because she simply looked at what was in front of her and did her job, she could see mistakes nobody else saw. She wasn't the fastest, but she was the best, and after a few weeks she was promoted to analyzing aerial photographs.

All the same, one day without warning her dream job suddenly turned into a living nightmare. She couldn't believe he was actually doing it. Or, she didn't want to. She found out he'd spent every day since he was hired destroying everything she'd created over the seven previous months — all on principle. Chloe wasn't naïve, but she'd never met anyone that vindictive.

Get out of there, right now! I told her.

People who live on principle first destroy themselves, becoming inflexible, then try to destroy everybody around them because deep down they're miserable and they want to make everyone else feel miserable too, to prove they're right, to justify their choice for misery, to validate their principle. But she didn't want to leave.

Nate quickly worked his way up as the darling of the growing team that analyzed aerial photographs and immediately started to undermine Chloe. Initially he just stared at her — first because she's so beautiful, but also in stunned amazement —

shocked at how accurately she did her job. Despite he could never dream of doing it so well himself, he couldn't even bring himself to compliment her. He was socially retarded, like so many Americans who grow up cut off from civil contact and treat other people like blips on a screen.

Still, she enjoyed her work. If there was one niche in the world she felt she could carve out as her own at the time without going back to school for her PhD, that was it — analyzing aerial photographs. Nobody else could even compare. And then Nate ruined everything.

As soon as he recognized her skill he set out to destroy her. Where in the world do people learn things like that? From their psychotic parents? It's not human nature. At least it wasn't for Chloe. We don't all try to annihilate whoever we find the most beautiful, or the most excellent.

The first thing he did only two weeks after being hired was ask to be promoted. Sounds harmless enough. Nate's dad, a Vietnam vet, told him to do it, and despite the quality of his work was worse than everyone else's on the team, Jaster and Justin (the "Data Manager" directly beneath Jaster), like knee-jerk dead robots, were "impressed" by Nate's "ambition".

Jaster was a "creaky talker". He said everything in a dry creaky voice as if he'd just woken up, or were deliberately sub-vocalizing to be unassuming, or to speak in confidence... or maybe he was just in love with the creaky sound of his own voice. Whatever the case, Justin started speaking like that too, and soon Nate followed, all creakily communicating like three reptilians that because Jaster was soon to take a two-week vacation to Zimbabwe — and because Justin secretly didn't want to take over

Jaster's work load — he would "award" it to Nate, since he'd asked for a promotion. Nate creakily accepted. Of course it would mean more responsibility, but he'd get paid more and he'd be in absolute control of the data for as long as Jaster was gone. Done.

Chloe was aware of Nate's maneuvering and had a nagging feeling in the back of her mind like an index finger scratching that she should do something about it, but she hesitated. Although she was the best in the office, the thought never crossed her mind to position herself above everyone else only for the sake of it. That's what birds do — try to find the highest spot simply because they can. They descended from reptiles. Nate looked like a gecko.

Chloe only wanted to do her job well because for the first time in her life she could walk to work; it was ten blocks from her apartment, and it was a job she liked, right off Harvard Square. The pay wasn't that good but she thought most people at Nimbus were pretty cool, and the project was for a good cause — they were analyzing data from the Mobil oil spill near Juneau, Alaska, in order to provide evidence to the NOAA for a lawsuit against Mobil Oil to repair the damages and repay local merchants for their loss of revenue. Good karma.

Nate lived closer to the office than Chloe, but he drove to work every day, on principle — or rather, rode — regardless how much energy it wasted or pollution it created. To him, driving was about social status, and even if it was on the dorky one-cylinder motorcycle his dad bought him, he thought it was satisfying. Everyday, after cruising by the Proactiv anti-acne vending machine, he slouched at a black metal patio table for lunch, ten feet from the black metal racks where he parked his

bike — the smallest version of a café racer for
adults on the market, which looked ridiculous. But
he sat there no matter the weather, gazing proudly at
his little yellow one-popper, with one exhaust pipe
coming from the one cylinder, poking awkwardly
back out over a slick tire, and he actually mocked
Chloe for walking to the office, saying nonchalantly, I hear you *walk* to work...

He was a Sketcher — all of life was a sloppy
sketch to him. "Done" is better than "Done Well".
Because well done takes too long. He absolutely
refused to do anything thoroughly or completely or
accurately because that meant you're "anal" or
"uptight". In restaurants he'd point to the menu and
whatever was under his finger he'd order, because
"it doesn't matter". When he bought a new couch,
the salesman tried to show him the quality of the
construction but he wasn't interested. It looked
good. He'd end up throwing it away regardless. And
in fact it was a piece of junk — sloppily stapled
together pieces of particle board, foam, and
polyester. He preferred "distressed" leather jackets,
"acid-washed" jeans, "pre-broken-in" shoes, no
matter if they would all fall apart in months — a
world of trash; disposable. Friends, even family —
all throwaways.

Obviously he didn't particularly care about
anyone he worked with. They were all only stepping stones to the ultimate goal — his personal
aggrandizement. At first blush, though, one might
misconstrue him for someone who saw the
underlying impermanence of things, and chose not
to cling to material existence. He loved it when they
thought that about him. But strangely, he didn't see
himself as disposable.

The project didn't particularly matter to him either. An environmental disaster only meant he'd get paid, so actually, the more the merrier. Let's see more oil spills, acid rain, and toxic leaks — the perfect line of work for someone who studied Environmental Conservation. You could always count on people polluting, so why not get into the business of cleaning up the environment? Reverse Intelligence. Like a Swedish arms dealer. Meanwhile millions get killed. Chloe teased him when he first arrived, calling his major "Environmental Conversation" because of his total lack of conviction, which sent him into a silent rage with glaring glassy gray eyes and a plastered smile on his zit-pocked face with gritted teeth, and chest puffed out. Maybe that was what turned him against her. But he was "livin' the dream" as far as he was concerned.

The bike was like kinky sex to all the geek boys at Nimbus who hadn't touched a girl in years. Like first timers at a strip club, or amateurs in a drama workshop, one by one, they each came over to Nate's desk and gushed over his new Kawasaki, told him about the one guy they each knew who owned a bike too, and how much they wanted one; how cool they thought it was to ride, etc... Nate basked in the heat of their brownnosing, leaning back in his chair with a casual smile on his stubbly, grayish face, with a proud glint under droopy half-stoned eyelids, and greasy limp hair almost to his shoulders like a lizard Shaggy in Scooby Doo. Chloe sat right next to him in the big office so she had to endure the parade of adoring nerds everyday.

Maybe she would have retaliated against his underhanded attacks if it weren't so hard for her to simply fathom the fact that an unshaven, mouth-breathing, stoner snowboarder, who wore plaid shirts, dirty jeans hanging halfway down his butt, torn up Air Jordan's, and a polyester "Volcom" trucker's cap — cocked sideways! — was getting the best of her. Volcom is for morons, she thought. He and his friends even made up a name for snow-boarding: "Shibbling". How disgusting.

"Dude, you shibblin' Saturday? You were so shibblin' last weekend, dude!" It made her skin crawl. Maybe she was a bit proud. After all, it never escaped her she was intellectually superior to most people — speaking five languages, having a Master's Degree in Theoretical Physics she paid for herself.

Nate was actually scared of her. He twitched nervously having to sit next to her every morning, and clutched his stomach, cold in the pit, and routinely evacuated his bowels practically on the hour. Hundreds of times a day he jerked his head around to abruptly glance at Chloe, expecting to catch her staring at him. Chloe only noticed because she has panoramic awareness — and she was well accustomed to guys being afraid of her. She's mixed race — African-American and Hispanic, with some Native American on both sides, adopted by an Italian stepfather (which is where she got her last name) — and looks like a dark Bo Derek in the movie "10" with hazel eyes, the corn-rows and everything. Plus, an IQ over 140 meant most guys left skid marks as soon as she said a single word.

Since his first promotion Nate only spoke to Chloe when Justin told him to ask her to do some-thing, and even then stuttered through every sentence, barely able to finish the request. Recently, she'd been ignoring his assignments though, because he'd ask her but then quickly tell her he'd do it himself, or assign it to his friend Shawn, either of whom would screw it up royally. That was the main reason Nate had a problem with Chloe: her work was better than his and he knew it — and so did everyone else. The Associate Directors at Nimbus already coined a phrase. When somebody got proven wrong after asserting they were right, they said you got "Chloe-ed". And everybody in the office came to Chloe when they had an issue.

Nevertheless, Justin and Jaster didn't seem to care her work was the highest quality, until one day. She first understood she was in trouble when she got promoted to "Data Quality Control". As soon as he heard, Nate ran to Justin's office — like a holdout toddler to the toilet — and insisted if Chloe got promoted then he had to be promoted too — only three months after his first promotion — to be "Lead Quality Control": her superior. Justin was completely spineless so he agreed, but then he asked Chloe to do an assignment he didn't think anyone else could do. He kissed up to her, saying Nate was "ninja" but he needed "Jedi", and the name that kept coming up in the office as the right person for the job was Chloe.

Justin looked like a pink-eyed white lab rat with pop bottle John Lennon glasses he constantly pushed up on the bridge of his long greasy pointed nose. He was skinny, and hunched over, and wore "cool" drab thrift store clothes meant to scream "retro", and listened to Death Metal all day long in his glassed-in office. He had a Master's in Social Work, and despite his lack of any natural skill with people, he was hired as manager of the team simply because of his advanced degree. It could have been a Master's in Underwater Basketweaving.

But what really set her apart was her sense of humor. She knew because of her darker skin everybody already half-expected her to be funny — when she told a joke they were usually laughing long before the punch line — and she had them doubled over in pain cackling their heads off when she made up a satirical news story and sent it around. All except for Nate who thought she was mocking him.

"Massive Oil Spill Results In Heretofore Unseen Wildlife 'Viscosity'". A Mobil supertanker ran aground Monday near Juneau, Alaska, spilling more than 6 million gallons of crude oil, greatly improving the viscosity of local marine life. The spill, the world's largest since the Exxon Valdez, coated over 600,000 birds, fish, and seals in quality, medium-weight lubricant that will provide them with valuable protection and will keep important animal parts running efficiently for months.

Local wildlife officials were excited about the spill. "A thick coat of oil should help these animals tremendously, especially with the cold coming." Said Ginny Fordman, Secretary of Alaska's Department of Fish and Wildlife. "Last winter, over 3,000 sea otters suffered severe thermal breakdown from the weather. When temperatures get to 58 below, sea otters actually need a quality oil like Mobil to keep their fangs and claws and other parts moving smooth."

Particularly enjoying the Mobil spill was the local flounder population who, excited by the oil cascading to the seafloor with dispersant, flocked to local beaches to play. Several thousand were spotted enthusiastically flopping about among thousands of tar balls, gasping for air from all their playful exertion. Many of the fish were so tired from frolicking they stopped moving altogether.

Mobil public-relations director Rob Stanfield weighed in on the serendipitous petroleum release, rubbing his belly. "For years our products have provided A-1 protection for millions of car owners. Now we've shown the world we can offer that same protection to Alaska's birds, fish, and other wildlife."

Chloe delineated the new segments, but now that Jaster was on vacation Nate doubled his efforts to sabotage her. He literally worked overtime, coming in an hour early and staying two hours late everyday in order to wreck all the work she did, not just on the new assignment but on everything so far for over seven months, changing it all from the precise delineations she made into his sloppy sketches without all the "unnecessary details". And spineless Justin approved all his extra hours. She looked over at him, and she could almost hear his tiny reptilian brain teeming as he relentlessly messed up her work in the database, What century does she think she's in? What is she, Japanese? What a bitch!

The atmosphere in the office changed from a calm quiet focus to a boisterous frat house exuberance because Nate was approving sloppier and sloppier segments. Nate was the hero now and everybody paid him court, greeting him in the morning, slapping him on the back, buying him lattes, laughing and cracking jokes, streaming on their computers while they "worked" — cartoons, music videos, sitcoms, MMA, movies — kicking up their dirty feet on their desks like he did on breaks; everybody actually started dressing like him, in plaid shirts, filthy jeans and trucker caps — even girls. Justin dubbed it "Team Nate". ..."StagNate", Chloe called him in her mind.

Shawn came over to Nate's desk one day and they started a harangue about Africa, pretending Chloe wasn't sitting right next to them.

Dude, did you hear about that new invasive weed, the African mustard? They say it'll infest 90% of the crops in the south within a year. Shawn said.

Those Africanized honey bees are spreading up the coast too; they're going to be here by next summer. Nate chimed in.

They're not like normal bees.

Hell, no! They'll attack you and kill you.

By 2050 half the world's population is going to be in Africa. And they're going to turn on us, dude, because of all the shit we've done to them. Shawn asserted.

And the Chinese are making deals with them. Nate added. It's going to be China and Africa against Europe and America.

When you buy a house you're going to need a private army to protect it.

That's what's good about America — the police and the military are the private army for white people. See this?

Nate showed Shawn a photo Jaster sent from safari in Zimbabwe.

That massive dent on the front of the Land Rover was made by an African elephant's junk, dude! Nate whimpered.

Chloe wasn't going to dignify any of their tittle-tattle with the slightest reaction.

She asked herself the age-old question: "Do you want to be right, or do you want to be happy?" The tables have turned. She thought. I'm sure that question was originally asked by people like StagNate to relate to others who weren't sloppy Sketchers.

And it made her question if she wasn't the one being inflexible.

Maybe I should be more open-minded...

Now the focus wasn't on accuracy, but on speed, speed, speed, and more and more speed, and Justin sat hunched over his computer screen every night after everyone left, "getting high" (in Justin's own words) on whoever "cranked out" the most segments that day, however sloppily. Chloe's new name for him was "Juspin" — it was a take on the slang "spun" for a crystal meth high, and it mirrored Jaster's name. She finally accepted the reality, found a job that paid almost twice as much, and quit.

On her last day, she faced Nate at his desk, and said, You don't have to try to build mistakes into experience, mistakes will happen naturally; sloppiness may make you feel less threatened, but precision doesn't have to be such a big hassle all the time. I'm moving on to better things and I honestly wish the best for you.

He grinned in nervous shame and said, Okay? And glanced around at everybody as if to ask, Come on, you thought that was weird too, right?

Nobody thought it was weird. Chloe left. When Nimbus delivered their research results to the NOAA, and when they brought it to court, the Attorney General ruled the evidence incomprehensible, and they had to start all over again, spending another five million dollars to get it done properly. Nate got fired, of course, and shortly afterward he face-planted on his little one-popper, teeth spread post-modern artfully on the curb, and bled to death in the gutter — not paying attention and not wearing a helmet. Justin got fired too, and ended up doing actual social work, counseling recovering drug addicts while becoming addicted to crystal meth himself, chopping the gritty white powder nightly with an expired credit card, shoveling it into his nostril with a sharp inhale, and slipping into tweaky wired oblivion. Last Chloe heard, Jaster was living in his dad's basement on Brattle Street, playing around on Ameritrade and with his X-Box. But at least he finally came out of the closet and admitted he was queer. Chloe was shortly after discovered as the Second Coming of Christ.

2

Ghosting

"Anything that's going to be created involves shattering what was there before. You need to be dismembered metaphorically in order to lose your fixation on this little instance -- uncontrolled by reason, only the wild dynamic of Nature. The energy that shatters in order to bring forth is death to purely material animal existence, and the birth of the sacred world."

— Chloe Pentangeli, Trance Dancer

It was the fin de siècle, 1999. A century was dying and another was being born. The French found it romantic last century's end. Now everyone was just afraid. I know so many people who stockpiled food and water, even weapons, as if Armageddon were upon us. Intelligent people. Exactly what the nihilistic powers wanted them to think. And the whole Y2K Scare of "worldwide computer meltdown" turned out to be a colossal dud.

I was on Christmas break from teaching. Why not get out of Colorado? I had a plane ticket to New York City and was packing my bags, feeling delicious butterflies — the distinctive rush at the prospect of travel. I'd get to see Chloe, and Max, and hopefully some of our other college friends too.

Venetian blinds drawn shut over the bright winter day laid the bedroom gray, and behind the blinds, the bouncing buzz of a fly bumping up against the burning glass of the south-facing window banged out a binary staccato message from beyond. I opened the screen a crack so it could get out before I locked the front door behind me, and ghosted — down the long dark hallway past the mailboxes, toward the brilliant sunshine of the windows by the building entrance beckoning me away from the dim exit light farther on down the hall...

I pulled my black rolling check-in along the quiet rural Fort Lupton street through the dry dreamy Colorado winter heat past cookie-cutter pastel-colored 1970's prefab houses, parked cars, newly planted saplings lining the curb, and the pervasive stench of cow shit wafting from nearby stockyards. The airport shuttle stop was only a few blocks away at The Branding Iron — a greasy spoon relic from the 1950's under an electric plastic sign on two tall metal poles with the name in red on a yellow background, easily visible from the highway from either direction, even at night, right on the main east-west, at the only exit ramp in town. The low boxy ranch-style brick structure had a flat roof, plate glass windows wrapped around three sides, and a parking lot filled with giant, jacked-up, gas guzzling, American 4-door 4-wheel drives. Waitresses wore tight pink uniforms with hard plastic nametags pinned to them, and served coffee in inch-thick white porcelain cups that hadn't broken probably since the place opened; and the clientele sported more than a few felt Stetson's, long sleeve western-cut shirts, huge shiny oval-shaped rodeo belt buckles, skin-tight Wrangler jeans and cowboy boots.

Truck stop meets grandma's homemade farm décor. Good old fashioned comfort food, if the prospect of cardiac arrest wasn't too discomforting: $5 steak and eggs every day. The cow was probably local, shot and butchered less than a mile away, served up in Grade A inch-thick cuts — although

the biggest rancher around had his cattle flown in
on jets from Argentina after grazing on the grasses
of Punta de la Agua. Imagine that. Some look
forward, others look back, a few do both; hardly
anybody does neither.

For December it was absolutely balmy; I
waited outside by the front door and the aroma of
fresh brewed coffee wafted by every time a person
left or entered. The shuttle pulled right up to me,
and I settled in behind the five other passengers, put
on my head-phones and some Trance, relieved to
say goodbye to Fort Lupton. I felt lighter already,
like the van was pumped full of pure oxygen.

* * * * *

Max's New Years Eve party would make every
other seem like the lame stilted Catholic Youth
Groups we used to go to when we were in junior
high. Except while I was waxing philosophical
about whether God existed or not — and wondering
what these boring get-togethers where everybody
was desperately pretending they weren't really just
horny little tweens had to do with it — he was
usually off in some dark unused linoleum-floored
storeroom making out with a girl in the musty cool
church basement, skirt hiked up and zipper undone,
warm hands on coldish naked flesh, getting hot with
heavy breath. He always told me about it on the
way home.

A few days earlier I bumped into a hardcore
raver in the checkout at Safeway, the only grocery
store within a 10-mile radius — a high school kid
with a fake ID; spiked hair dyed black, piercings in
his face, and tats, wearing a sleeveless black t-shirt
and huge black baggy pants — loading up on 3.2%

beer, hand sanitizer, and cough syrup. I know
nobody calls them raves anymore. That word was
so demonized by the media in the 90's people
stopped using it, despite the same kind of parties
have been going on successively since they started
in the 1980's, but there's no simpler way to indicate
"electronic dance music parties and the subculture
that's part of them" than the word rave.

He said a bunch of his friends were going to
commit suicide en masse as the clock struck twelve
on New Years. …I don't know what I'd do if I were
stuck in high school out here in the middle of
nowhere, close enough to wish you were in Denver,
far enough it's a pain to drive. …Chloe told me
once, Everyone's life is a process of repeatedly
flirting with death, and retreating — we have no
right to deprive them of that.

The shuttle dropped me off at the United
terminal under the shade of the weird white circus
tent roof of Denver International and immediately I
was hit by that eerie "weightless" feeling of airports
because so many people are in-between. Rolling my
check-in over the glossy gray-brown marble floors
imported from Italy, I checked my bag, got a boarding pass and drifted with all the other displaced
travelers to the gate, settled into a seat on one of the
thin black leather airport couches perpendicular to
the floor-to-ceiling windows and watched the planes
take off and land.

And then she appeared, as if to highlight the
fact I hadn't had a girlfriend in two years. I'd never
seen her before but she smiled like she knew me a
hundred feet away, big blue eyes sparkling, long
blond hair matted and dirty with a lot of hairpins in
it; walking with crutches and a black Velcro
cast/boot on her right ankle, most likely a snow-

boarding accident on winter break from college. It may have been dry on the plains but they had snow-making machines up on the slopes. She headed directly toward me, sat right across from me, looked me in the eye, smiled again, and propped both her feet up on the seat.

Of course it's obvious what that does — she was practically spread eagle. She had a pretty face, her cobalt blue sweater was wrinkled like she'd slept in it, and her black wool tights had dingle-berries all over them, as if they'd never been dry cleaned, and the weave was loose so her skin was visible underneath through the veil, and she was clearly not wearing underwear. She kept glancing at me and smiling as she incessantly talked on her cell phone.

I have nothing against flirting for the fun of it, but I'm not seduced by every fresh blossom that blows along either. Within a minute of seeing her I felt no chemistry, though. Some people argue I can't possibly make a definitive character assessment after only a minute, but I haven't been wrong in ages, and whenever I do engage someone contrary to my first impression I usually end up regretting it. Unlike Max or Chloe my rule of thumb is I won't get sexually involved with someone unless I feel like I could give my heart to them completely, otherwise I might as well be with a prostitute. Yet, even though I didn't feel any connection with the injured snow bunny, this is how the Mind trips...

First I thought of moving to the empty seat next to her, asking where she was coming from, intro-ducing myself. Then she'd tell me her name, we'd have a couple of laughs, and when the plane boarded we'd sit next to each other. Once we were in the air at cruising altitude, I'd nonchalantly mention the Mile High Club. She'd tell me to follow her to the front lavatory — not to the rear one because that's where all the flight attendants hang out. Once we were alone at the front, she'd go in first and leave the door unlocked. After an accept-able interval, I'd go in too and lock the door behind me.

I snapped out of it and she was still sitting on the airport couch smiling across from me. Another plane takes off and lands... She boarded early among the people in wheelchairs and with infants, I passed her seat on my way to the back of the plane, she smiled once again, and that was that.

* * * * *

At Newark I rushed through the airport as the sun was setting, got my check-in, followed the signs to the connected AirTrain station, rode the raised tracks to the local NJ Transit stop, and as soon as I stepped out into the open air for the first time since arriving on the east coast, I was filled with a deep sense I wasn't home anymore — I could smell the dank salty ocean. I couldn't see it — the station was surrounded by junkyards and a tangle of freeways; there was a gravel parking lot filled with hundreds of brand new cars, protective white plastic stuck to parts of the exteriors, waiting for transport, next to a low dirty abandoned brick warehouse with gaping black broken window holes — but the shore wasn't far; I felt drunk from the scent.

It was unseasonably warm there too, in the low 60's, and darkness fell by the time the train pulled in. I rode it into Grand Central, gazed up at the hundred-foot-tall teal ceiling with the zodiac embla-zoned on it; took a second outside to appreciate the majestic façade blasted by flood-lights, the gleaming Chrysler building looming behind, and walked down 42nd Street to briefly let in the spectacle and glare of frenzied Times Square. Thousands roamed under towering flashing multi-colored billboards like daylight, advertisements splashed everywhere, even all over people, and the city roared, a dazzling pageant of opulence, while only a few blocks away down a side street homeless people slept on the sidewalk under the scaffolding of a building front being repaired — not the ragged habitually transient, but people who were relatively well dressed, who I could imagine holding jobs, all in a row, like a dotted line ready to be signed against the edifice on cardboard mats, but left blank, bodies half-covered with coats pulled over their heads, anonymous. Strange — a whole group of them, men and women, as if they'd communicated about where they'd all sleep. It could happen to anybody.

I caught a cab through heavy traffic in lower downtown past landmarks and storefronts, and transitioned from the packed concrete cattle chutes of Manhattan to the space and wide open vistas of the Williamsburg Bridge, suspended in air over shimmering black water between two banks. Weightless. Quiet. Alone in a city of millions.

* * * * *

Turning "ghost" into a verb is a visceral way to depict the transition from discontinuity to contin-uity: one thing ends completely, and the same thing continues, but it's not entirely the same, like an affinity of one for the other — which reminds me of a butterfly for some reason, a fluttering notion — an

affinity of the Present for the Past and the Future
(because we're only ever in the present); maybe
because of the two 'F's in the word affinity, like
wings — a visual thing — or evolution from an egg
to a caterpillar; from a chrysalis to a winged beast. I
remember Chloe's shape-poem, like a cocoon:

Flicker...
Hoping, Fearing
Provoking Past and Future
Did I do my best? Will it be enough to...
Overlook an abyss, cliff to my back, a foothold?

Imagine vertigo eyes of a color unseen,
Unbearable sadness of unheard siren songs,
Seductive golden blossoms of an alien scent.

Relish cool juice of plump fruit never tasted,
Or satisfying opulence of untouched curves.
Think a thought no one ever thought before.

In solitary cinema we reminisce and project
Reflections of every becoming moment.
Mysterious faces mirrored on
Circular watch crystal;
Spinning hands
Endlessly
Dance

* * * * *

When the cab dropped me off at his apartment
on the wide end of a triangular three-story building,
as soon as I opened the taxi door I heard the pounding beat of electronic music and a roar of voices in
excited conversations echoing down the street. The
party was powered up.

I got buzzed in by somebody and walked awkwardly pulling my check-in through the dark crowded apartment jammed with hundreds of his New York artsy friends, and all of their friends, all whooping and cracking up with gigantic rolling eyes, swilling from brown beer bottles snatched from the big tin ice tub in the kitchen. There was only dim lamp light in each room, and I couldn't find anyplace to put my bags, so I finally stashed them behind the couch in the living room and pushed back into the party.

The apartment twisted at odd angles from a lounge, dining room and kitchen on the ground floor, up to a bedroom, a bathroom, and another living room on the second; to a painting studio, a photography studio, and Max's bedroom on the third floor, and ended in a stairway that gave access to the roof of the entire building. His roommate Toby was a photographer at the Village Voice, and his pictures of Manhattan street scenes were phenomenal, hanging on the walls all the way up. His parents supported him for years while he interned and volunteered, waiting for a paid position. He was out of town but didn't want anybody staying in his room so I'd be sleeping somewhere else.

Stumbling up the narrow wooden stairwell packed with people in jean jackets and t-shirts with "cool" sayings, shouting over the blasting House music, pounding from the ground floor up to the top floor, I pushed my way toward the roof for some fresh air, and bumped past Trevor, one of our college friends; both of us turning with recognition, him still in his signature thick blond curls.

Dude? What's goin' on? He said. We grabbed hands.

Ghosting

Hey, Trevor.

It's live up there, dude... Check out the video.

Then he spaced like he always did, eyes going vacant.

I'll check it out.

He bolted, no doubt doing his Casper routine — disappearing on his girlfriend Lily. Chloe nicknamed him Casper because you could be in the middle of a conversation with Trevor and pause to look at something, and when you looked back he was gone. It was more than ADD or ADHD, it was a special talent or a skill. At first it pissed Lily off to no end, but I'm sure she was used to it by now.

I walked up that last creaking flight of hardwood stairs, through the battered black steel door flung wide onto the roof. A cool wet breeze rustled around me for a second and I walked to the edge of the warm dancing crowd, everybody on the roof bouncing up and down to the beat, with a heart-rending view of the Manhattan skyline behind them, and I felt the ancient wooden beams flexing under my feet. Whoa. That was somebody's ceiling.

Max didn't need to worry about cops or the neighbors. None of them gave a damn about the noise. Landlords griped about property taxes rising, and yuppies and artists moving in, but lots of them were looking to sell. Gentrification. Good for the city. Good for the neighborhood. Good for them. Good for everybody. The cops let the artists party, and couldn't care less if the poor got evicted — the crime rate was already dropping. The only sting was homeowners everywhere could see their stories ending, their histories fading — families that lived there two hundred years... The Williamsburg they knew and loved was ghosting, and so were they. Right then I felt a hand whack my shoulder.

I turned and Max said, Xavier! Good to see you, man! He hugged me and slapped my back, It's been like, what, two years?

It has.

Max looked like Michelangelo's David, the same Jewish-Italian mix as the sculptor's model. Every woman I knew who met him remarked he was beautiful.

How are you, man? He said.

I'm good. Glad to get out of Colorado.

How's the party? He asked.

It's great.

This is only the pre-party, dude. Wait till you see where we're going after this.

Is Chloe here? I asked.

…She's here. You're such a sucker for the babes. He chided. We'll find you someone.

Max knew how long it had been since I had a girlfriend so he wanted to get me laid. He was dismissive about Chloe because, although they were good friends now, they tried to hook up once in college but they were so similar it felt incestuous, and they repelled each other like north poles of two magnets when it came to sex. I think in reality they each found their equal in the other, but were both afraid to have a real relationship where they weren't simply toying with inferiors. But then again, both of them would say they never wanted what I call a real relationship.

He put his arm around me and said, Welcome back, man!

Thanks.

We plunged into the darkness and the roar and the sea of flashing faces. I got caught up by the dance floor and he disappeared.

Ghosting

* * * * *

Last time I visited we went to the Whitney Biennial. We were stunned speechless at the display — oversized canvases of a cartoon white explorer searching through ruined stone pillars with a flashlight; a graphic video of open heart surgery projected onto a giant screen over a bed with bloodstained sheets; huge flat designs of circular dinner plates with floral motifs...

Almost everyone I graduated with quit making art.

It's expensive. I said.

Lynn stopped because she said what she painted was never like what she saw in her head.

It's always been that way. I commented. A few people are born with a voice or a vision and everybody else has to work to find it for years.

We're getting more scattered and restless. The ones who were the least talented in school are the most successful now.

That explains why it's so soulless.

It feels like they're trying to be someone they're not, like they're ashamed.

Most people's experience doesn't fit the ideas we've been fed, so we learn early to fake it — to make a show of how it all works together like we've been taught, so we don't feel left out.

Good thing some of us still have some balls.

He set his big shoulder bag on the floor, knelt beside it and unzipped it. I'd wondered why he brought it along but it didn't seem important to ask what's in the bag. He took out one of several rolled up paintings on paper, spread it face down on the floor and started brushing the back with poster glue

34

from a big jar, as hundreds of museum goers milled around us.

What are you doing?

Watch me give it away. He said.

You're going to get arrested!

Haven't you ever been in jail?

Hell no!

It used to be a badge of honor back in my dad's day. Anyway, these zombies are so numbed-out, I bet none of them even say anything.

Did you not get accepted to the show?

Are you kidding? I'm not going to pay their ridiculous submission fee.

I felt like any second security would converge on us.

What should I do? I asked.

Nothing… He closed his eyes, took a deep breath, exhaled slowly, and said, I am invisible, I am invisible, I am invisible…

He stood and affixed the first painting to the wall, and then proceeded to glue the rest clustered around it one-by-one. A few people glanced at him curiously but no one said a word. We didn't have much to say either on the way out, flowing with the herd toward one of the exits where two security guards stood in navy blazers and gray trousers. One perked up when he saw Max, and cut through the crowd toward us.

Sir?

He touched Max's arm. We stopped.

Will you come with me please?

Why? Max asked.

Just follow me, Sir.

Max said, I'll meet you outside.

Ghosting

He took him to a small room, empty except for
three long folding tables, and two other security
guards watching silently, standing against the wall.

Place your bag on the table and open it.

Max complied and the guard took out the one
remaining painting on paper and examined it.

I'm just carrying it around. Can't I bring a
painting into the museum?

The point is you can't take them out.

There's my signature. You want to see some
ID?

Max handed him his license; the guard
compared the photo to Max's face and the signature
to the one on the painting, scowled, and handed it
back.

You can go.

It felt like I'd been waiting in the cold for hours
when Max came out.

What happened?

We joined the throng streaming down Madison
Avenue.

Whatever you think are your limits are only
there because you're thinking them. He said.

* * * * *

There'd been a brief rain shower since I was
inside, and the black tarpaper roof and all the
writhing bodies were glistening wet. Tall black
stacks of speakers now blasted spacey Middle
Eastern sounding Drum 'n' Bass. Hundreds of warm
steamy bodies twisted to the sad tweaky groove,
and I watched the video of semi-abstract images
projected from one of the third floor studios onto
the white-walled building across the street.

A pretty girl with pale skin and dark brown hair wearing an elegant short dark blue and red silk print dress and black flats, came over, smiled and started dancing near me, facing me. I knew how this worked. I started dancing too. After a minute she smiled and turned her back to me, still dancing. That was the signal to move in and I held her waist as she rubbed her ass into me. I've never liked twerking. I mean, it feels nice at first to pretend like you're having sex, but then there's no more mystery or intrigue. So after a few minutes, I said thanks and walked away. In no less than 10 seconds a guy with a goatee, wearing a half-cocked orange Yankees baseball cap, oversized white t-shirt, baggy jeans hanging halfway down his butt, exposing his red plaid boxers, pants bunching at his ankles over orange Fila high-tops, swooped in and was behind her, knees flexed, with his fists extended, corralling her.

This is what we've come to: Oedipal Dressing — that is, if you buy into the Freudian psychosexual theory to describe a boy's feelings of desire for his mother and jealously and anger towards his father. The girls look like sophisticated young ladies, and the boys look like shady little children playing dress up in their teenage brother's dirty laundry. It must appeal to a woman's maternal instinct to nurture a toddler because if it didn't attract them, guys wouldn't dress like that. And conversely, the "dudes" seem to go for the "hotties" that look more refined and adult — like their mothers.

I saw Max sitting next to a girl on the ledge at the edge of the roof and I pushed through the crowd, slipping between wriggling slick figures toward a tiny open space next to them lit by a streetlight, and sat down with the hissing street traffic to our back. Her face was pretty, smoking an organic American Spirit cigarette. She had heterochromia — one amber-brown eye, and one pale blue-green eye — blond hair to her shoulders, long thin torso, and she wore a blue and green vintage 1960's taffeta dress. I could smell her sweet Egyptian musk from there, a fragrance popular with the neo-hippies in Boulder which they usually over-apply, as is also the case with patchouli, but which in my opinion is a far less offensive scent, so I was used to it. Definitely a hippie though, through and through, but also tough, wearing a game face throughout, a thorough New Yorker I thought.

Max looked around at people dancing, and said to her, You don't seem like you're too into this...

I like the music. She said. Just not the dancing.

What do you mean?

I'm not going to go out there and grind my ass up against somebody I don't know. I actually can't believe that's become socially acceptable. She said.

I felt a little embarrassed. Maybe she saw me dancing? Someone I could potentially relate to though, once Max took off.

By the way, Gaia, Xavier; Xavier, Gaia.

Hi.

Earth Mother?

My parents were hippies. She added.

I thought, How typical: the daughter of liberals turned conservative.

So you don't like men and women touching each other when they dance? Max teased.

She blew organic smoke, I mean when a man and a woman who don't know each other start dancing next to each other and at some point it becomes okay for him to grab her from behind and push his crotch into her ass without exchanging a single word!

What's so horrible about that? Max asked.

She held out her fingers to count the ways. She's shamed by social convention into not protesting, because if she does she's a "bitch". And he's egged on by social pressure to be sexually aggressive, otherwise he's a "pussy". It's all about instant gratification. What ever happened to a man asking a woman to dance, or her asking him… taking your time?

That still happens. He replied. But if they hook up on the dance floor and they're both having fun what's the problem?

Um, well, let's see. It's about life for story value, bragging rights, collecting trophies. They're both objectifying and dehumanizing each other; it's not about getting to know someone; it's shallow and won't lead to friendship or intimacy, only empty sex. How's that? She said.

…Those are some big opinions. He responded. What if once you leave the dance floor you do talk to each other, and get to know each other? And what if you see each other again and your relationship does turn into a friendship? What if you do become intimate and eventually make love. That's possible. Anything's possible.

I wondered why he was suddenly talking in the second person. Shockingly, she had nothing to say, and turned away, and took a drag of her organic cigarette.

She exhaled, and said, Whatever…

I've got to make the rounds. Max said.

This is your party?

Yeah.

She smiled at him, So, you're *that* Max…

Give me your phone number; we can talk later.
He responded.

Her eyes sparkled and she told him her number.

He put it in his cell, and touched her shoulder,
Let me know if there's anything you need: a
different drink, a blindfold, a shotgun...

She laughed briefly, I'll let you know.

It was good to meet you. He leaned in toward
her and she turned to face him, and for an instant,
they kissed.

Max was incredible. Stunning! How in the hell
did he do that?

I followed Max through the crowd over to the
DJ wearing a fuzzy white hood with tall rabbit ears,
set up on a folding table under a canopy tent.

Max leaned close to him and said, Robot Girl.
And he walked away.

I was into the track the DJ was playing so I
stayed and listened and looked out over the dancing
crowd and the brilliant towers of Manhattan across
the water. He mixed the next track and it was a train
wreck. The beat didn't match, and he switched to
Techno. I turned and looked at him and he grinned
at me deviously. People on the dance floor noticed
too. A few left. The next mix was a train wreck too
and the track actually sounded dorky. More people
left the dance floor. The following several tracks
got dorkier and dorkier until the only person left
was a tall drunk girl with short red curly hair in a
white tank top, gray skinny-jeans, and green
Converse canvas sneakers, dancing "the robot" —
clowning, laughing, and glancing over at her friends
waiting impatiently for her by the stairwell door.
Robot Girl...

* * * * *

Later, after everyone left I flopped in a bristly old burgundy armchair that would have been velvety decades ago in the second floor living room, and sipped a beer. Max came in with Gaia (surprise, surprise). Trevor followed, now with Lily; I stood, gave Lily kisses and hugs, and they sat on the chairs and couch next to me.

What's up, bad boy? Max said. He slid a magazine across the coffee table between us, Check out this cover I did...

I picked up the magazine and squinted at it. The cover was a pixilated fuzzy image of a woman putting two hard penises in her mouth, superimposed by the magazine title.

It's a lesbian magazine, so of course the first thing I thought of was a girl sucking cock. He said. I did it with one first, but the editor said she couldn't print that. So I did it again with two and they published it. Two heads are better than one, right?

I chuckled and slowly shook my head, Only in New York... I don't know if I can make it to another party.

Considering the time difference and the altitude you should be up all night. He retorted.

It was a long day. I replied.

I've got a little somethin' somethin'.

Max fished in his pocket and handed me two clear capsules with tiny American flags on them and white powder inside.

You know I quit doing that stuff years ago.

Come on. How often do we all get together? He cajoled. Let's party!

I don't think so... I said.

This can be a one off. Then you can go clean again.

Gaia chimed in, Come on, Xavier. It'll be fun.

Trevor said, What's wrong with you, dude?

It'll be alright, 'X'. Lily promised.

Peer Pressure... I sighed, popped them in my mouth, and washed them down with a swig of beer. America's an experiment. ...I was willing to experiment.

He grinned. You want to know what that was?

Not really. I replied. They all chuckled, like the soundtrack of a sitcom.

Let's head over to Organism.

And we all stirred...

* * * * *

Now, I don't condone habitual compulsive drug use of any kind — case in point, I quit — but I have to be willing to get dirty if I'm going to dig deep in this story. I'm one of those people who's "pot sensitive". The first time I ever smoked a joint I vomited for an hour, and ever since — because I have friends who smoke and I don't want them to feel bad about it — whenever I take a hit, I'm either talking all night or I'm asleep. Neither of which I like. Usually asleep. So I prefer to let it go. But I'd be a liar if I said psychedelics didn't make a difference in my experience. If you do get high though, make sure whatever you take is pure. If you're not sure get a test kit from dancesafe.

However, that initial try smoking marijuana was when I understood how interconnected we are. Take Max and Gaia for example. When they met she said, "So you're *that* Max..." meaning they have a mutual friend who told Gaia about Max. Once Gaia tells him who that friend is, they can both imagine that friend, and Max can then tell him/her when they see each other again, "Hey, I met Gaia."

And it goes on like that because Max and Gaia and the mutual friend each have people they know who know Max, Gaia, and their mutual friend. So all of those people share common memories of each other which means they have an ongoing link, because memory only happens in the present. Right?

The first time I took acid I could follow every single thought from its origin through all its logical permutations to its final conclusion, and then for the first time in my life I noticed space — non-thought... My virgin trip on mushrooms I laughed for hours; I'd never been that happy before, ever. And I'll never forget walking with Chloe high on mescaline one summer night under a blazing crescent moon and towering gnarled cottonwood trees through lush Norlin quad, bursting with the freshness of insight permeating everything, turning to her and saying, We *are* God!

Obviously I'm not the first one to say that, but I really felt it at the time, and I never had before. Psychedelics can jolt us out of our supposed reality to see the truth every once in a while — as long as we're not doing them like we're trying to fill a hole — especially "the first time". Zen Mind Beginners Mind — we master it in an instant, but then if we let them, the cultural and existential constrictions creep in and cripple us. Granted, most people if asked why they get high will answer, Duh... 'cause it's fun. They're just doing it to get numb. But if you ask the question "What is fun?", you reach the answer, "out of control", and see the basis of "spontaneity", and understand that's because our nature is to "create". You see a flower blooming, and it's all flowers blooming, beyond Time... but only for people with eyes for that sort of thing, and the flash is only ever temporary. Impermanence...

The hole never gets filled until there is no hole to fill. And after a while one may prefer to get where they want to without drugs.

3

Organism: Chloe's First Epiphany

"The Devil is only a repressed demon, one who hasn't been allowed to play into your life, who hasn't been given his due, and so becomes a violent threat. And a demon is only one of the unconscious impulses that are the dynamic of your life. They're a gift, really, because without them we're dead robots."

— Chloe Pentangeli, Selected Talks on The First Cycle

Next we were staggering down empty Williamsburg cobblestone streets — parts paved over with asphalt lit by pink streetlights; buckled sidewalks glimmering with shattered glass pushed up by centuries-old elm tree roots. A tall chain link fence with bright green weeds at the foot, glistening at the edge of the walkway, guarding an empty parking lot, followed by dark rows of ancient three-story redbrick walkups, marching beside the old cobblestone showing through thinning tarmac in places; then the blacktop finally giving up letting the old hand-laid stone rule. Like a baby teething... or the original intention refusing to be denied. First thought, best thought.

Max stopped, and said, See this?

We all stopped. He held the big fan-shaped leaf of a small tree right next to the street. It looked like Gingko.

It was around before the dinosaurs. He said. It survives in the city because it could deal with the all the carbon monoxide after the meteor hit and choked the reptiles to death. This is prehistoric!

Organism: Chloe's First Epiphany

We all went, Whoa... And walked on.

I sighed and looked up at the streetlights streaming down in glistening rainbow tendrils, feeling my body tingle from the drugs. It was a big night in Williamsburg. An illegal New Year's Eve Witches Sabbath for artists called "Organism" at an old abandoned mustard factory near the waterfront, just across the black river from Manhattan. And there was no cover. I recognized groups of people from the party at Max's — some getting out of cars, some arriving by foot, and lots of new people. We all formed a loose dark procession toward the entrance over shiny brown brick-laid streets and greasy granite slab sidewalks, flowing silently past the rusty corrugated tin fence glowing orange in the streetlights around the gigantic abandoned factory. Nobody spoke because we were all overcome with the sense that something big was about to happen — or at least I was.

Inside the main building Beg for Eden played screaming lyrical guitar riffs — easily as good as My Bloody Valentine and even more melodic. It takes so much more than talent to be successful in music. Balls. Drive. Luck. Karma. In any of the arts. They were way more talented than shoe gazers like Ride who got famous, but you had to be there to hear them. Cans of imported beer on ice and bottles of water were for sale for two bucks apiece in front of a 50-foot-long fuzzy-looking mural of a naked young couple strolling a meadow under tall trees like a blurry early Matisse Max painted on one of the old brick walls with a broom, a ladder, and 10-gallon tubs of house paint. Paradise... And people walked around selling ecstasy, mushrooms, acid, pot, GHB, etc...

* * * * *

Gaia stood with Max at the back of the line waiting to buy beers on the side of the packed main building opposite the stage. Chloe spotted Max and came over in her essential "little black dress".

Hey, have you seen Xavier?

He was just here. He's around somewhere. This is Gaia... Chloe...

Nice dress. Chloe said, referring to Gaia's 1960's taffeta.

Thanks.

It's hard to find things like that anymore, unless you want to pay an arm and a leg vintage. Chloe added.

I know. Thrift stores were all shopped out in the 80's. I got this from my mom. I think the whole Grunge-look started because there weren't any more cool clothes left to buy second hand for cheap.

That makes sense. Chloe turned to Max, I'm going to go find 'X'.

* * * * *

In another huge room hundreds of watermelons hung by wires from the twenty-foot ceiling over sweat-drenched hordes writhing to sexy Techno blasting from a massive black wall of speakers while a DJ spun at a booth on three decks, bubble headphones over his red tuque, bobbing his round shaved head to the beat, surrounded by hundreds of paintings, sculptures, and drawings lining the walls of the entire room. At random the watermelons exploded overhead one after another and showered pink flesh and green rinds onto the crowd. They had M-80's planted in them.

Organism: Chloe's First Epiphany

Outside at a booth on the wide main stage a DJ spun IDM warming up for the headliner. Next to the side of the main structure, a row of ten swing sets stood over puddles of different colored paint, and as people got swinging they dragged their bare feet through the pools and smeared them on the dark walls making abstract foot paintings. There were 50-gallon metal drums with fires at various places in the yard where a few people warmed up, despite that it wasn't too cold out. Organism was prepared for anything.

As the clock struck twelve after the customary countdown, thousands cheered, kissed, and made out as several men dressed in skin-tight all-white plunged from the tip of the 200-foot-tall phallic mustard seed silo on thick white ropes, rappelling while videos of chimpanzees mating, bison rutting, and snails entangled shooting love darts and copulating — sexual organs extending from their heads — were projected over them onto the curved metal tower.

"Candy ravers" sucking lollipops and pacifiers, wearing cut-up t-shirts and immensely baggy pants with chains and multiple zipper handles dangling, shuffled around — there for the drugs and the fashion — along with dreadlocked neo-hippies in loose hemp fiber earth colors with primitive tats — into the tribal vibe. Yuppies and business people in dark suits, tuxes, and cocktail dresses — looking to get their minds blown and to blow off steam — mingled with yoga instructors with their perfect bodies in tight pastel colored stretchy clothes, "embracing the feeling" that they were still a part of life outside the studio. Pale Goths in leather and black vinyl with spiked hair and black and white makeup reminded everyone that there is a separate darker reality parallel to all the others, while ex-hippies in their 50's wearing rainbow-colored tie dye and face paint wished for a flashback to their better days. A few gang bangers in baggy athletic apparel strutted cagily past some dude dressed as a cowboy, with a Stetson, a Carhartt jacket, skin-tight Wrangler jeans, a big oval 4-H rodeo belt buckle, and classic low-heeled boots — in New York City! People of all races, ages, and persuasions commun-ed.

Raves always have the widest cross-section of the public — one of the few places we can all come together. Makes you wonder why so many people are against them. The beat pounded.

* * * * *

A lot of conventional-minded people can't handle the raw sexuality of the beat. I'd been to a couple of raves in Boulder where a few frat boys showed up, and on both occasions freaked out, mocking the music and dancing. Once, three of them surrounded a guy grooving by himself and they all started mimicking him, making fun of the way he moved to the beat. He left. The other time, two frat boys snuck up and actually slid their palms onto the backsides of two straight guys dancing next to each other, not because they wanted to come on to them (maybe covertly), but to piss them off. They all ended up pushing each other till people broke it up. Now we have Dubstep — music so asexual nobody even knows how to dance to it, where train wrecks are normal and expected. I can appreciate it — Dubstep is to electronic music as Punk is to Rock & Roll; I get it — but I don't see the point in hopping around like a bunch of castrated squirrels.

At least with Punk there was slam dancing, which I imagine was like rough sex.

I have a DJ friend who says that's why there was such a deliberate effort to destroy disco in this country, because social conservatives couldn't handle the sexuality of the rolling beat — that and the fact it was made by and danced to by mostly black people. It's astounding that Racism, so deeply woven into the fabric of America, has become the biggest elephant in the room so many people want to pretend isn't there. Radio stations had DJs rake the needle across disco records on air in the 1970's; at professional baseball games owners actually allowed groups to smash thousands of disco records with a tractor in the middle of the field for the cheering crowd after the game; all across America people sold "Disco Sucks" bumper stickers with a vengeance. Meanwhile in Europe disco never lost its popularity, it just evolved.

Most of the people at Organism seemed open-minded enough to handle it, though, and nobody was playing Dubstep. That same DJ friend told me, "Like it's reggae roots, Dubstep only reaches the lower two chakras, the rest you have to make up in your head." The power of the beat travels mainly through the earth. House, Trance, and Techno can reach up to the heart center, but only Psytrance reaches all the way to the crown chakra.

* * * * *

Chloe spotted me in the crowd, ran and threw her arms around my neck.

Xavier! I was looking all over for you at Max's!

Where were you till now? I asked.

I got some cash from the hotel.

How did you know where this was?

Max gave me a flyer.

…Chloe Pentangeli… Her long slender torso felt like it belonged in my arms, and her scent was sweet lilac; I only wanted to hold her and forget everything, but she always said she didn't want a boyfriend, and she was clear about it up front with everybody. Chloe thought relationships were basically people trying to freeze a fleeting moment to make it last forever. By nature they're stuck — dead fish bobbing in an eddy, caught in a spiraling sidetrack going nowhere, outside the flood of change — because humans, like all mammals, are not naturally monogamous or sexually exclusive.

It's so good to see you! She said, sounding surprised, and kissed me.

Good to see you too.

How's teaching ESL out in the boonies?

I still like the job…

Are you writing?

Not really.

How long are you here?

My return flight's in a week.

She beamed into my eyes, You should come up to Cambridge. I've got a room for rent in my new house.

…Interesting.

Her eyes sparkled, Do you want a beer?

Sure.

I'll get us some.

Here. I handed her some money.

I'm buying. She said. Wait here.

And she disappeared into the crowd. I didn't know what to do with Chloe except go along with being "just friends". We all have only a few people in life who are unforgettable, people who changed our lives irrevocably — the ones we learned from, the ones who splashed down like meteors sending ripples through time all the way to the beginning and all the way to the end, exterminating the dinosaurs, giving rise to humanity — and she was one of them for me. I wouldn't call it unrequited love, because she loved me in her own way, but I knew we would never be together.

Crash Worship played on the outdoor stage, and as their three drummers built up a thundering primal rhythm, they stripped down to only loin-cloths and banged on the platform to the rhythm of the drums with crooked wooden staffs, hubcaps nailed to the tops like cymbals — men and women naked-legged and bare-chested; mud and straw smeared all over their skin, some wearing Native American spirit masks. The guitarist loosened the strings as he played to get the eerie low groaning sound he wanted, and I recognized his dark dirge version of Ring Around the Rosies behind the roar of percussion.

Ring-a-ring-a-rosie
A pocket full of posies
Achoo, achoo
We all fall down

Children sang it during the Black Plague because the first sign of infection was rosy little rings. Dark images of medieval woodcut prints of massive 4-weeled horse-drawn carts lit by torches, bearing statues of Jagganath — a title for Krishna in his role as World Ruler — with people throwing themselves under the wheels getting crushed to death were projected onto a giant screen behind the band. Infected men and women all over Europe and

Asia joined those travelling rituals, ingested hallucinogenic mushrooms, went wild with dancing and promiscuity, and ended their lives in a blaze of glory rather than suffer a creeping death by plague.

Lightning flashed, thunder boomed, and the crowd roared; it started to drizzle again, like the band did a rain dance that worked. They picked up tempo. Pyrotechnics exploded; towers of flames shot into the wet sky lighting up the stage, and thousands roared again. Women in the crowd tore off their shirts and jumped half-naked onto the slippery platform, bouncing with the band. It was like a pagan orgy. A writhing juggernaut... Fire and flesh under a deluge. A Dionysiac. A Panic. A feral lament. The psychedelic frenzy of plague victims ecstatic for release from miserable lives throwing themselves under the rolling flaming wheels. A shooting star into the black. The death of a century.

I recognized Gaia on stage in her classic taffeta, the only one with all of her clothes still on, shaking her wet blond strands spreading water in luminous rainbow arcs under the lights, kaleidoscopic in the rain, shimmering as she swayed to the pounding beat. Max walked up to the foot of the stage with a bottle of beer in each hand. He said something to her and set the beers at her feet; she got on her knees excitedly, grabbed his wrist, pulled him up on stage with her, and immediately put his hands on her breasts as they danced. He threw his head back and laughed with abandon. She grinned mischievously. Two other women naked from the waist up joined Gaia and Max on stage, and formed a small dancing circle. Max took off his shirt, stuffed one end in the back of his jeans, and wrapped his arms around all three of them.

Chloe came back holding two brown bottles glistening with moisture catching the reflections of the lights and handed me one.

¿Una vuelta?

¿Por qué no?

Here's to you coming to Cambridge. She said. Cheers.

We clinked bottles and sipped the cool golden fizziness and wandered through the carnival throng.

Where are you working these days? I asked.

She sighed, got a far away look in her eyes, and said, This place called Stellar. It's a technology distributor.

What do you do?

I'm in Inside Sales. I talk to resellers with existing accounts and book their orders. No cold calls.

What's a reseller?

...Okay, this is what they call "The Channel". The Distribution Channel. You have the manufac-turer, like Sun, then the distributor, like Stellar; there's the reseller, and finally the end user. The manufacturer says to the distributor, This "whatever" costs say $1000 — which probably only cost them only $500. The distributor says to the reseller, This "whatever" costs us $1100, and the reseller understands they're inflating the cost, so the reseller goes to the end user and says, This "whatever" costs $2000, but I'm willing to work with you. The end user usually says — if they're smart — I want it for $1400, and everybody else makes out with a profit. It's like a gentlemen's agreement, The OBC.

The what?

"The Old Boys Club".

Why doesn't the manufacturer just sell it directly to the end user for $1400?

They don't think like Steve Jobs who wants to keep the whole process in house. In their view the cost of a distributor, an Inside Sales team and an Outside Sales team would cut into their profits, and they don't want to diversify, they want to concentrate on only manufacturing. The guys at the top think specialization is the best way to market their products and can't stand the thought of all that extra information. Like, "Crazy making".

She waved her hands briefly in the air by her ears.

They can't focus or make a commitment to anything despite that's all they really want to do. Literally, they rename the divisions of the company every three months and move everybody's desk — as if that's going to improve performance — to impress the share-holders. I've had eight desks since I've been there and my division's had three different names, but I still do the same old same old and profits are plunging. …I'm going to go back for my PhD soon. She said. I feel sorry for most of them.

Robby is this stocky ginger-headed semi-pro golfer who's always cracking jokes — the class clown everybody likes. He turned a corner when he realized an endless email inbox means you never have to organize anything. He brags that he never cleans his apartment — let the landlord deal with the mess when he moves once a year — and that he only eats fast food — to hell with that organic crap. He sounded a little guilty, though, when he told everybody Easy-Mac was his favorite, and described making it, how you just microwave the noodles with water then add the processed cheese packet, like he secretly understood it degraded the

whole process of cooking and eating. He tells
everybody, Recycling is for pussies. And all he ever
talks about other than himself are TV sitcoms. Most
people should just unplug their TV's, I swear. Once,
after the laughing died down, after one of his
comedic rolls, he got serious, leaned close to me
and whispered, I don't think anyone would even
believe I was depressed.

...Wow. I said. As we meandered through
thousands.

Kirsten is the smartest one. She's tall and
blond; built like a Viking. Everyone goes to her if
they have an issue, even the mangers. She has a
photographic memory, and she's pretty helpful
despite she secretly hates everybody's questions.
She wears tons of cheap perfume that exudes in this
eye-watering cloud, like she jumps in a vat of it
every morning before work. She came over to tell
me something one time, and I must have wrinkled
my nose trying not to sneeze from the perfume, and
she asked me, What? Do I smell like a whore? I
thought, If you think you smell like a whore why do
you buy the perfume in the first place, and then
douse yourself in it? But I didn't say anything.

Her mom died when she was thirteen, and she
always gets dodgy when she talks about her dad.
She made a point of letting everybody know she
was "sexually inexperienced", but constantly speaks
dripping erotic innuendo, and one time told me the
only thing that gets her off is sleep porn, where
someone always supposedly surprises somebody
who's asleep. Occasionally she even lets it slip that
she hates her dad because he was "too intimate".
She's married to this browbeaten short guy she met
at church, and whenever he comes to the office to
pick her up she henpecks and badgers him in front

of everybody. Probably fifty times a day she says,
I'm such a terrible person. I'm such a terrible
person. I'm such a terrible person.

It sounds so sad. I said.

Buddy, the Director, lumbers around with a
bullhorn barking orders like a drunken JV football
coach, "Sell above cost! One order, one booking!
Canadian order means Canadian dollars!" He's
trying to be funny, and it's stupid, but ultimately he
really means it. It's the typical corporate environment where management has a secret agenda and
quotas that they won't tell employees. They say,
"Quality is what matters; we're not concerned how
fast you go." But at the end of the day all they really
care about is speed and numbers. Michelle, the
manager beneath Buddy, showed me a plastic jug of
McCormick vodka in her desk drawer one day, and
said, Why do you think I have this?

There are the mimickers who knee-jerk sneeze
or cough whenever anyone else sneezes or coughs,
and the people who compulsively say "Bless you!"
or "Gesundheit!" whenever it happens, as if that
fulfills some magical purpose. The swallowers
noisily gulp whatever — diet soda, water, coffee,
their own saliva — all day long in the library-like
atmosphere. Everyone hears Karen in her office,
yapping on the phone, sounding like her mouth is
full of food and lisping, spelling out names —
David: 'D' as in dog, 'A" as in animal, 'V' as in
veterinarian, 'I' as in immunization, 'D' as in doo
doo — I mean…

She's one of those friendless people who only
talk about their dog, misconstruing the animal's
obsequious affection for unconditional love. She
even bought her puppy a fake ID so he could come

to the office because it's only legal to bring a pet to work if it's a service animal, like a seeing-eye dog.

Renny, a religious fanatic — one of a herd in the office that all go to the same Evangelical Christian church — plays church music every day and sings along with it while everyone around her cringes. She even did missionary work in India and Nepal but learned nothing at all and only feels superior. She said, They think we're fat just because we eat cheese. Ha. I never eat cheese. But she's at least 70 pounds overweight — a stress eater, snacking all day on greasy chips and sugar, always telling everybody about the new diet she's on.

They're constantly getting sick, coming down with colds, the flu, strep throat, pink eye, coughs. Maybe it's Sick Building Syndrome — I don't know — but for whatever reason I never get it. And they all have their treatments: Ambien, Melatonin, and Valium to sleep; Paxil, Zoloft, and Wellbutrin, to stay upbeat; Allegra, Claritin, and steroid inhalers for their allergies; Nexium, Zantac, Procrecia, and bottles and bottles of chalky white tablets to keep their stomach bile from backing up their esophagi into their mouths; Zelnorm for their irritable bowel syndromes; Maalox and Gas-X to keep from belching and farting clouds. Who knows what else they're taking…

I added, in a TV announcer's voice, Side effects may include thoughts of suicide, sexual dysfunction, internal bleeding, narcolepsy, or even death.

She rubbed the back of her hand across her forehead and sighed. God! Did you take any of those pills Max had?

Yeah.

I am so high right now! She said.

Me too.

I held out my hand and she took it in hers and they were both clammy.

What was in them? I asked.

She laughed, You're so funny!

She laid her head on my shoulder briefly. She thought I was joking.

I asked her, How does it feel to be named the Second Coming of Christ?

It feels great, of course, but there are lots of people who deserve it more than I do.

I disagree...

...It sounds ridiculous, doesn't it? It was just some website... You can say whatever you want on the Internet. There's a kind of intimacy online if you're sitting alone in your room, and you say what you really feel, and talk about whatever you want; and what comes back seems meant only for you, more private than TV which comes into your living room, and way more personal than movies you see in public with strangers. But people forget they're always broadcasting to potentially billions — and it's a permanent record.

It's been un-PC to talk about religion for centuries. I commented. The social stigma of even saying the word "spirituality" is on par with writing the word fuck, or publicly showing pornography, or smoking a joint in a room full of teetotalers.

The day Christianity became the official religion of the state people took it literally to avoid government persecution. She responded. Greeks never thought there were actual immortal beings living on top of Mount Olympus! But suddenly, in complete contradiction to experience, they tried to imagine the Christian deities as real, because with a Roman sword to their throats they weren't about to say it's just a metaphor. And then they became

ashamed of the ancient religion where Zeus lusted
after gods and mortals, Dionysus intoxicated
himself and the world; and Orpheus enraged women
with his lascivious songs — ashamed of those
things in themselves because the new religion didn't
provide for them except to be confessed as sins.
Religion became a moralistic legal matter.
Materialistic duality corrupted and possessed the
infinite sublime.

So there developed a split. I said.

To most people there's the material world and
all the "real life" rules that come with it, and then
there's religion, which refers to a world completely
separate from this one with another set of rules that
don't really apply to material life.

Like a parallel universe.

It's beyond me why so many people have a
problem with that concept. It's widely accepted as a
good thing to play make believe for an hour once a
week, imagining a fictional idyllic world parallel to
this one, because it makes most people feel temporarily content, and somewhat stems the tide of
hatred and aggression we pour into the real world, a
consequence of the lack of a spirituality that reflects
all aspects of ourselves, which results in the self-
loathing that goads us to attack others. Religion
became like an inside joke — easier to go along
with it than to come right out and say it's bullshit.
People who take it seriously are secretly seen as
idiots because deep down we know.

It only relates to a fragment of us so it makes us
see our potential as limited. I said.

Exactly. Nobody starts out feeling that way. If
you give a child a paper butterfly, she'll imagine it
fluttering to foreign continents conversing with all
kinds of beings. Imagination is limitless. Whether

60

we acknowledge it or not, it insults our intelligence to accept a pool noodle or arm-floaties when we face circumnavigating the globe. That's why there's such a massive decline in religious membership, and an equal rise in fundamentalist posturing to try and re-legitimize dying religions.

In your case it's more like they're clicking restart.

I won't play into all that. ...I'm not going to waste the opportunity, though. You know, you see those movies where somebody suddenly gets super powers, but then all they do is hoard a bunch of money from the stock market or Vegas and fuck a lot of people. What about improving life for everyone else on the planet?

Max would say the two aren't incompatible. I added.

...I guess they're not. She mused.

I wasn't suggesting anything.

My body was tingling, and all the wildly dressed people in the decaying factory shimmered with rainbow halos around them.

It looks like everything is made of colored light. I commented.

Nothing is really what it seems. She replied. If something were really what it seemed all the time, then drugs wouldn't change anything. I've been studying Dark Matter. They call it Dark because we can't find it with any instruments available, but the only explanation for the behavior of known matter is there's 99% more of it out there. This whole world, everything you think is real, everything you see, hear, taste, touch, smell, and feel is only 1% of what's really there — right now, right in front of your face!

Our shoulders intermittently touched as we walked which sent shivers of unbearable pleasure through my body. What's the other 99%? I managed.

Well, there could be billions and trillions of particles between you and me right now, even entire universes, but they're more than four dimensional, and four is all we can experience. There could be as many as twenty-three dimensions. All of space could be teeming with particles and universes. Another theory is that Virtual Particles are constantly popping in and out of empty space, and Bubble Universes within Bubble Universes are constantly popping in and out of existence.

The air all around us sparkled when she said that.

So the number of universes is infinite? I offered.

They're theories. She replied. Dark Energy is even wilder. The expansion of the universe is accelerating and we can't find any measurable force driving it so we call it Dark. But the force it would take to do that is a magnitude of 122 more than the strongest force we can measure. That's a one with 122 zeros behind it. That's how much more poten-tial energy there is right at our fingertips, way more powerful than an atomic bomb. Some call it Zero Point Energy.

What does that mean?

...The multi-verse is like a thin layer of foam on a bottomless ocean. Everything we experience is the movement of that layer. But the foam only moves because the endless ocean beneath it moves, and that fathomless sea of power is everywhere, and available all the time — at Point Zero. If someone discovered how to access that unlimited power...

we might even be able to manifest mere thoughts
into physical reality.

The backs of our hands brushed against each
other's, and suddenly I heard a brief wave of sound
as if all the musical instruments in the world played
simultaneously.

The wildest thing is we've detected some
objects so far away... I'm not talking about this far
away, if this is the universe and this is the object...
She balled one hand into a fist indicating the
universe and held the other hand six inches away
indicating the object. I mean this far away. She
moved her hand away from her fist arm's length.
Space had to expand faster than the speed of light
after the Big Bang for that to happen, and we don't
know how. People don't like to talk about this stuff.
Physicists, anyway... The speed of light, the one
last constant everybody thought would never
change is gone. There is no law. No rules anymore.
Everything is groundless.

In a flash I was ticklish and dizzy as if the earth
dropped from under my feet; when I held her hand
to steady myself, I suddenly felt drunk, and the air
instantly filled with the scent of chrysanthemums.

It's true with everything. She said. We can
watch videos from Iceland, or South Korea, or from
our next door neighbors. We have instant access to
music from yesterday or fifty years ago, made by
anybody, all over the world. I get perfume from a
shop that makes custom scents — tomatoes, new
car smell, dirt — anything I want. The insights of
all the psychological and philosophical traditions in
history are at out fingertips. My mom says there're
lots of books she wishes she could have read but she
had to focus on science. I tell her, You can read
them now. It's a mindset. Instead of complaining

you don't know something you can do a search and find 100,000 pathways to it in less than a second.

The time is Now… I chimed in.

Let's write some poems. Short ones, like haikus. We'll trade line for line. She suggested.

I shrugged, and said, Okay.

As we sailed through the throng, for a second I zoomed out 50 feet above my head and saw myself below walking hand in hand with Chloe through the dark crowd, and thought, Why have I ever worried about anything? And then I zoomed back.

Somehow we found a martini bar in a remote corner amid the bustle and sat down. The bartender in a white shirt, black vest, and white bowtie, with a waxed moustache and his dark hair slicked down 1930's style, served cocktails in chrome glasses that swirled with rainbow iridescence.

Chloe asked him for some paper and a pen and we wrote pseudo-haikus, as Psytrance blasted.

Outside of myself
On Psytrance and who knows what
A world comes and goes.

Night of derailment
Train wrecks and luscious gravel
My body everywhere.

Stumbling onto Mind
Tripping over my Self
Into recognition.

Rolling in intoxicants
The road is paved with our thoughts
Sweet mountain sage.

You're one in a billion, Chloe. I said.

Why?

Because you're fully alive. Most people only want to find a place to hide and watch the light flash by like time-lapse — night, day, night, day… You're like the sun.

* * * * *

Next thing I knew, Chloe was pulling me by the hand, through the crowd and drizzle outside, into a wide open loading dock door of one of the smaller buildings. Inside it was deathly dark and completely empty but there was an old stairway against one wall leading to the roof. We climbed the rusty brown metal stairs, startling several pigeons that flapped and squeaked noisily away; pushed open the creaky metal door at the top, and stepped into the open air.

She led me by the hand to a spot in the middle, took off her clothes, and looked up at the sky, feeling the soft rain on her brown skin smiling. Music from the stage echoed faintly. We kissed and her mouth was hot and tasted like drugs. I could give my heart to her completely as simply as petals fall from a rose. I took off my clothes too, and laid her down on the gritty tarpaper roofing, and we made love. Distant street-lights flashed in the rain looking crystalline through a haze of water under the spidery lights of the Williamsburg Bridge. Her spine arched and she dug her fingernails into my back and squeezed me as she shuddered in orgasm. Then she seemed gone, but after a few seconds she was back, and she laughed, astonished at herself.

What? I asked.

I just had an epiphany… I completely stopped my thoughts and relaxed there for a second, and then there was only white light... Like an explosion, and limitless... As soon as I thought something — I thought, What is this? — the white light disappeared, and I was looking at you again. ...That's what we are. She said. White light.

* * * * *

I woke up on a futon on a floor covered with paint-splotched canvas glowing pale in northern light from tall old windows. The white walls were spattered with multicolored pigment. There was a thick old wooden table streaked with drips, and on it a big tin coffee can full of heavily-used brushes of all sizes; it smelled like linseed oil, turpentine, and pine resin. I saw a painting leaning against the wall in the corner, and sighed, relieved. Max's studio. He painted some serene fuzzy landscapes everyone said were "kind of Zen", and he was gaining some recognition — with a small 'r' — in "The City".

I looked next to me and there was Chloe naked under a pale blue down comforter, breathing softly, deeply sleeping. Traffic hissed outside on the wet street. I knew better than to trip out about what happened the night before. It was what it was — a beautiful moment. I was infinitely thankful, and now it was gone. It didn't portend anything for the future; Chloe and I would still be friends, as ever. I got up, put on my boxers and t-shirt, and headed downstairs.

Max sat at the kitchen table in a burgundy, white, and light blue vertically-striped satin robe, leaning over a steaming cup of coffee and the Village Voice, with a rolled cigarette smoking in his mouth. He used to say the truest test of your mental stability is if you can roll a perfect cigarette tripping on acid standing in the rain. Gaia sat next to him wearing Max's over-sized white terrycloth bathrobe with one of her organic smokes dangling, reading the lesbian magazine Max did the cover for.

She looked up, Hey, Xavier.

Hi.

Get some coffee. Max said. There's some scrambled eggs and bacon. Toast… He gestured toward the kitchen with his head.

Thanks...

I went into the kitchen and poured some coffee out of the Krups. The whole place was spotless and pale light streamed in through the open windows onto the scrubbed checkerboard linoleum floors and white walls, porcelain sinks and counters. He must have stayed up all night. There was a plate of buttered toast on the counter. Max made it the best, crisping the bottom side first in the gas oven, taking it out, turning it over, laying chunks of butter on that side, and putting it back in to melt the butter and toast the unbuttered side. Thick-sliced bacon on a raised rack in a shallow metal baking sheet on the stovetop made my mouth water; the scrambled eggs in a big cast iron skillet next to it looked good too, and I piled a plateful, warmed it in the microwave for a minute, and took it to the table.

Did you get some rest? I asked.

Not yet. How's Chloe?

Still out...

I expected him to be annoyed that I brought Chloe home but he seemed profoundly unconcern-ed. I sat down in one of the '50's style pale blue vinyl and chrome chairs at the pale blue Formica table with chrome legs on the hardwood floor, and dug in.

So are you excited for the new millennium? I asked.

He chuckled and said, A week ago I was walking and I was going to cross the street when I noticed this weird little black dog and stopped. Right then a taxi blew by me honking and slammed on the brakes and somebody jumped out at the curb. …I thought, Thank dog.

* * * * *

I went back up to the studio and found Chloe pulling her little black dress over her head.

How did you sleep?

I wouldn't really call it sleep. She answered. More like unconsciousness. How long have you been up?

Half an hour.

I found my pants and shirt on the floor and pulled them on.

There's bacon and eggs and coffee downstairs.

Mmm. Sounds good.

…Thank you, by the way. I said.

You're welcome.

She kissed me briefly and walked to the door. I followed her out of the pale light of the studio into the dark hallway, and we ghosted.

4

The Daisy Cutter

"Thought is the highest expression of energy, but there are different levels of thought. "Unconscious Thought" or Animal Instinct is the lowest. Almost any woman physically capable will want to get pregnant without consciously thinking about it. "Conscious Thought" — like reason or scrutiny — is higher, but it's limited. You can't think your way out of death. The highest is "Superconscious Thought", beyond animal impulses, beyond analysis; beyond religion and philosophy, beyond discursive thinking altogether."

— Chloe Pentangeli, Trance Dancer

     I took Chloe up on her offer and went to Cambridge on the train — not to stay, only a visit. Be more flexible. Her new house was a huge dark brown Victorian three-story with lots of windows and a balcony under a giant elm tree out on Fresh Pond Parkway right next to the water. The landlord lived on the ground floor so we climbed a flight of stairs he built at the back on the east side, passed through the laundry/mud room and entered a long spacious linoleum-floored kitchen, with a tiled counter under two tall windows ending at a double sink and a gas stove with a big hood.

     A doorway to the left opened onto a living/dining room with two bay windows. The walls were white and the living room part had a Hunter's Green wool rug covering most of the hardwood floor to about a foot from the graven baseboards. Ornate woodwork surrounded the windows and doorways too. There were two pea-green armchairs, a beige couch, a coffee table and a few standing lamps, a bookshelf, a black stereo on a low wide stand, and tall speakers on the floor. The wooden dining table with fluted legs and six matching high-backed chairs stood on the bare hardwood under a crystal chandelier right next to the French doors of the sunroom where I'd be staying, each individual window pane covered by a red sheet of Japanese rice paper so I could have some privacy.

There was a frameless futon on the floor in the sunroom under a wall of south-facing windows, a dresser against the west wall, and on the north side, a closet and a door to the short hallway leading to the bathroom directly across, back to the living room on the right, and left to the balcony at the front of the house, only big enough for two old wicker chairs overlooking Fresh Pond. Winding oak stairs led up to the third floor where there was another bathroom above the first, and three bed-rooms, one off to each side and one at the back for Chloe and her two roommates.

We spent the afternoon at Elizabeth Evarts de Rham Hospice Home on Chilton Street, only a few blocks from her place. Chloe was a volunteer and went from room to room singing songs from the Cole Porter Songbook — whichever ones the dying patients requested. She wanted to have continual contact with the process of death, so the imperma-nence of things became a living experience, not just an intellectual idea. The hospice was comfortable in a stuffy old Victorian way, and most of the patients seemed content, but it was a little poopy smelling.

They were all terminal so the hospice let them do whatever they want. They had a smoking room, someone rolled around a bar cart offering whatever kind of alcohol they asked for, and lots of them were on morphine drips. I did my best to sing with her — "Just One of Those Things", "I Love Paris", "Night and Day", "I Get a Kick Out of You", "Ev'ry Time We Say Goodbye". The patients smiled and even joined in. How would we live if we reflected daily on the fact we're terminal? A patient who died got rolled out on a gurney through the long dark hallway, limp body flopping on the thin mattress under a white sheet. When the corpse passed, Chloe quoted the Pixies, singing under her breath, "This monkey's gone to heaven... This monkey's gone to heaven..."

Chloe and I sat at the dining table the next morning and quietly sipped Earl Grey with heavy cream, sweetened with apricot jam in pale winter light.

I've got to do something good for the world. She said, out of the blue.

Because of your epiphany?

We all have a sense of the totality of our being. You know what I mean. As a writer you feel compelled to say something important and unique even if you're not doing it right now. You're aware it's there hidden, and you sense how fulfilling it would be to find it and show it. Just knowing it's there is why we push through all the doubts and fears and failed attempts to bring it out. Somehow there's confidence we *can* change and offer something good. It's why we don't get caught up in connectivity and endless information, stuck in a maze of holes to jump and branches to duck, because we know one day the world will reveal itself to us in total simplicity and we'll have a purpose.

Some people say by just being we've already reached our full potential.

Yeah, but are they completely aware of that and content, or are they secretly depressed and too lazy to affect change, or living in fear?

It's better than trying to force change that only benefits a few.

That's a coward's way out — glorifying being a loser.

…Why don't you tell me how you *really* feel?

Well, it's simplistic to blame everything bad on trying to accomplish something. Ex-hippies who rail against America while hiding in Mexico to live out their dying days on their dead parent's inheritance are no different than racist conservatives badmouthing oversized government who rally for ballot initiatives to secede from the union — both acknowledge it won't change a thing. Is whining and complaining the ultimate fulfillment of our lives?

Obviously not.

Then there's something good we each can do for the world. I was five when I first understood that, but I couldn't wrap my mind or body around it.

What happened when you were five?

You want to hear the story? She asked.

Of course.

She took a deep breath.

…We were moving to southern California — me, my mom, and my stepdad. He got a research position at the Salk Institute in La Jolla to study the chemical origins of life so he took a sabbatical from the University of Nebraska; he insisted on driving through Death Valley. He's obsessed with death.

We stopped in the middle of the salt flats to look at the little brine shrimp squirming in evaporating shallow pools. It was 120 degrees outside. He pointed at the tiny sickly-pale animals writhing in inch-deep salt water.

See! Life can spring up anywhere! Even in the harshest conditions!

It was his way to prove he hadn't done anything wrong. He enlisted in the Army when he was twenty-one after his first chemistry degree, joined the Chemical Corps, and was sent to the South Pacific to test atomic bombs. He described it in detail — how he squatted in a trench twenty miles from ground zero, facing away from the blast with protective goggles on, his arm covering his goggles, just in case. Ha, ha. When they detonated the 50 megaton hydrogen warhead, he said the light was so intense you could see right through your arm like a moving MRI in vivid color — all the bones, and blood flowing through arteries and veins, even capillaries.

Entire atolls were vaporized — dead sharks floating on cloudy calm water like burnt out match heads on melted wax. They went around in swift boats with Geiger counters and measured the radio activity. Now everybody in his unit is dead of cancer or leukemia except him. He feels like any day his number will come up.

Anyway, I complained about the heat and we piled back into the Chevy station wagon and took off again. My mom met him when she was a sophomore at UN Omaha. She went to his office hours for Chem. 101 and as soon as she sat down he thought she would make the perfect wife — docile, bookish, Catholic — despite the fact she had me. He hadn't been married before and was feeling the urge to reproduce like most men in their forties, and she wanted a father figure. So, he waited till the semester was over, asked her out, and pretty soon she gave up her dreams of a career in academia and they got married. …You can probably imagine his exasperation when my mom told him she couldn't have another baby — "Why didn't you tell me before we got married?!" She reminded him, "You never asked." His dreams were crushed, and it seemed like he took it out on me.

Even then I knew it was my karma to be a physicist. I was fascinated by how things worked. My obsession at the time was door hinges. There's that Zen saying, What we call "I" is just a swinging door that moves when we inhale and exhale. I have no idea what that means, but I'm curious, and I was the same way with real doors when I was a kid. When my stepdad opened the back door of the station wagon the next time we stopped, I stuck my fingers in the crack near the hinges moving the door to try and figure out how it worked, and he promptly slammed it. He did that every time he saw me fooling around with door hinges. He figured it was the only way I'd learn it was dangerous. Of course I cried and held my bleeding fingers. My stepdad ignored me and my mom accepted his harsh treatment as something she'd contracted into — she'd support him no matter what.

My mom never knew what to do with a crying child. The smelly little thing with mucus and blood and secretions coming out of it… It all meant germs to her. Whenever she kissed me, if you could call it a kiss, it was always only on the forehead, and she tucked her lips inside her mouth so she wouldn't contract anything, and she pressed her tight face to me like that. Most microbiologists I've met are germophobes. Then she gave me a tissue to hold my bloody fingers and strapped me in tight with the seatbelt in the back, and said, There, now you're safe. You're ready for anything.

She's from a traditional small-town New Mexico family, and her ancestors are actually Jewish — Conversos, forced to convert to Catholicism or be executed — who left Spain in the 16th century to avoid persecution, and settled in what's now New Mexico, a century before the Mayflower even got here. She slept in the same bed as her mother — her father had a separate room — till she left the house to go to college at sixteen. That was normal in rural New Mexico, for a daughter to sleep in her mother's bed till that age. To protect against incest? Or as a form of contra-ception? Or just plain parental control? Who knows, but she said she hated it. No wonder she got pregnant from her first boyfriend. My real dad. I've met him and I love him but he could never get along with my mom.

The crazy thing is it wasn't her choice to have only one child. She had six brothers. But seeing a seventeen-year-old unwed Latina mother in 1974 Omaha, Nebraska, when the white doctor performed the c-section, while she was under he took it upon himself to give her a hysterectomy as well. Can you believe they still call them that?

My only response was, God… I felt ill from the sheer indignity.

She never said anything. Chloe added. Didn't even complain. She just accepted it, feeling shipwrecked and alone on a massive ocean of terrifying lethal waves. Ironically, that was the last time my stepdad ever slammed my fingers in a door too. I stared at him so hard that by the time we got to La Jolla there wasn't anybody staring any more. One look in my eyes in the driveway of our new house and he recoiled afraid. I said, I'm more intelligent than you; you'll never break me. He stumbled away and started unloading the bags.

Chloe paused and sipped her tea.

She said, Let's take a walk. I want to get outside before it turns cold again.

* * * * *

Indian Summer was there too. We caught the bus on Huron Avenue, rode it to Harvard Square, and I took off my leather jacket as we strolled the brick-laid sidewalks. Algiers served real Arabian coffee, thick with grounds, in a basement location filled with light because two of the exterior walls were glass and around them the earth was excavated several yards away, shored up by terraced wooden beams the thickness of railroad ties all the way up to the edge of the sidewalk at ground level. Brick paved the space between the windows and the wooden retaining wall, and black metal outdoor tables and chairs furnished the patio.

An old Persian lady sat at a table with a little handwritten card-board sign that said "Fortune Teller $5". She told Chloe's future by the sludge in the bottom of her white demitasse. Gazing down into it for several minutes examining the black streaks in the bottom, she finally looked up with dark mysterious eyes that seemed to reflect the whole world.

Forgive those who have let you down. She said. I see you can do that fairly easily, but more importantly, forgive yourself for letting yourself down. That will be more difficult, but if you do, you will get everything you truly desire.

Chloe didn't quite know what to make of that. We walked on tree lined cobblestone side streets littered with fallen leaves down to the lawn beside the Charles River, sat on the dead grass and watched white seagulls and fluffy clouds loll across the blue. A gentle breeze rustled the barren branches of the tree we were sitting under and one of the last clinging dead leaves fell.

One leaf falling is all leaves falling, through all eternity. Chloe said. You should reconsider moving here.

I want to stick it out for a while. I responded. See where it takes me.

You'll have way more fun here than in Fort Lumpy.

It's not ideal, but I like my job and I have time to write. Not that I'm doing a lot of that these days, but the potential is there. ...I can't force it. It's always crappy when I force it.

You could teach ESL in Boston. There are tons of Brazilians. She said.

A big cloud passed in front of the sun and suddenly there was shade everywhere.

I don't know. I responded. I have a feeling any other ESL job would be a lot more time consuming.

Sounds like you better start writing then. She replied.

Don't remind me.

* * * * *

For dinner we went to Pamplona, another basement location, but slightly higher than Algiers. Window wells surrounded old mottled glass panes half above ground. Inside, the walls and ceilings were white stucco; the tables had white tablecloths and straight-backed carved wooden chairs with rush seats from Spain. We shared a bottle of Rioja, and a bowl of paella.

Mmm... See how the saffron rice is light and dry? Chloe said. I don't know why so many people try to make it wet and greasy here. The peas are fresh — they burst; the carrots are still firm; chicken, sausage, mussels, squid, clams, shrimp, and white fish chunks... The best I've had in the US.

We ordered flan for desert and drank Palo Cortado Jerez.

Taste how the aromas of caramel and candied orange peel mirror the flan? And yet it's dry with that long intense hazelnut finish that complements it. Mmm.

I want to hear the rest of your story. I said.

She sighed and continued.

My stepdad invented a poisonous gas that could be used in artillery shells — the two components necessary to make the poison were kept separate in the shell and only combined to become lethal once the shell exploded. Very ingenious... The War Department of France bought the patent. He invented the explosive chemical slurry that fills the 10,000-pound bomb nicknamed The Daisy Cutter — the most powerful non-nuclear weapon in existence.

He started down a path and figured he'd follow it to the end like a kamikaze on crystal meth — which was invented by the Japanese and widely used by suicide pilots. After all, we'd already imprisoned ourselves with "The Bomb". Every country that has them will never get rid of them because they're afraid their enemies will develop them. But who would ever use nuclear weapons?

He decided the future was in advanced conventional weapons.

At that age I was quiet, and my parents never talked much, so I had hours of silence to reflect on things in the back seat of the station wagon — my stepdad didn't believe in listening to the radio either. Staring out the window at the white salt flats speeding by and the ghostly gray hills skirting the horizon, wondering why I was ever born, something happened. I remember it as a falling star, a point of light dropping from the sky and landing in the center of my forehead like a kiss, and a thought came to me — "You have to do something good with your life. You have to help people, because there is no God who's going to do it for us."

After a while I said out loud, If there is a God then the world is like an old music box, and He just wound it up and let it go.

My mom shuddered; she shifted uncomfortably and glanced fearfully at my stepdad. He cleared his throat — a nervous tick he still has — clenching and unclenching the steering wheel, and glancing intermittently at my mom with bloodshot eyes, not wanting to take his stare off the road. As usual, neither of them said anything to me, but from that moment on, my mom secretly vowed I'd become a Catholic nun.

They were holding two contradictory ideas in mind simultaneously — God and Science. Remember Keats called it Negative Capability: "…capable of being in uncertainties, Mysteries, doubts, without any irritable reaching after fact & reason—"?

Cognitive Dissonance is what they're throwing around these days. I said.

Right — confusion, anxiety and stress caused by holding two conflicting ideas at the same time. Most people live with "an acceptable level of stress" so high they'd actually deny they feel any anxiety at all despite that they're mentally and physically falling apart.

There's no conflict between mysticism and science, though. Most physicists I know recognize the Hindu vision of the expanding-collapsing multi-verse as accurate. It's the infantile view of God in Heaven and the Devil in Hell and humans stuck here or there or in Purgatory that contradicts science.

They were both raised culturally Catholic, but their parents didn't go to church, and neither did they. Now they took it up earnestly to make sure I became a nun — and for my stepdad to assuage his guilt for creating so many weapons of mass destruction. They started acting like zealot converts, even though deep down, religion for them was a superstition like putting an arm over their protective goggles — just in case — as they crouched in a trench twenty miles from ground zero, waiting for an atomic blast.

Converts are always the most faithless and the most fanatic, because in the back of every convert's mind there's a big doubt — they have no confidence things will work out, that karma will be karma; and no conviction their principles will produce the results they desire (that's why most of them switched religions in the first place!) especially when they see heathens all around them getting what they want — so fanatics bleed trust of the untrustworthy by lashing out with blind dogma, imposing control in order to make safely predictable the organism, to ease their own insecurity.

They took me to church with them every morning before I went to school, before my stepdad went off to work. Chloe said. They got me up at 5:15, in the darkness, to make the six o'clock mass, and brought me to nighttime prayer meetings twice a week after dinner, treating it all as some kind of rote duty.

* * * * *

At night we headed to Central Square, a neighborhood in Cambridge she called "the war zone" because of all the crime, but where all the best clubs were. Her favorite was The Cantab, short for Cantabridgian, the name for somebody who lives in Cambridge. It was tiny, dingy, and dark, with condensation dripping down the red lacquered walls from the sweat of the dancing crowd, and smelled like spilled beer and cigarette smoke. One of her roommates, a skinny red-headed northern Italian named Atilio played wailing guitar blues with his pick-up band The Tumbling Dice, while his girlfriend, Sofia, a buxom brown Umbrian fawned like a groupie.

Chloe's other roommate, Colin, came with his girlfriend Colette. They were both Irish. He was a Harvard grad student in Political Science, and he looked the part with his longish sandy hair, his rough gray tweed jacket and long black cotton scarf wrapped twice around. Colette was studying Irish Literature at Mount Holyoke, and could've stepped out of a 19th century portrait with her porcelain complexion and dark chocolate tresses in a vintage beaded black silk gown.

That dress looks beautiful on you, by the way. Chloe said.

Thanks. I was lucky to find it. You know the vintage store round the corner? There's that old wooden trunk I'd walked by a hundred times, but yesterday this little voice said to me, Take a gander, and I found this at the bottom.

I'm so jealous.

Don't be. You can borrow it.

Colin and Colette were both super patriotic, yet affable as they were, it wasn't too far a stretch to see them setting a bomb that blew the roof off a Belfast pub, English arms and legs flying every-where in a pink mist of blood. We sat at a table right next to the dance floor, drank Murphy's and John Powers and watched about thirty people work up a heat to the music in front of the band. Colin and Colette asked me all kinds of questions about who I was and where I came from and what I was doing there — I was exotic to them.

Chloe and I took a cab home with Colin and Colette. Atilio had to pack up his gear, and Sofia would wait for him, so they'd come later. We all sat in the living room; Colin put on some David Holmes, and broke out a bottle of Jameson, and we sipped it on the rocks, got absorbed in the Irish Trip Hop, and took some bong hits, which made everyone a little philosophical, resulting in one of those conversations where everyone's interior monolog strangely somehow seems related.

I've never met anyone "like me". I said. I've met people similar to me, or people who agreed with me, but never anyone "like me". Maybe it's the simplest truth in the world. That you'll never find anyone "like you", and that's what relationships are — dealing with someone who's not like you. But it doesn't diminish the fact it's one of the hardest things about this age.

Any age. Colette said. Lots of times in history there've been writers' movements and artists' movements where creative progressives meet and talk like they're all in it together. Now most artists act like any other artist is their enemy, unless they're one of the rare loners who don't even think about it.

She spoke in that Irish way where they aspirate the 't' at the end of a word.

…Which still doesn't negate that there's no general convergence or community anymore. She continued. We're all in it for ourselves.

Colin said, Actually, we're all in it together. Catholic, Protestant… Muslim, Jewish… They're just overlays to separate one group from another. We're animals. We were born and we're all going to die and go wherever animals go when they die. Simple as that.

I used to say we're only animals, but it's not true. Chloe replied.

That sounds so apocalyptic Christian anyway. I said. "We'll all abide in the bosom of the Lord by and by", so what does it matter that we defile the planet if we don't get what we want?

I never got the whole French "Petit Mort" thing. Colette said. I mean obviously people are dying every moment. It doesn't take sex.

Yeah, but when you say people die every moment that's *them* dying. Petit Mort is *you* dying. I responded.

To the Mind if someone leaves the room, they die. Chloe added. No big deal. "Wha's a come an' a go?" As my cousins would say.

I want a combination of Mormon afterlife and Islam. Colin joked. Mormons get a whole planet when they die. I'd be the God of the planet and the seventy-two virgins would worship me.

Colette smirked and shook her head.

But I could call for you if I wanted to. That's the only way a Mormon woman can get to Heaven, if her husband calls for her.

Who says I want to marry you? Colette responded.

You joke about it now. Chloe said. But everybody believes in God when they die — Oh, God! Oh, God! …Trust me, I've seen it.

Language separates us from animals. I said.

That depends on how you define language. Chloe retorted. Apes can sign.

I thought it was money. Colin interjected.

Not really. Chloe answered. The Primatology Center in Rome determined monkeys can assign value to tokens that represent different quantities of different foods — they can apply reason to symbols; that's money.

We're the only animals that cook. Colette asserted. People who eat junk food are like animals foraging, too lazy to prepare a meal.

It's clear there's a natural hierarchy among humans. Chloe concluded. Some have understood humanity is more than being an animal. More than grabbing all you can, getting all you want, and dying like a pig.

Colin chuckled.

I know it's not "kewl" to take spirituality seriously but when you get older, when you're dying, you're going to wish you'd gotten over your shame and fear and intellectual laziness. Chloe said. Your friends will probably scoff at you, or try to convince you not to be curious, or stop being your friends. But you'll find new friends. She added.

…The point is to acknowledge beings of higher intelligence, take part in their legacy, and see them as examples so we can evolve as a species rather than justify all our faults with rationalizations blaming our animal nature. Otherwise, we're just a bunch of walking corpses.

A deep silence fell on the room. Then Atilio burst in with his guitar case and Sofia in tow after packing up all their gear from the show.

Whazzup niggaaz?!

* * * * *

Everyone else went to bed and Chloe and I quietly listened to The Orb, when she suddenly blurted out, You can get a job at the Museum of Fine Arts! That would be perfect for you!

I sighed, and said, I'm going back to Colorado, Chloe.

Her expression lost some joy.

Then I asked, What about you? What are you going to do after your epiphany?

She collected her thoughts and replied, I'm going to give orgasms to as many people in the corporate world as possible.

5

Candy's Dead

"To be free of the past we have to go through it. The only way out is through. But for most people it's not enough to simply say, 'The past is gone, don't let it affect you.' It's true memories are only recurring thoughts with no more intrinsic weight than any others, but our bodies react to thoughts, and more to repeated ones we give more credence. That conditioned reaction is what needs to be undone in order to be free."

— Chloe Pentangeli, The Second Cycle

Sometimes it's best to be like a tree. A tree that isn't dead. It feels the sun and moves with the wind; its leaves change color with the season, fall off when snow comes, and grow back in spring — and it doesn't react to anything we say. Part of me wanted to tell Chloe, That sounds insane — going from corporate job to corporate job, from city to city, giving orgasms to as many people as possible. Who couldn't think of a hundred reasons to tell her not to? But a question is often more effective in getting to the heart of a matter than giving knee-jerk advice based on judgment. Anymore, I don't give advice to anyone unless they request it.

At first I simply asked, Why? As we walked the two-and-a-half mile loop around Fresh Pond.

I used to think sex was purely chemical. She said. Dopamine activates your reward circuitry in the mammalian brain nestled right beneath the rational neo-cortex. When you engage in any activity that furthers your survival or the continuation of your genes — whether it's eating, taking risks, achieving goals, or drinking water — your brain gets a shot of dopamine. And orgasm produces the largest dose of dopamine possible. So, I concluded we're all basically drug addicts. But now I see.

Because of your epiphany?

...Orgasm is a moment when the rational mind stops grasping, when the discursive mind completely shuts up — more powerful than any drug. That's our solution as Americans: just take a pill. Orgasm is an unequaled opportunity to cut through all the conventional selfish delusions and recognize the true limitless nature of Mind, to glimpse the ultimate truth that this world is a construct of our own creation, and all our greed and self-interest aren't going to amount to anything, so we might as well be kind to ourselves and to each other, and enjoy this hallucination.

You want to stop their minds?

We need to evolve as a species, Xavier, if we're going to keep from destroying ourselves and the planet. And we can only evolve if we're happy, because that's when we're not bogged down in memories or pining for an imaginary future, or even obsessing on the present. When you're completely happy doing something, are you thinking about anything at all?

...No, actually...

That's what athletes "call the zone". That's why time flies when you're having fun. Time is relative — if it even really exists at all. And that "no mind" is when we grow and change as human beings.

It sounds like fun for them, but what about you? That's going to be like mind rape.

...Not really. What's the first excuse anybody makes when faced with becoming part of the solution rather than staying part of the problem?

I don't know.

That's half of it: "I don't know what to do." People always claim they don't know where to start.

What if they really don't? I asked.

It's simple. She said. Be generous. Generosity makes us drop the conceptual barriers we erect to keep other people out, and for some "strange" reason that feels good.

I know lots of people who claim life isn't about being happy. I said.

The mantra of the miserable... She replied. Everybody works for what they think will be a positive outcome. Even if they're destroying themselves and the world, they're doing it because they truly believe it'll produce the best possible result. Call it what you want, but it's simplest just to say we want to be happy. And it's dawning on us happiness isn't only about what we can take, or what we can get. Look at all the file sharing on the Internet —music, videos, movies, literature. The surge in generosity is evidence humanity is evolving, and it's the impetus for further evolution. For the first time on this scale in history artists of all kinds are giving their work away, and that's part of the expression. There are more web-sites offering free things than there ever were brick and mortar institutions doing the same.

But that's only a tiny part of the picture. I retorted. Don't you think things are getting worse overall? If we stop carbon emissions tomorrow we'll suffer the effects of global warming for a hundred years. Wall Street and big corporations are making record profits but the world's teetering on the edge of another financial disaster that won't affect them at all. All kinds of violence is on the rise worldwide. I could go on and on.

…Well, in degenerate times the opportunities for personal transformation increase exponentially. It's now or never, I'm afraid.

But why the corporate world? I mean, I guess you could say they need it the most, but I can think of better places to start.

I always say start at the beginning. She answered. This goes way back. Plymouth was the first Puritanical colony, and they marched out with guns and bibles to conquer the "savages". But 30 miles north in what's Quincy now, 10 miles south of here, Thomas Morton founded Merrymount, where they made peace with the Algonquins, and accepted them as part of the community, and because of that, became richer than Plymouth, which pissed off the starving Puritans to no end. When are we ever going to learn Elitism, Racism, and Moralism are just bad business? Britain would still have their empire today if they shared the wealth instead of hoarding it. Merrymount didn't have the same restrictions against racial integration, drinking alcohol, having sex, or dancing, and the Puritan regime used that as a pretext to attack and destroy it, denouncing them as debauched pagans and licentious atheists leading degenerate lives. That was the moment we became a nation of moralistic sexual cowards, guilty self-destructive bingers, and self-interested malicious nihilists. They stomped out happiness.

Until the 60's when it exploded again. I offered.

But which was stomped out again by Hoover, Nixon, and Reaganism. Chloe added. Probably not to the same extent, but in general people are still so ashamed and guilty they don't even think they deserve happiness. I have to be careful when I say "happy". In the overly-caffeinated "Excited States" most people think happiness means "keyed-up giddy laughter at everything like a primetime sitcom soundtrack". I'm talking about relaxed joy with a good sense of humor. Joy is the vaccine against the Puritanical Virus. Everybody feels joyful after an orgasm.

That's true…

It's not like their ultimate goal is to be miserable. It's easy to think a corporate executive of a pesticide company who's responsible for polluting rivers and ruining the livelihoods of hundreds of small farmers, who believes happiness and well-being are delusions, takes pleasure in being malicious, but he's got a mandate to make profits for the shareholders no matter what, at any cost, and he honestly believes he's doing the best thing he can to maintain his own livelihood.

Come on… I said.

I know it's outrageous, but if you really look into it you'll see it's true. Don't get me wrong. I'm not one of those namby-pamby new agers with insipid smiles who can't say something negative about anybody or anything, as if that's less egotistical than pretending everything is cake and frosting. If you refuse to recognize someone as a corrupt asshole it doesn't help to call it snow when you get shit on. And if you insist a poop sandwich is the same thing as chocolate cake, then you better be willing to eat poop and be glad about it. There's nothing enlightened about being a Pollyanna doormat. The longer you avoid recognizing the world as it is, the harder it becomes to be honest with yourself, and the more stuck you become. Lots of love and light sycophants won't admit or can't feel they're completely miserable. And lots of corrupt assholes are happy as can be, or in any case think they are. And that's the problem.

That dirty executive would probably liken human beings to animals, citing self-preservation and caring for his family as his motivation to destroy others and profit from poisoning the earth, but that's where he'd be wrong. A monkey given access to a key will unlock the cage of an unfamiliar primate when food is brought, to share it. Even lab rats share food with unfamiliar rats that are restrained. No animals, not even reptiles, kill members of their own species in order to secure a food supply. Only human beings destroy each other again and again; and we have the means to eradicate ourselves completely with atomic bombs, the pinnacle of scientific imagination and creative intellect. Despite there's always been more than enough food for everyone on the planet, and even though the cold war has been over for more than a decade, the US and Russia still keep nuclear arsenals on 24-hour standby alert, ready to incinerate humanity at the touch of a button. But it's not human nature or animal nature to intentionally destroy our own kind.

The Puritanical Virus didn't start with the Puritans... I commented.

Every living thing on earth — plant or animal — shares the same DNA, except viruses. They have no DNA. They have to penetrate and corrupt a cell with healthy DNA in order to reproduce them-selves, so A), They can't simply mind their own business if they want to survive, and B), They want to change everyone different into what they are, which means, C) They won't stop until either they are destroyed or all other life forms on earth are

destroyed. They're not even strictly alive by
definition — they're called pseudo-living, like The
Undead. Puritanicals think happiness is irrelevant
and untrustworthy; and that possession, control, and
uniformity are the only true satisfactions in life, no
matter how miserable they are, and the corporate
world is the most pervasive outbreak of that
contagion.

I guess it would be easier to infiltrate the
corporate world or Wall Street than the government;
and they control government more than the
government controls them. I said — weirdly
beginning to catch her drift.

Politicians are notoriously sluttier, but I could
definitely reach more people in the corporate world,
which is important since what we've always faced is
a tiny fraction of humanity that holds power over
the majority — and they're desperate now to
perpetuate their dying strain as more and more
humans see the light.

I wondered if I could wrap my mind around the
whole thing.

It is mind blowing to think sexual freedom is a
force so powerful the government tries to control it
with laws and censorship. I commented.

Well, as you expand your consciousness you
begin to see the world in a new way and things you
would have accepted without challenge become
questionable. She continued. Once you start to
explore sexuality you feel empowered, which is
why government tries to control it, because if
you're sexually empowered pretty soon you start to
question the political authority trying to box it in.
That's exactly what happened in the 60's.

…I'm sorry, but I keep picturing that Vietnamese monk setting himself on fire to protest the war. I said, and my voice shook a little.

She held my hand and looked me in the eye, I'll be fine… I like the comparison though. This body is temporary.

So you're really going to try to give them all orgasms? I asked.

I'm going to give them all some love.

…Buy lots of condoms.

Of course I will. Call me crazy but do not call me stupid.

Cupid…

Gray clouds massed in the west over angled rooftops and barren trees; the wind gusted and skimmed mist off the water's surface, getting choppy with the coming turmoil.

* * * * *

When did you first learn about sex? I asked. Not necessarily your first sexual experience, but who taught you?

It was something I'd always wanted to know about her. I mean, my parents told me about sex when I was four years old, and I had no idea what the hell they were talking about, but they felt like they'd performed their duty — case closed. Wash their hands. Whew!

My parents never told me anything. She said, reading my mind.

Who was it? I asked.

She smiled, remembering.

Her name was Candy. She was the first and only person I've ever fallen in love with. She didn't teach me everything — I learned a lot on my own afterward — but she was my first instructor, so to speak.

I grew up on the west side of Omaha, where mostly white people lived. The town is racially divided. Voluntary segregation… It's unpopular to admit it these days but still, after all the civil rights upheaval of the 60's, if you're white and go too far into the black side they'll beat you up just because you're white. If you're black and go too far into the white side, the cops will arrest you just because you're black. I got both reactions at different times.

I was going to an expensive private school on the west side where everybody was on Ritalin and Adderall and Vyvanse. The main office was like a pharmacy with hundreds of little white paper bags stapled shut through the prescription note filling an entire 12-foot-long counter because everybody's doctors had their drugs sent directly to the school for easy pick-up. If somebody wanted to make a little extra cash around exam time they'd sell their supply, and the buyers would have these all night study sessions focused like lasers.

When I was twelve my mom decided I was growing up without any sense of ethnic diversity, so she insisted we move to "the ghetto". My stepdad found this abandoned white mansion on a hill on the east side, in what used to be a wealthy neighborhood half-a-century ago, that since became lower middle class when all the white people evacuated to the suburbs.

At one time the area was filled with palatial homes, but most of them were torn down and replaced with cheap boxy apartment buildings, and the rest were either abandoned or chopped up into separate units. He bought it for a steal and had it fixed up. It was three stories tall with a slate shingled roof and white pillars supporting the portico over the front porch, surrounded by a huge yard, a rough stone wall topped with tall bushes in front, and an old-fashioned black wrought iron fence all around. Inside, my stepdad had the floors and stairs carpeted low-pile gray because he thought hardwood was cold. He left the original woodwork, though, and had the walls painted off-white.

Our neighbors immediately stole our riding mower out of the free-standing garage in back. They stole my pet rabbit Walter that I kept in a hutch outside. They stole my stepdad's dog, Princess, a little Pomeranian that liked to stray to the street end of the long semi-circular driveway that curved around the house to the garage in back. They broke into the house as soon as we weren't there and stole the TV before we had the alarm put in; they pelted us with rocks whenever we were standing on the porch or in the yard in plain view. A real cultural education. The welcome reception lasted about a month.

One day I made friends with a mixed-race girl down the street named Terry. She was pretty, with vanilla-colored skin, part Asian, part white, straight dark brown hair cut short, and freckles. She was a cute tomboy, my age, and pretty soon we did everything together. We were instant best friends. My parents left me alone after church on Sunday when they went to visit their church friends. The only reason I liked Sunday was because I had hours to myself, or with Terry.

I remember getting into a fight with her over building an igloo that winter. I wanted to pack the snow into a kitchen pot and make blocks and then stack the blocks to build the dome. She wanted to make a giant pile of snow, pack it down, and then hollow it out with big serving spoons and a trowel. Every time I stacked up blocks, Terry dumped snow on them and belly-flopped on top to pack the pile down. It didn't take long till we were pushing each other and shouting. We couldn't really hurt each other in our big down coats and mittens; I tackled her and we wrestled in the snow, aggressively at first, but soon our movements slowed like we were moving through molasses, and our bodies started to tingle and pulse. We laid there sweating, breathing steamy breaths into each other's faces, gazing into each other's eyes. She smelled like a bowl of vanilla ice cream left out too long, or like eggnog. Her scent made me dizzy.

Then Terry jumped up and said, You know what? Build it yourself! And she stomped home through the snow.

The next weekend Terry came over to watch TV and pop popcorn, and for the first time she brought her sister Candy... I was mesmerized... Candy was tall and lanky, sixteen-years-old, with long wavy dark brown hair, small breasts; the same French Vanilla skin, but a little bit more Asian looking. She sat on a cushion on the floor like a Thai princess, with both legs to one side, and looked so euro-cool in a black mini-skirt and a long-sleeve navy and white horizontally-striped sailor's shirt. She seemed older than sixteen and I wondered what she was doing hanging out with two twelve-year-olds. Maybe she wanted to feel like a kid again?

Her facial features were cat-like, and she moved and behaved like a cat: demure, graceful, solitary, somehow inviting, yet ultimately unreach-able. There was something wild about her too, like an animal that hadn't truly been tamed, that hadn't had its killer instinct bred out of it. Most dogs will scavenge, or find a new master, or simply die if you throw them out. A cat will immediately start to hunt.

She turned and looked me in the eyes, smiled, then glanced away and stared at the TV, put a piece of popcorn in her mouth, and chewed with her head held high. She was so beautiful I could barely form a sentence, too afraid to sound stupid. Plus I didn't want to make Terry mad. Even then I had a sense Terry had other girlfriends who she'd introduced to Candy, and as soon as she did they forgot all about her. It felt like a test, but as soon as I saw Candy I failed, like all the other girls. Terry shifted and sighed on the couch as I couldn't take my eyes off Candy.

Finally, I asked her, Do you have a boyfriend?

She said, Yeah. His name's Otis. He's a lot older. Except I guess he's not really my boyfriend. Otis is my pimp.

It felt like a plug got pulled somewhere and my insides ran out, my heart the last thing to circle the drain and disappear, leaving me an empty shell. Then I thought, I could still kiss her at least...

I asked nervously, Do you want to come over sometime if it's just you and me?

She looked at me and smiled and shrugged one slender shoulder, Sure. You're cute.

Terry sighed, exasperated, and rolled her eyes, Gyod!

She got up and stormed out the front door, and slammed it behind her. I felt bad about making Terry mad, but all I had to do was return my gaze to Candy and I forgot all about it.

Pretty soon Candy left too, turned to me at the front door and said, Call me next Sunday.

Candy's Dead

That whole week was glacial. School, homework, eating, watching TV, church, prayer meetings, my parents — it was all a blurry background behind the only clear image I could see: the picture of Candy in my mind as I opened the front door, let her in, she smiled, stepped inside, and I closed the door and locked it behind her.

It happened just like that on Sunday. Mesmerized by her hips swaying in a black miniskirt, feet in black flats, wearing a fuchsia t-shirt with a black skull-and-crossbones that read "Bow Wow Wow" as she came inside; a black spaghetti-strap purse dangling from her shoulder. I led her upstairs to my bedroom, we sat on my white comforter, and I glanced at her nervously.

I asked her, Do you like ABC?

She smiled like I was cute in a pathetic sort of way.

They're alright. Put this on.

She handed me a Cocteau Twins cassette, "Head Over Heels", and I played it.

Where do you go to school? I asked.

I dropped out last year.

Oh…

I'm teaching myself. I'm studying French right now. I like the way it sounds.

Then I didn't know what to say. I tried to think of something. She seemed like she enjoyed watching me squirm, adjusted the pillows and relaxed.

Finally, I said shyly, Let's take a bath together.

She let out a short laugh. Her look said, You're such a little girl.

After a second, though, she responded, Okay.

She strode to the bathroom taking off her t-shirt as she went and I followed. She must have seen it when we walked up. She slipped out of her white bra, miniskirt and pink panties as the tub filled, and got in.

She arched her eyebrows and looked at me as I stood there frozen, and said, Well?

I undressed fast and got in the tub facing her.

I want you to wash my back. She said.

Okay.

I stood up quickly and got in behind her. I soaped and lathered my hands and rubbed her back reverently like she was a priceless marble sculpture. I filled my cupped hands and rinsed her back and then reached around and gently folded my fingers around her breasts, each one just a handful, and held her like that with my cheek against her spine, feeling the life energy pulse through my hands up my arms and through my whole body. Candy looked pensively down at the water, and we breathed in unison: long, quiet breaths.

Finally, she straightened up, and said, Let's go back to your room...

We got out and each took one of the meticulously folded maroon bath towels from the racks, and dried off.

She sat naked on the bed, looked me in the eye and said, I'm going to show you everything.

I was stunned, and tried to figure out what she meant. I pictured her opening up her chest and showing me all her internal organs, and the whole picture dissolving in a blaze of white light. She reached out and pulled me toward her and kissed my mouth passionately. Her mouth was hot, and her silky skin steamed from the heat of the bath, and she smelled sweet like the calendula soap, but there was something cold about her. I didn't care. She took a strap-on out of her purse and I gave myself to her... I had my first orgasm. It felt like the whole universe was exploding.

When it was finished, she closed her eyes, and her expression changed to a calm, innocent, contented smile, and for the first time, she looked as young as me. We melted into a single pool of warm golden honey, and just breathed.

I asked her, Why are you a prostitute?

Because my mom needs the money.

She makes you do it?

She sighed, and said, Yeah.

I was quiet.

She's crazy. She Said. She can't work. My dad's not around. Crazy hippie... Went to live in some Hindu monastery in India...

I was still quiet.

Then she blurted out, Don't feel sorry for me. If you're working you're a whore. It's only little kids and crazy people who aren't.

Just then I heard the front door open downstairs and my stepdad calling for me, Chloe?

I leapt out of bed, Get your clothes on!

She ran quickly to the bathroom to get her panties, skirt, and t-shirt; I dressed frantically.

That was the end. I felt like telling her to run away, to come stay in our basement, to do something — anything — but then I thought, What can she do? She's only sixteen; she has to take care of her mom and Terry. And somehow I could tell that was the last time I would ever see her. Because I was in love with her, and I didn't know why, but I knew she wouldn't stand for that.

* * * * *

It was spring, and my heart ached constantly, and everything seemed excruciating: the vivid blue sky and white feathery clouds through my bedroom window, like a framed moving painting on the off-white walls, as I lay on my bed listening to This Mortal Coil's version of Tim Buckley's "Song to the Siren". I wandered aimlessly in the yard, touching the trembling little buds on the mulberry bushes lining the fence by the street, laden with small patches of wet snow, feeling the frigid gentle breeze kiss my warm neck, inhaling the musty smell of melting icicles, glistening in rainbows, dripping liquid light — it all took my breath away and made cold ecstatic tears well in my eyes. My whole body vibrated with unbearable joy like an electrified sponge, and I felt alive for the first time in my life.

I called Candy incessantly for weeks; she would always make some excuse about why she couldn't come over, or say she would but never show up. At least twice I waited all day Sunday with a bathtub full of hot water gone cold, until finally I pulled the plug and let the water drain out.

Did you try going over to her house? I asked.

I wasn't allowed to, although I probably could have snuck out on Sunday when my parents were gone. But I was way too romantic. It was more tragically beautiful to never see her again.

Well, you had to at least have seen her from a distance. She lived close by, right?

Occasionally I saw her from the back window of our station wagon as we got home from prayer meeting at night — waiting by the bus stop with too much make-up on, wearing black patent leather go-go boots reflecting the pink streetlights, in a skin-tight t-shirt, and a dark miniskirt so short you could see the bottom part of her ass cheeks... going down-town.

* * * * *

I tried to get in touch with her freshman year and Terry answered the phone. She told me Candy was overseas but she'd be back in a few weeks. Their dad came home from India and somehow he'd made a lot of money over there. Chloe explained. He bought a house in a middle-class part of Omaha in the no-man's land between the white and black sides, and sent Candy on a trip. Their mom was in an institution now, and Terry and her dad lived in the "new" house as he fixed it up, and so would Candy as soon as she got back from abroad.

She invited me to Candy's Welcome Home party. Chloe said. I met a woman in the library — my work/study job — who was driving to Omaha for Christmas break that wanted somebody to share gas, so I got a ride in her old red Saab 900. She played Bob Dylan the whole way, and smoked Camel unfiltereds. I heard "Lay Lady Lay" about a billion times.

When I got to the big red brick house, Terry let me in and as soon as I walked through the front door, there was Candy descending the staircase in the glow of track lighting, everything else dark around her, like a music video. Long wavy brown hair blown by some inexplicable breeze, maple eyes glimmering, gently smiling, wrinkled white long-sleeved cotton shirt fluttering, loose field-gray linen cargoes, the scent of jasmine, and a faint white glow around her — "Lay Lady Lay" still echoing in my mind. My breathing slowed just to see her, and my heart pounded. All I wanted was to feel her warm breath against my neck again.

She hugged me, and said, It's good to see you! What've you been up to?

I'm in school in Boulder, studying theoretical physics.

How's that going?

I like it.

By the way, I'm going by my full name now — Candice.

Candice fits you.

How are your mom and stepdad? She asked.

They're alright I guess. We rarely talk now that I'm in school. Like they're glad to get rid of me… It looks like you and your dad have a whole new relationship.

He's totally different. It's like I'm meeting him for the first time.

Are you still…

A prostitute?

I didn't want to…

It's alright. I've come to terms with it. It's not how I survive. I don't have a pimp. Every now and then if I need some cash I'm not opposed to it — like having a one night stand — but I'm the boss; and I charge a lot more for it.

There were about 30 other people there, and it was pretty low key — people sitting on couches and chairs in the shadowy living room to the left of the stairs, a girl sitting on the bench at a baby grand piano, talking to a guy leaning against it next to her, everyone sipping drinks; ambient electronic music playing.

She was friendly, and sweet, and gazed into my eyes as we spoke. She traveled all over England, France, Spain, Italy, Greece, and she went to

wineries, and beaches, and every great art museum.
She heard music she'd never heard before, ate food
she'd never tasted, bought perfume you can't even
find here, and got tons of beautiful clothes. She had
to buy another suitcase to bring it all back.

Did you meet anyone over there?

Lots of people. They're so much more forward
than we are. Men *and* women.

Who was your favorite?

She sighed. I was walking on Paradise Beach
on Mykonos, trying to find a place to sit. This was
in August so it was crowded, and everybody who
had a spot was completely naked. I found an open
space and lay on my towel and took off my bikini,
and in the distance I saw this dark handsome guy
with thick dark curls, smiling and walking toward
me with an open bottle of wine in one hand and two
glasses in the other.

He was naked too?

Not yet. He still had his shorts on, but they
were some little tight Speedos. You know what I
mean. He sat down right next to me and said in
English, Would you like to share some wine? I said,
Okay. And he poured us some chilled dry rosé.
Really good; not like that pink Zinfandel swill you
get here.

I don't care about the wine! What about him?

His name is Hassan. He's Moroccan, going to
school in Toulouse studying architecture. Really
sweet... he invited me to dinner.

Where?

It was this seafood taverna right by the marina
and we sat outside with the lights of the town
reflecting on the water. I had grilled langoustines—

What's that?

They're halfway between a lobster and a shrimp. They have little claws. He had sea bass and we drank a bottle of white wine, and then went to his place — he was renting a house with a couple of his school friends — and we made love outside in the pool under the stars and a palm tree.

Was it really sweet like making love, or was it wild like fucking, or "just business" like having sex.

It was definitely making love. He was gentle and beautiful. His name means beautiful.

I sighed, and asked, So, what's next?

I don't know. That's what I'm trying to figure out.

Terry came over and said, Why don't you guys go up to my room? You can have some privacy.

Candice's room wasn't ready — she didn't have a bed yet and it was all taped up with drop cloths laid down ready to be painted — so we followed Terry upstairs. Terry put on "Pleasure of Love" by the Tom Tom Club, and left. Neither of us knew what to say. She took my hand gently. Then spontaneously, I held her waist, and we slow-danced close under low lamp light, everything white glowing golden: the walls, the curtains, the down comforter, her pillows.

She asked, Is this okay?

I said, Yeah…

It felt like we were both radiating wavy energy streams entwined in a shimmering rainbow halo around us as we breathed in each other's long hot out-breaths. I saw a vision of the two of us over our heads dancing gracefully, turning in a circle at arm's length. I kissed her — the longest, most tender kiss I've ever had. She pulled away, short of breath, and blushed. I felt my whole body tingling and vibrating and was trying to catch my breath too.

Candy's Dead

Sorry... I have to sit down. She sat on the edge of the bed and asked, Do you feel that?

I said, Yes.

I've never had a physiological reaction to someone before.

Neither have I.

This is weird.

She stared at me with big glassy eyes.

* * * * *

We called each other and emailed everyday for months until one day hers just stopped. After a week of worrying I called Terry and asked her if anything was going on with Candice. There was silence on the other end of the line...

Finally she said, Candy's dead...

...What?

It was a freak accident. She got out of the shower and dropped the blow dryer. She was electrocuted...

I could hear in her voice that she was really upset but I didn't want to believe it.

I said, They're supposed to shut off if they hit water.

Hers didn't. Terry continued. It was only a couple of drops... I'm not kidding. Candy's dead...

The silence built till it was a roar in my head... I skipped class, stayed in bed and cried for two weeks.

6

If You Don't Know You're Alive...

"She was like Arthur on his quest for the Grail. In a wasteland of people leading inauthentic lives the heroine enters the forest at a point where only she had chosen — a self-directed, not over-mastered field of action — where it was darkest, and there was no path... the corporate world. Only she could see and enter the Holy castle of the Grail because she alone had the spiritual readiness. Her "sword" represented that energy of clarity and knowledge and decisiveness — that penetrating insight. Only she could cross into the world of the Goddess who informs all things."

— excerpt from a Time interview with Xavier Ibarra

It was the best job I ever had in my life. Aims Community College was a mile east of town and I rode my bike to work. The majority of my students were from Mexico, but some were from El Salvador, Nicaragua, Colombia, even Peru; and I got to speak Spanish everyday. I felt like I was traveling when I went to school. Granted, they thought we were insane with our total disregard for family, the terrible food we eat that makes us obese, our constant scrambling only for money, our delusional desire for romantic love, our lack of real spirituality. And they told me about the countries they loved, their food, their families; their histories. But they liked the US too, and felt like we didn't even like it as much as they do, with all our complaining and political fighting. I actually looked forward to going to work everyday.

I was lucky because the text for ESL was a Picture Dictionary which required no lesson plan. I had zero preparation for class, no tests to give, and no homework to grade, so when I left the classroom I dropped the job completely and had all my free time for writing. Out in the middle of nowhere there was nothing else to do.

Fort Lupton is flat in every sense of the word, population 6,787, spreading out on a grid from the stoplight at the main intersection of County Road 12½ and Denver Avenue on the plains that stretch east from the mountains 200 miles to the border. Once I went to the local bar out of utter boredom and a little curiosity and ended up striking up a conversation with the bartender, Tracy. She was thin, flat-chested, and pretty, with long brown hair, wearing a white wife-beater and black skinny-jeans, twenty-three years old. There were only two other guys in there at the time and they both sat several seats apart from each other — and me — hunched over pints of beer, drinking slowly as Toby Keith twanged and jangled on the jukebox. I ordered a pint of Fat Tire and it had barely any fizz in it.

Sorry, hardly anybody drinks that. Tracy said. The keg needs to be changed. Almost everybody's a Bud Light or Corona man around here. She added. After a while she sighed and said, I want to get pregnant again.

Why? I asked. Taken aback after the little small talk we'd made where she'd already mentioned she was a single mom with two kids, sipping a beer. Working at a small town bar, why would she want more kids?

Because my boobs got so big! I want to get a boob job but I can't afford it.

...I didn't go back after that.

* * * * *

I asked Chloe if I could chronicle her experiences as a temp as she traveled around working for different companies and she agreed. We scheduled a call every Sunday — a phone date — and she'd tell me what she'd been up to for the past week. I got one of those phone recording devices so I wouldn't have to worry about deciphering my notes or messy handwriting and we could talk freely.

Chloe signed up with a bunch of employment agencies in Boston and waited. She let her long corn-rows out and got a haircut that was elegant, sophisticated and professional. Within a week one agency got her a job, and several more after that.

The company you're with is called Discovery? I asked.

What an innocuous name! She said. They're professional corporate spies! They get paid by big businesses to turn up information about their competitors. They had me cold-calling companies asking about their profit margins on certain products. Of course the people who answered wanted to know, Who is this? Who wants that information? One of the middle managers told me, Tone it down. Be more nonchalant. Make them brag. This crap really goes on…

That's what I was warning you about. I reminded her.

I didn't prove to be too good at it so they switched me to entering data about product placement in stores. Post Cereal wanted to know if Safeway was putting their product on the top shelf instead of Kellogg's, because where it was placed affected how well it sold. So somebody in Discovery went to hundreds of supermarkets and recorded that Kellogg's was in fact on the top shelf

in the majority. So, Post would then call Safeway
and tell them to put their cereal on the top shelf.
And then Kellogg's would retaliate. The nightmare
life of a stock clerk…

* * * * *

One day Chloe asked her boss Rick out to
lunch, and they walked to one of those Japanese
places where they cook the food in front of you. It
was his favorite place. He liked to watch the chefs
work because that's all he ever did — work. They
sat next to each other facing the chef as he whirled
knives around, and chopped up shrimp and steak
and vegetables and grilled them. The place was
wide and dark except for lights over the chef's
stations, and decorated with framed Japanese
calligraphies, and samurai swords on racks over
dark green tiled pillars, and large exotic plants in
big dark pots on the floor. Rick was handsome in a
Channing Tatum sort of way — but way smarter —
with a casual wardrobe straight out of Nordstrom.
He was good humored, and cooler than most people
in the office, albeit kind of high strung.

His heel bounced nervously on the floor as they
ate; he fiddled with his napkin, bit his fingernails,
and talked incessantly.

He said, We wonder why the company's
struggling when executives and managers all over
the country fly down to corporate headquarters in
Florida in thousand dollar suits for a meeting over
hundred dollar plates and twenty dollar cocktails,
only to say, Yes, we all agree on the new strategy.
When we could just as easily send an email…

Rick gulped his beer and told Chloe he studied
drama in college and always wanted to direct plays

or films, but decided to be more practical. He was stressed to the limit as the company tried to squeeze every ounce of productivity out of him, and he hated it, but at the same time he felt like he had to do it because he was going to get married again in six months. It would be his third attempt, and this was supposed to be for the long haul...

Chloe ordered a bottle of white Bordeaux to help him relax and he acted shocked at first, but he had no trouble drinking it.

She asked him, How old are you?

Thirty-four.

You know Joel Schumacher?

Yeah, he directed "Batman Forever" with Val Kilmer.

He was thirty-five when he first went to Hollywood — with no experience in the film industry. It's not too late. She said. If you don't know you're alive you might as well be dead.

He changed the subject, What about you? You studied theoretical physics?

I'd have to get a PhD if I wanted to do anything professionally. I'm taking a break from school right now.

As they got tipsier Chloe got more forward, briefly touching his hand as they talked, laughing at his jokes, touching his knee. It's so easy for a woman to seduce a man. Men have libraries full of books on how to succeed with women. All a woman has to do is let a man know she wants him, and say yes — generally speaking. And the fact Rick's fiancé was Russian, living in Russia, definitely worked in Chloe's favor.

After two divorces, Rick's friends got together and chipped in for a vacation to Russia, sort of as a joke, where the sole purpose of the trip was to find a wife. It was a two-week package deal of twelve prearranged dates with Russian women each looking for an American husband. Rick thought he had nothing to lose. At the very least he would have a dozen nights out in beautiful St. Petersburg with beautiful women who all wanted to marry him, fly home, and have a good laugh with his friends. His third date was with Katya, a brunette with green eyes, and the next day he cancelled all his other dates and asked to see only her for the remainder of the trip. When it was time to go, he proposed to her, and of course she said yes. As soon as he got home he picked out a $10,000 engagement ring and sent it. Now he was in the middle of a mandatory two-year waiting period. He could go visit her, but she couldn't legally come to the United States. He would be a pushover for Chloe.

Out of the blue, she put her hand on his thigh and he blushed, turned away, and talked nervously about work and mundane things, looking down at the tabletop, pretending her hand wasn't really there. Chloe soon discovered prolonged physical contact with no context or explanation is a door opener in most situations.

He said, Do you think we should get another bottle? I mean, I don't know, it's really good, but I don't want to get drunk. I have work to do, and you've got all those spreadsheets… And he babbled on.

Chloe grinned and asked, Do *you* think we should get another one?

He waved to the waiter.

* * * * *

They were both tipsy, and alone in the elevator back up to the office. Chloe pushed the button for the top floor, and as soon as the doors closed she pulled Rick close and kissed him. He responded wholeheartedly and slid one hand up the inside of her thigh, hiking up her short skirt.

Things definitely took a surreal turn for Rick after that. Chloe shattered his everyday perception of the workplace by doing something completely unexpected — first, all the wine; and then kissing him in the elevator. It made it seem to him like anything was possible after that. And that was all that really mattered to her — him feeling he wasn't really stuck.

They stepped out on the roof; he took a deep breath and surveyed the Boston skyline, and surrounding waters.

She took his hand and led him to the elevator room where the electric motors that raised and lowered the elevators were housed. They were Japanese-made and ran quietly. It smelled like dust, machine oil, and sparks — that metallic electrical smell.

She sat on the edge of the counter next to the elevator control panel and breathed in his ear, Go slow...

The elevator motors went off and on, wheels and cables spinning back and forth, cars moving up and down through dark shafts, bringing people back to their offices after lunch, or taking people down for late lunches at one of the hundreds of restaurants downtown.

Watch your mind when you come. She whispered. Matter, Energy, and Mind are every-thing in the universe, they're interdependent; that's why anything you can imagine for yourself is possible.

Afterward, shaking violently, he staggered away from her, and leaned up against the wall, trying to catch his breath. She smiled and slipped off the counter.

He didn't say much in the elevator back down to the office — still in a dream world — but he did manage to ask, How much longer are you here?

Trying to hold on. Clinging to the safe and familiar, refusing to take risks or be flexible was the fast track to the grave in Chloe's mind. It basically came down to a mathematical equation for her. We always have three options to find satisfaction: to accept something, to reject it, or to ignore it. That's a 33 $\frac{1}{3}$% chance of getting what we want. However, if we accept something, odds are we'll become dissatisfied with that choice over time. So, if later a similar situation arises where a choice between the same three options is available, and we don't ignore it, it's best not to cling to our old position because if we accept the new situation, the odds of finding satisfaction jump to 66 $\frac{2}{3}$%. Simple math.

Chloe would later discover a fourth option that would guarantee 100% satisfaction, but she was a long way from that yet.

You know this probably won't become an exclusive or a regular thing. She said.

Oh, I know. He replied.

He looked at her as if he may have really understood. Rick was the seventh man in the office she'd given an orgasm, and she had ten more men and six more women to go, to complete the job.

* * * * *

One executive, Nancy Maugham, came back after a week off for emergency surgery. Chloe overheard her talking with Cliff, one of the other executives. She'd been depressed and weak, and at first the doctor told her she had liver cancer. That's a bad one because she would have six months tops if she really had it. Lucky for her, it was a mis-diagnosis.

It's like Russian Roulette with these doctors! She said. I wanted to kill him!

Good thing he was wrong. Cliff responded.

You They didn't even put me under. He gave me a local, cut a hole, stuck in a tube, and sucked it out.

Be glad it was only an abscess.

You don't think I'm glad?

You sound upset.

He scared me to death!

It made Cliff uncomfortable to talk about emotions, so the thought of consoling Nancy never even crossed his mind. The urgent compulsion to quickly change the subject overrode everything. The topic of conversation was death, so he moved on to the next item.

Did you hear about Lloyd?

No. What?

This happened while you were gone. You know he had chronic fatigue ever since he got divorced?

Yeah?

His wife was the one that wanted it. Cliff said. She whined about how they never slept together anymore, and all he cared about was making money, and she wanted to "really enjoy life"... and some other eastern spirituality bullshit. Now *there's* somebody who *really* doesn't know what's going on...

If You Don't Know You're Alive...

That's what Cliff really said. He conceived of
life as an ugly brutal war under a requisite whitewash of civility. The saying he repeated over and
over was, "The ultimate expression of appreciation
is to acquire." The more possessions he piled up, the
more wealth he secured, regardless at whose
expense, the more victorious he thought he was.
Nancy didn't buy into that nightmare, but she didn't
want to push back. She didn't have the strength to
argue with Cliff after what she'd just been through.

Okay, I get it... She said.

Cliff was the one who told employees they
didn't have to turn off their computers or the lights
at night. Global warming is a hoax. He laughed a
strained nervy laugh about his cruise vacation near
the Cayman Islands where the ship's crew dumped
tons of garbage overboard in plastic bags, and he
smugly likened it to the fact that Boston discretely
built a pipeline fifty miles out and pumps its sewage
directly into the ocean. Ha, ha... From your ass to
the sea... Humans are the only land animals that
consciously shit in their own water supply.

Remember he took a week off right before you
left? Cliff said. One of his neighbors smelled a
stench coming from his house and called the police.
They found him dead cooking on a heating pad.
Chronic fatigue turned out to be fatal fatigue.

His blasé description irritated Nancy to no end.
She decided to challenge him.

And how did that make you feel?

Her question startled him and confused him.

What do you mean?

I mean what emotions did you feel when you
heard Lloyd was dead?

...I didn't feel anything.

He sounded defensive.

Nothing at all?

I felt nothing. He confirmed.

You could yell at him, you could slap him, you could spit in his face, you could stab him or shoot him, and all he would do is stare back at you with those numb dead eyes.

You're like a dead tree, Cliff. One day you're just going to fall over and rot! Nancy shouted.

Cliff was dumb-shocked. Nancy stormed out of his office looking shaken, stopped abruptly, and collected herself with a few deep breaths. Chloe straightened up and looked busy to give the impression she hadn't been hanging on every word of their conversation. Nancy walked slowly toward Chloe's desk. She stopped again when she saw her, having a moment where she noticed things she usually didn't.

I haven't seen you here before. Nancy said.

I'm a temp. Chloe Pentangeli.

She held out her hand and Nancy shook it.

Nancy Maugham. What are you working on?

I'm working on some product placement spreadsheets for Rick, and helping out IT a little. Chloe added.

Good to have you. Nancy smiled and blushed; her eyes twinkled, and she walked on.

The following week Cliff got hit by a truck walking back from lunch, crossing the street while texting, not paying attention. He was crushed to death a block from the office, his skull exploding on the asphalt like a ripe cantaloupe under the truck's front tire, brains spraying all over the pavement.

Nancy didn't take it well, but now she smiled every time she saw Chloe, and made a point of passing by her desk several times a day. She asked her to do a PowerPoint presentation for one of her meetings. Chloe never used Power-Point before but it wasn't hard to figure out. She gave her a full color presentation with company graphics and Nancy gushed over it. She was pretty for fifty-five, with gray eyes and auburn hair, and her Jackie-O Chanel suits, but she didn't let anybody close to her. Chloe found out she'd divorced her husband three years earlier and hadn't had a partner since.

Finally, on Friday Nancy stood over Chloe's desk with a red face and said, You know, my home computer's been acting up. I went online the other day, and the firewall was disabled, and it kept saying a DLL file was missing...

You got hacked. She told her. I can fix it for you.

Do you think you could come over on Saturday around three o'clock?

Sure.

Nancy blushed again and said, See you then.

She handed Chloe her card, and walked away. The card already had her home address and personal phone number written on the back. Chloe put it in her purse and continued with her product placement spreadsheets.

* * * * *

On Saturday, she got to Nancy's house right across from Boston Common on Beacon Hill, and heard loud music inside. It was a beautiful brown-stone with a wide stairway up to the black lacquered front door. Surprisingly, she found it ajar. She went in and locked the door behind her, and called Nancy, shouting over the blasting "Gypsy" by Fleetwood Mac. The place had all original antique woodwork and paneling painted glossy white, and

118

an authentic gilt-framed Renoir hanging in the foyer over a giant white Chinese vase with two cobalt blue dragons on it illuminated by rays of sunlight from a nearby window. She heard a faint reply from upstairs, and went up the wide blue carpeted flight listening to the hiss of the shower getting louder and louder. Steam poured out of the slightly open bathroom door near the top, backlit by a circular window at the far end of the hall. In the sweltering white bathroom there was a claw-foot tub and a rounded sink with classic nickel fixtures and the floor was tiled with little white hexagons, all lit by two tall old windows; she watched Nancy's pink figure moving slowly behind frosted glass as she set down her shoulder bag, got undressed, and took out the gleaming chrome strap-on.

Chloe didn't see any fundamental difference between having sex with a man and having sex with a woman. We all have buttons people can push. It didn't matter to her who pushed her buttons — whether it was a man or woman — and she didn't mind whose buttons she pushed these days either as long as she gave them an orgasm. She believed the more evolved a person is, the less specifically male or female they were anyway. And she had no qualms about having sex with herself. She knew a few hipsters who liked to conflagrate masturbation into some kind of sweeping shift in consciousness, "A 'new' centrality of Self resulting from the death of Family, Society, God, and the Couple, leaving us with self-sexual gratification as a higher form of self-love." Please… Chloe thought they were socially retarded wankers who preferred to hide at home and shamefully touch themselves, not out of some kind of "advanced evolution" but a juvenile fear of putting themselves out there and actually meeting a sexual partner. To her masturbation was no more than a viable temporary alternative.

She said, Hi Nancy, it's me, Chloe... And then opened the door to the shower.

Nancy glared at the strap-on and gazed up at Chloe with big round eyes. As they made love Nancy ran one hand shakily through her wet hair, and then in a jagged line over the glass leaving a streak mark through the condensation punctuated by peaks marking Chloe's thrusting rhythm as she pressed her cheek up against the cold translucent pane. Soon, though, Nancy started hyperventilating, and said, I've got to get out of here. I can't breathe. In the cool air outside, on the chilly white tiles, Nancy wobbled on her feet, a little weak in the knees, and held onto Chloe. Wait. She said. I'm getting a head rush.

Chloe put her arm around her, and Nancy kept running her hand shakily through her wet reddish hair. After a few deep breaths they went to her bedroom. Nancy laid on her side on the king size bed. Chloe got out some more equipment.

Have you ever done it DP? Chloe asked.

Nancy looked mystified.

Double Penetration.

Nancy slowly shook her head, staring.

After Nancy had several more orgasms, she curled up, arms wrapped around herself in fetal position with her eyes closed, shivering.

Chloe asked her, Are you alright?

She nodded slowly.

Chloe saw Nancy's laptop on the desk in the bedroom, and asked her, Is that the computer with the problem?

Nancy nodded again. Chloe folded the bedspread over her, and then sat at the desk, and in five minutes fixed the laptop. She sat on the edge of the bed and was a little worried because Nancy kept shaking.

Are you sure you're alright? Chloe asked.

Nancy grinned and slowly nodded again. Chloe kissed her on the cheek, got dressed and left.

* * * * *

On the way back to Cambridge on the 'T', she stopped at Phu Ket, her favorite Thai restaurant in the war zone for some take-out, and at the package store for some Singha beer. When she got home she sat at the dining room table next to the French doors with a bowl of Tom Kah Gai and some sticky rice.

Mostly I cook something simple. She said. But when I eat out I usually get something I wouldn't normally make at home. Tom Kah Gai is the measure of any Thai restaurant. If they can do that well, they can do anything. It's basically chicken mushroom soup, except the mushrooms are fresh, and the broth is coconut milk, with red chili flakes, lemongrass, water chestnuts, baby corn, cilantro, garlic, and white onions. If it's too sweet it's not right, and if it's not sweet enough, it's not right either. It has to be timed. Throw in the most delicate ingredients at the last second, like the mushrooms and cilantro. The one at Phu Ket is orgasmic. I can always taste each individual flavor without one overpowering another. And with a sip of Singha it's absolutely sublime.

Bear in mind. She said. I love food, but it's not about what I eat or where I eat; it's not about me or my self-esteem — to show off or put myself above anybody. It's about 'tasting'. The phenomenon. It's what makes us alive. Like art is about 'seeing'; not

what you think about it or how much it's worth.
Music is about 'hearing'; not how genius you think
what you listen to is. ...Or you could eat frozen
pizza, junk hamburgers, and microwave burritos
everyday...

* * * * *

The job at Discovery was over, and Chloe had
given orgasms to thirty-three out of forty-one
people in the office. She finished all her assignments, everybody raving, saying they wanted her to
stay on, that they'd find things for her to do, but she
told them she'd already bought her plane ticket. It
was time to move on and start over again. Nancy
was absent when she said goodbye. The rumor was
she quit to find a less stressful job.

It was almost September, and Chloe wanted to
see the aspens turn in Colorado. There is no more
spectacular display of Life and Death simultaneously than the aspen leaves exploding in a riot of
color just before they drop from the trees, all in the
span of a few weeks. If you catch it at its peak,
you'll never forget it. She called up agencies in
Denver and set up appointments so she could hit the
ground running, packed a few bags and
disappeared.

7

The Birth of Venus

*"We're in a freefall toward an unknown future, but all you
have to do to turn your hell into a paradise is make your fall a
voluntary act — joyful participation in the sorrows — instead
of resisting and complaining and lashing out."*

— Chloe Pentangeli

Although she seemed to be helping almost
everyone at Discovery, it occurred to her giving
orgasms to the people in one office out of an entire
office building wasn't enough. Chloe wanted to do
something to help everyone, even the ones she
didn't have sex with. So she started giving little
going away presents, so to speak, and you might say
housewarming gifts. She giggled to herself for half
an hour on the plane, holding it in so she wouldn't
look like a lunatic, remembering her last day at
Discovery when she scrambled the elevator
controls.

That's why she began to always make friends
with the building engineer. He's got keys to everything and knows the whole building inside and out:
the roof, the basement, abandoned offices — useful
for a midday rendezvous — and entire empty floors.
Remember the conspicuously unlocked door to the
elevator room on the roof with Rick? She usually
found him hanging out at the security guard's desk
inside, or outside in front of the building if she
came in early. He's proud he got the building up and
running for the day and wants to watch people's
reactions as they walk in. Isn't the temperature just

right? Don't the doors open and close perfectly?
Don't the elevators run like clockwork?

Well, they didn't run like clockwork the day
she left Discovery. People got on, pressed six and
found themselves in the basement. When they
pressed seven, they wound up on thirteen — one of
the empty floors of naked steel beams and dusty
bare concrete. They were in a panic, thinking they'd
entered a parallel universe or something.

People fought in the elevators about which
buttons to push; some became confused and
hyperventilated, others wept. An administrative
assistant pulled the fire alarm. The entire building
was evacuated via the stairs. On the sidewalk, the
chief security guard ushered people away from the
emergency exit toward a nearby pedestrian square
where hundreds gathered, several held each other
and sobbed. It would take some of them days to
recover — jolted out of their habitual numbness.

* * * * *

The Captain's voice came over the PA, and
said, ...We've started our descent into Denver. We
should be on the ground in about twenty minutes.
Weather in the Mile High City is mild, scattered
clouds, about 70° with a light breeze and 20%
humidity. Local time is eleven-o-five...

She glanced out the window and saw the gray-
blue Rocky Mountains getting closer and closer, got
up and walked back to the toilet with her shoulder
bag. In the bathroom she pulled out a loose ream of
8 ½ x 11 sheets of paper, bent the whole ream
lengthwise, and crammed it down the toilet past the
spring-loaded stainless steel flap. She took out a
plastic liter water bottle filled with yellow-green

antifreeze, dumped it into the bowl, and flushed the blue liquid behind it. She stuffed the empty bottle through the swinging door of the trash receptacle, washed her hands, and returned to her place. The plane was heading on to Los Angeles after Denver so there was a good chance she could get a front row seat for the action.

As soon as she got her check-in from baggage claim, she ran out and caught a taxi to downtown Denver, had the driver stop at 17th and Larimer, sat at an outdoor table at The Market café/gourmet food store, ordered a Borgia and a cherry Danish, and savored the orange zest and orgeat in the mocha. The weather was cool and dreamy, like September always is in Colorado, and the low humidity brought out the contours of white fluffy clouds, sharply defined against sapphire skies as they lolled wispy past crisp angles of dark skyscrapers. It felt unusually quiet and lazy; office workers loitered near fountains and around little open squares; they didn't know or care what to do with themselves, and took their time getting back to work after lunch. Something about the change of season in Colorado zaps people.

She smiled when she saw a plane drift across the lazy sky, climbing high, marking a white vapor trail west. According to procedure, the pilot would dump the toilet waste to lower their weight and increase fuel efficiency for the flight. Normally the waste comes out in a misshapen lump of ice, frozen by the chilly air in the upper atmosphere. Traveling at 500 miles an hour, the frozen lump usually breaks up into smaller and smaller pieces due to friction as it descends, eventually becoming a fine spray of piss and fecal matter that gently mists the city. But with the anti-freeze, it would spew out like diarrhea, still liquid, droplets streaking back on the fuselage, and hundreds of 8 ½ x 11 leaflets stained with blue disinfectant would waft out all over downtown Denver, drying as they descended. She giggled to herself as it happened just like that. Office workers in sunglasses looked up and smiled whimsically and turned to their co-workers and pointed as pale blue pages fluttered gently down, and settled onto dusty streets and sidewalks.

One administrative assistant in a white long-sleeved shirt and khakis, leaning against a low wall surrounding some plants in a little paved square, set down his sandwich in the white Styrofoam to-go box, and bent to pick one up. He held it in both hands and read it, chewing slowly, and then the earth stood still. He stopped chewing, and his face went blank, part of his sandwich hanging from his lower lip. There was no thinking about the past or the future in that moment, only the words in front of him, and he didn't even think about those at first. He stood there holding the fluttering leaflet, shaded by a tall office building. A gentle acrid breeze smelling of car exhaust and piss rustled his mouse-brown hair, and the stained bluish page. It read, "WE THINK ABOUT TODAY, WE PLAN FOR TOMORROW, WE REFLECT ON YESTER-DAY... NONE OF THESE ARE REALLY LIVING. LIFE ONLY HAPPENS IN THE PRESENT MOMENT. ABANDON THE SELF TO THE SENSES."

He stayed suspended like that for a few seconds, the truth dawning on him, and looked up at the sky, disoriented. Then time kicked in, he smirked and resumed chewing, wadded up the pissy little note, walked to the nearest trashcan, tossed it, and headed back to the office, leaving the rest of his

sandwich for the birds. Chloe had reached him...
That was enough for now, even if only for a minute.
She walked to the curb, hailed a taxi, and went to
another college friend of ours Luis' house in
Boulder.

* * * * *

I don't blame her for not wanting to stay at my
place out in Fort Lupton, and I was happy to drive
to meet her once a week. Luis had a little guest
house in his backyard right up against the foothills
at 4th and University. His parents were smart. Luis'
older sister went to college at CU too, and his
parents figured, Why throw away all this money on
rent when we could buy? So they mortgaged their
house in Burlington, a small town on the eastern
Colorado plains, and bought a little run down two-
bedroom bungalow built from rounded river rocks
with a freestanding garage, before the prices in
Boulder skyrocketed. He and his dad fixed it up and
converted the garage into a separate apartment/
guesthouse. And in between after his older sister
graduated and when Luis went to school, they
rented it out to other students.

Luis got a Bachelor's Degree in English and
wanted to stay in Boulder, so his dad signed the
house over to him. Now he's a manager at Whole
Foods and trying to write a novel. He'd been at it
for years, and he'd shown me chapters before. It
was all about family, and really sad — he had a
dark cloud hanging over him — not the kind of
thing I was really into. It was okay, but it was
probably going to take him decades to finish. Luis
never slept with Chloe in school, but still, he was
always cooking for her whenever she came over,

like he was trying to prove he'd make a good husband.

The guesthouse was a one bedroom cottage with southwestern decor his mom chose — everything rustic in a New Mexico style, all the furniture asymmetrical, made of gnarled wood; the floor tiled in terra cotta with Navajo rugs thrown down. It felt kind of homey to Chloe, even though home growing up was nothing like that. Maybe since her mom was from New Mexico, it was the lingering familiar. She always got kind of sentimental about Colorado anyway because she went to school in Boulder.

She settled in and went to the main house to have dinner with Luis. He cooked chicken Molé Poblano — that dark Mexican stew with three kinds of red chili, and chocolate, with a long list of other ingredients that takes an expert to do right — made fresh corn tortillas, and they shared a bottle of Tempranillo in candlelight.

At some point, he looked at her, his brown eyes sparkling in the flicker of the flames, and said, I feel trapped here... Boulder's changed. I can't relate to anyone anymore. They've got no souls... It's like everyone thinks they have to be somebody they're not. And they feel ashamed if they're not who they think they should be. It makes me sick...

You can move. She said.

He smiled ironically, and shook his head, I can't right now...

Well, just avoid the assholes.

It's not only the people, it's the city itself. Boulder's not like New York, where the environment is so harsh it challenges you, and no matter how solid you think you are, at some point you have to question that, just to get along. Or even like a small town, like Burlington, where you have to deal with all the wide open space, and the silence, and the serious lack of entertainment. People in Boulder never have to change or question themselves, and they're all so smug about it.

It was true. Boulder had become different since we went to school. It went from a laid back pseudo-hippie liberal enclave to a politically correct speedy upscale mini-Aspen, everything clean and precise and planned, with a doubled police force — infamously inept though they may be — and endless fear-mongering to keep the community insular. Some scraped by, living in houses with tons of roommates because rich families had their college student offspring buy all the low income housing, but most poor people left. Boulderites called Longmont — the town to the north — "Wrongmont"; Lafayette and Louisville to the east were "Laugh-at-it" and "Loserville". To the south Broomfield was "Dumbfield"; and the worst was the name for Denver — "Denvoid". Everything west up in the mountains was jauntily "up the hill".

...I just want someone I can relate to. Luis said. And beamed at her with his dark jewely eyes.

She touched his hand, You'll find somebody...

He sighed, and got up and started running the dishwater like a good husband would.

It's hard to find a long term partner in Boulder because everyone just wants to play, or they want to carve out the perfect life with the perfect partner and invariably nobody ever fits the bill. Expectations are so high because there's so much money. It's a town for serial monogamy. In college I complained to Chloe once that all I really wanted was a serious girlfriend, but what I always ended up

doing was dating for about three months and then
breaking up, with never any lasting connection.

Chloe shrugged her shoulders and said, That's
Boulder...

But she didn't want to shatter Luis' dreams.

* * * * *

The next day all they did was sit in front of the
TV, drinking tequila, watching images of the
smoking World Trade Center towers crashing to the
ground over and over and over again.

This is The Year of the Snake in the Chinese
calendar. She said. Two holes in the ground are like
a snake bite. ...The snake is a liar, though, in our
mythology. It doesn't look real.

Don't get all metaphysical on me. He said.

I mean it looks like a controlled demolition.
Physically, the only way any building can collapse
straight down on itself is with explosives planted
throughout the whole thing. And those buildings
were designed to take several hits each by commer-
cial jets because they're so tall. We studied it
freshman year. ...On top of that, jet fuel burns at
700 degrees and steel melts at 2,500. You could
burn jet fuel forever and structural steel would
never melt. Look it up. That's why your stove is
made of steel. It's literally impossible for them to
collapse like that from an airplane crash.

He sighed, Who knows what's fake or real
anymore?

That's exactly what the nihilistic powers want
you to think! She scolded. As long as you claim you
can't tell what's real or fake you'll stay complacent!
The only good thing about that is ultra-conservative

morons won't ask questions either, but you should know better.

Luis looked ashamed.

Even if by some freak physical anomaly the jet fuel on those planes burned hot enough to melt the steel on a few of the upper floors, it would look like this.

She dropped a box of American Spirit organic cigarettes on top of a tall thick unlit candle on the coffee table, and the cigarettes simply rested on top.

It's not enough weight to crush all the rest of the building. The bottom is designed to hold the weight at the top.

Do you really think anyone will want to believe that? Luis asked.

* * * * *

Chloe went in for interviews with the temp agencies she called from Boston and by the time she got back to Luis' house one agency already sent her an email saying they had a job for her in down-town Denver. She took the bus from Broadway in Boulder right to Market Street and walked to work. Her new boss Amy was pretty, tall, and athletic like the swimmer Dara Torres, the same short blond haircut, cool skinny glasses, and buff, like she worked out daily.

They got along right away. She was the big sister Chloe never had. Amy was an overworked soccer mom, divorced, and fishing for a second husband. She kept pictures of her kids on her desk in their soccer uniforms — Jimmy and Jamie.

Chloe said, Amy really wanted to believe in the myth your partner should be your best friend. But that's why she got divorced. She met some guy, a handsome ex-jock who sold vacuum pumps to meat packing plants — admittedly not too bright, which she didn't mind because she'd sworn never to go out with anyone who was smarter than her, and they slept together on the first date. Following her instinct to bear children, harboring all the romantic notions of a picture-book wedding, she still believed that to begin with they should be best friends. Forget about being lovers. Puritanical America. So first she set out to be what she thought his best friend would be like. Big mistake... She didn't even try to really befriend him, to be herself.

They went to Avalanche games and she showed off her knowledge of hockey rules; she hung out with him and all his guy friends after Rockies games, and drank beer with the best of them. In fact, all his friends were jealous he'd met a girl who could actually be "one of the guys". That confirmed to both of them they'd made the right choice, and wedding bells rang.

There was no getting to know each other, becoming intimate, developing trust. It was like shopping on the Internet. They both saw a picture of what they wanted — an image of the ideal partner they each coveted — and put it in their cart, only to find when it was physically delivered it wasn't what they wanted at all. Six months later, she was shocked after the huge effort she put into being his best friend, all he really wanted her to do was cook and clean like his mother did, while he worked and watched football and drank beer with the guys, belched and farted, and wasn't the slightest bit interested in her personal life, or romance, or communicating about girly icky feelings — the things she finally admitted to herself she really needed in a relationship. But it was too late by then.

She was already pregnant. …Still, myths die hard. She stuck it out with him for nearly a decade until she just couldn't take it anymore.

Chloe thought it would be next to impossible to help her though, for one main reason — she had young kids. She had no time. Simple as that. Something she began to notice. The way in which a person related to the concept of Time made a big difference as to whether or not she could help them. She followed Amy to a cluster of office cubicles where three administrative assistants, all about her age, sat at computers.

Everybody, this is Chloe. Amy said. Emerson, Trent, and Anika.

Anika looked up from her work and subconsciously stroked her hair.

Chloe's going to help the transition from paper to plastic. Amy glanced at Chloe and briefly bit her lip as she smiled, That's what I call it.

They all said, Great... Nice to meet you, Chloe... We could use the help... etc.

Amy led her away. Chloe briefly glanced back over her shoulder and saw Emerson and Trent leaning toward each other making silent dramatic gestures about how hot they thought she was.

She took Chloe all over the office and introduced her to eleven other people, and finally showed her to her desk. This was going to be a big project. Wilbur was a re-insurance company, meaning they insured insurance companies. If you think regular insurance companies don't like to pay a claim, these guys would rather sell their daughters, wives, and mothers into prostitution slavery than shell out a penny. She was going to be helping them convert all their paper files into electronic files they could all access from the company Intranet. Hardly any downtime for a midday rendezvous like with Rick back at Discovery. She'd have to pack a lunch, and do most of her real work outside the office after hours.

* * * * *

Anika was twenty-one, blond, and used to a lot of attention. She had big breasts, baby-fine white-blond hair, baby-soft skin, high cheek bones, and cat-like pale blue eyes — a prototypical Norwegian. She wasn't much younger than Chloe, but there's a world of difference between twenty-one and twenty-six.

Chloe thought it was ironic how they actually made their first connection. The main receptionist called in sick and they asked Anika to fill in for her. Amy asked Chloe to finish some letters for Anika that were on Anika's computer, so she had to sit at Anika's desk. Anika came back on one of her breaks, padding noiselessly on the carpet, and Chloe absent-mindedly reached for a letter coming out of the printer without looking, and accidentally found her hand right on Anika's ass.

Anika acted really shocked and made a big deal out of it. Her desk was within hearing range of Brad's office, the executive she was typing the letters for, so she said in a voice way too loud for the office, Did you just touch my ass? Oh my God! I can't believe it!

It seemed sort of out of character for Anika, but Chloe apologized, and said it was an accident, and explained she was just reaching for the letter, loud enough for everyone around them to hear, to allay the alarm. What a drama queen! But it was the perfect thing to laugh about later when they went out.

It was tricky asking out a straight girl. Chloe didn't want her to think she just wanted to be friends, because then any attempt to seduce her would come as even more of a shock than if she were straightforward about her intentions in the first place. Plus, if they started off as friends it could take forever to get around to sex, and that wouldn't serve Chloe's purpose. She had to seduce her and move on to the next one. Then again she didn't want to be too straightforward and come on too strong right off the bat because that would only scare her away. Anika wouldn't start with the assumption Chloe wanted to sleep with her, as she would if Chloe were a guy asking her out. But Chloe had to make Anika aware that sex was a possibility right from the start. To accomplish that, she would immediately talk about sex, but using a degree of nonchalance that wouldn't work for a guy if he were asking her out. In a man it would come off as disinterest, or possibly TMI, depending on who he's talking to, but between women it came off as intrigue.

First Chloe asked her if she wanted to have lunch together. They went to Green and got salads. Chloe's was pear, butter lettuce, macadamia nuts, and fennel with fresh lemon juice and grape seed oil. Anika's was romaine hearts with kalamata olives, cherry tomatoes, crumbled feta, and yogurt cucumber dill dressing.

Without any particular lead up, Chloe said, In high school I had an affair with a girl.

Really?

We were totally in love with each other... It's different being with a woman. She knew what I

wanted better than most men. She gave me better
orgasms too. Do you have multiple orgasms?

Well... not yet.

Hmm...

When the bill came, Chloe picked it up and
said, I'll get this. She put her card down and looked
at Anika, We should go for coffee this weekend.
The Market is always good.

I was going to go to the gym. Anika responded.

Anika never went out with anyone the first time
they asked. She was fresh out of college at Metro
State, and used to being hard to get. It would take a
lot of work, but Chloe was up to the challenge. She
asked again the next day, got turned down again,
and the third time Anika agreed to meet her for
coffee. But then she didn't show up. She said she
really just forgot. Chloe knew it was a possibility
she may be extremely late or not show at all, so she
brought her laptop.

As Chloe described it, Anika lived completely
outside of time. She pictured "The Birth of Venus"
by Botticelli, the goddess standing on her shell in
the middle of the sea, out of touch with everything.
The ocean knows no time. One wave crashing is all
waves crashing, turning mountains into beaches,
through all eternity. Anika wasn't overly concerned
with the past, the present, or the future — as if she
lived in an eternal Now. She was immortal as far as
she could tell. Forever beautiful, forever young, she
had nothing but time. All the time in the world...
Nothing ever changed for her concerning people
attracted to her. She was the blazing center of her
own solar system, and there would always be
planets, comets, and asteroids orbiting hopefully
around. So if Chloe didn't make her feel special, all

she had to do was wait, and somebody else would, sure as sunshine.

Some people say beauty is a curse. If not, it's definitely a spell. Chloe is beautiful, the most beautiful woman I've ever met, but she has the antidote to the spell — intelligence. Anika may have genuinely forgotten she had a date with Chloe, or remembered she'd planned to do something else at that same time before Chloe asked her out and decided to do that instead. It's like a side effect of growing up beautiful. Anika never experienced a dynamic where somebody didn't make her their top priority, so she never had to make anyone else a priority. She didn't know how to. She didn't have to remember any appointment because it was guaran-teed someone would remember it for her; if all else failed, her dad. She'd never met a guy who didn't tell her she was special and try to convince her that his feelings for her were special. But it wasn't a conscious agenda. She would never demand that kind of constant attention. Anika simply expected it without even thinking about it.

Chloe said, A few of the junior associate guys were mad at her because she turned them down or didn't show up on dates, but it didn't do them any good to be angry. She just thought they didn't like her. And then they slipped her mind completely. They would have to do something really spectacular to impress her and sweep her off her feet after that. And they could have, if they got over being mad and put in some more effort. Actions speak louder than words.

She asked her out again, and she said yes again, and this time she did show, but she was an hour late. They met at The Market and sat at one of the indoor cherry wood tables, with matching cherry wood chairs, and sipped mochas. Chloe said things like, Tell me about the last time you felt totally happy. Describe the most romantic date you ever had. Explain why Mark was your favorite boyfriend. I'm curious what it feels like when you're in love.

Never ask a question, always propose. Chloe told me.

Anika usually turned around and made the same propositions to Chloe. That was her knee-jerk response. Like when I tell people I teach English as a Second Language the knee-jerk response for the vast majority of people is to ask, What's the first? As if that's relevant. Chloe made sure to answer from Anika's point of view.

You know what it's like when you meet someone and you feel totally connected and safe, when they see you as you really are, and they think you're amazing... You can just let go and be yourself. It makes you feel like you're melting, and there's complete trust, like you've known each other your whole lives. It's kind of seductive. Imagine sitting under the stars, up in the mountains, with a cool breeze, and the scent of juniper, sipping a glass of good red wine, and then going out for a romantic candlelight dinner...

The power of suggestion.

Anika sighed dreamily. Chloe made sure to touch her hand briefly as they talked, and gazed into her eyes just a little too long, and let her eyes wander over Anika's body only briefly, so she'd know she thought she was beautiful without being too forward. Anika had to know Chloe was attracted, but Chloe couldn't be too attracted, otherwise Anika would feel uncomfortable. After about an hour Chloe said she had things to do, and asked her if she'd go out again next Saturday, and she said yes.

8

Tetralemma

"In Time there are only pairs of opposites — hope and fear, desire and aversion, nostalgia and regret. Putting ourselves in accord with rhythm of Nature we're not engaged in the field of time, and we can find rapture beyond difference."

— Chloe Pentangeli, Trance Dancer

Chip came into the copy room with a stack of papers in his arms and a dour face. He heaved a frustrated sigh when he saw Chloe using the big scanner, didn't look her in the eye, and shifted on his feet impatiently.

How much longer do you think you'll be?

I have ten more in this folder. She said.

He rolled his eyes, looked around the room, and glanced at his watch, extremely bored. He behaved the same way when they were introduced on the first day. He was obviously attracted to her but didn't want to show it.

Chip was way too serious, really thin, with underdeveloped pectorals, but mildly handsome in a conservative way, with dark green eyes, and dark brown hair, clean-cut. He could have upgraded from mildly handsome to mildly attractive if he ever smiled. One of those people who worked too hard and jogged too much, and never ate enough, he was a hypochondriac who planned out his entire life to satisfy his overbearing father.

She could hear him lecturing Chip. You've got to plan for the future. You've got to work your way up. It's never too early to start a retirement account. You've got to save 10% of every paycheck. You've got to keep on track, and don't get distracted by girls. If she really loves you she'll support your career. If she really loves you she'll share the same goals.

He was one of the special ones. In more ways than one. He thought he was special, first of all — too good for most women. And it would take a special effort to help him because there was a strong possibility he was closet queer, although that never stopped Chloe before. Straight or gay, anybody can have an orgasm, and she felt as a woman if she gave a queer man an orgasm it was actually more effective in helping him to open up than if a man gave him one.

Chip was one of those people who live only for the promise of the future. He was willing to give up any satisfaction in the present for the promise of satisfaction in the future. But you see the stupendous error in that way of thinking. Once you get to the future you're back in the present. So nothing ever satisfied him.

He also liked to cite the study that her former boss Jaster recalled, where the psychologist puts a cookie in front of a child and tells her, You can have this cookie now, but if you wait till I come back I'll bring you another one. Unlike Jaster, Chip really believed the kid who waited and got two cookies was smarter and more respectable, and the one who ate the cookie right away was pathetic and undisciplined. But what if one cookie was enough for her to feel full right then and two would be overkill? What if the child only wanted one cookie in that moment? Would it really benefit her then to hoard cookies for some imaginary future? She doesn't know what will happen, just as none of us can predict what will come, and cookies have always been available before. The study fails to account for that.

One may ask, What if there were no more cookies, wouldn't she be better off to stockpile them? Wouldn't that put her in a more advantageous position? But we can play the "what if" game forever. What if the sky falls, Chicken Little? Does that mean you need to build a concrete bunker? Would you want to live in a world where only the paranoid survived? How long would you last?

It becomes clear the root of squirreling off cookies is the super-ego, the delusion some more-powerful external force is judging us, and that degenerates into a paralyzing Fear of Failure, which in turn is a manifestation of a deeper seated Fear of Death, which arises originally from primordial ignorance — the notion of duality, that we are separate from whatever it is we perceive. Culture doesn't prepare us for death, and neither does religion. The only purpose of Culture as we've constructed it is to ensure that we remain consumers — of cookies or whatever — and the overriding purpose of almost every religion is to perpetuate itself by securing wealth.

Anyway, the first step for Chloe was to dress up. Chip appreciated a well-dressed woman more than most men because dressing well means money, and money secures the future. She wore dresses for three days before Chip actually approached her — she couldn't approach him first because then he'd think she wanted something right now, in the present. He was concerned only with the future.

On the third day Chip walked up to her in the copy room, looked her in the eyes, and for the first time, he smiled. Smiling at women they like is normal for most men, but it was a rare occurrence for Chip. Chloe smiled back and struck up a light conversation. The second step was to compliment him.

Are you a runner? She asked.

Yeah, actually. You could tell?

You look like a runner. You're so in shape. How many miles a day?

Well, I start the week with three, then go to six, then ten, and then back down to six, and three, and I rest on the weekends — a basic cross-country schedule. I used to run marathons but I decided it would be too hard on my knees in the long run.

Impressive. She said, and thought, Wow! He swallowed that little scrap along with my whole arm!

She knew Chip worked hard to stay thin and in shape because he was fighting against time. The ticking clock is the arch-enemy of the future, because sandwiched between the present and death, the future is always running out. The older you get the less future you have according to his thinking. Chronophobia. It was the conspiracy against him he didn't dare acknowledge because that would result in rampant paranoia. If time were against him then who or what wasn't?

It had to be a precise operation. If he received her compliments well, then she had to let him know he was special, he wasn't like the other men in the office; he was different in a good way. Then she could ask him out for a drink, or even for dinner — either one as long as he thought he was being given special treatment. It would be a huge mistake to ask him out with her and a bunch of other people. If he didn't receive her compliments well, which would be a rare occurrence, but could happen — because sometimes he got shy — then she'd just have to bide her time and keep complimenting him until he did receive them well. That would mean either he was in a self-esteem slump, or he thought he was so special he needed extra validation before he could give Chloe his attention, and she'd have to keep at it until he did.

If he did bite, when they went out she'd have to be willing to let him feel like everything was his idea. She might suggest a restaurant but she'd make sure to ask him where he preferred to go because he would already have it all nailed down in his mind — like a wooden bridge he built with his bare hands — which restaurants and bars led to the future he coveted. Some men like a woman to take charge, but not Chip. It was not the time to be spontaneous for Chloe. As it turned out, Chip did receive her compliments well and he asked her out for a drink.

* * * * *

On Friday, to make Anika feel special, Chloe instant messaged her saying, Don't tell anyone we're going out. It's a secret.

She replied, Why? What are we doing?

Chloe wrote, Wear running shoes, and bring a sweater, but have something nice to change into for later. It's a surprise. ;)

Later, when she was on her way to the copy room she passed near Anika's cubicle and heard her talking excitedly to Trent, I don't know, it seems so random. Wear running shoes but bring something nice for later? It's kind of exciting!

* * * * *

She went with Chip to his favorite wine bar where they had a hundred different champagnes to choose from, and they talked and laughed and had a good time, but she quickly understood he wasn't going to sleep with her that night so she had to wait till he asked her out again. He thought if she was willing to wait for it, then it meant he was special, because time was the most precious commodity in the world to him. It was like burning paper money for heat.

Chloe said, He looked at time as a permanent linear progression, and himself as a temporary traveler on that path, which terrified him, because it meant someday he would leave the field of time forever. Nihilism… But he acted like he wasn't temporary, like he was the same person from one day to the next. Solid. Inflexible. Unchanging. Permanent.

Time is change. Chloe said. None of us are the persons we were when we were born, even on a cellular level. The body that was born died a long time ago and was replaced with new cells. Consciousness has changed from when we were children too — our whole world view is different. We're always Becoming.

Chloe tried to look at it logically once upon a time, but it becomes absurd as it undoes itself. If you were exactly the same person today you were yesterday, then you'd never change, and nobody else would either — you'd be immortal. No change ever. American athletes who lose invariably say "Everything happens for a reason". But if everything is predestined then what's the point in trying to win? If there were no potential for change, drugs wouldn't work, therapy wouldn't work, exercise wouldn't work, diet wouldn't work, nothing to change your state of being would work.

Then again, if you were a completely different person today than you were yesterday, then logically you could be anyone tomorrow — Napoleon Bonaparte or Queen Latifah — and time would be random. Pre-history, 1000 years in the future, the Byzantine Empire, anytime anywhere. You'd be unstuck in time like Billy Pilgrim in "Slaughter-house Five", except you wouldn't be him all the time and it wouldn't matter what you did because the desired result wouldn't necessarily follow the chosen effort.

If today you were both the same and not the same person you were yesterday, then you would be everyone, and everyone would be you, like that scene in "Being John Malkovich" where everybody had his face and the only thing anybody could say was, "Malkovich, Malkovich, Malkovich." That's where most New Ager's are, worshiping the nautilus because it's spiral, the crooked path, and anything goes. But spiral is sneaky linear. They may sing "I am he as you are he as you are me and we are all together", but what they really mean is "me me me me me me me". It's all about "me" and they're still trying to get from point A to point B — they still covet a particular style of experience — just on a curvy path with smiles and hugs, dolphins and crystals, channellers and pastel-colored rainbow paintings. Deep down they still embrace the notion they're solid, which is black and white.

And if you were neither the same person you were yesterday, nor a different person today, then you're nothing — no you, no anyone else, a complete void — the basis for nihilistic behavior. It's all going to disappear in the end; the world and all of life is an open sewer because waste is the only thing we can ever produce, so desecrate the sky with noxious gases, defile the oceans with feces, despoil the earth with disease and toxins, and doom and all living creatures to agony, because nothing matters… We're left with a tetralemma, because Time is beyond logic.

* * * * *

One of the first times Chloe experienced time as nonlinear was when she jumped off the seventy-foot cliff at Gross Reservoir above Boulder. She drove up there on the curvy road through thick pine forests with Max one hot September weekday when neither of them had class. The sun was bright and sharp and the air so dry it made her nostrils sting when she inhaled as they walked over red rocky earth and crackling pine needles toward the cliff's edge. Max had been there before and he warned her not to jump from just anywhere — people died because in some spots the cliffs jut out at the bottom and you can't get enough momentum at the top to clear them — but he knew the place to jump from. On the way, tracing the cliff's edge, they saw several memorials to dead jumpers, some painted in white sloppy script on the red flagstones, or with dead dried up flowers in bundles, or clusters of weather beaten stuffed animals, or a makeshift wooden cross with a name carved into it stuck in the ground nearby. Finally, they stopped at a place with no obvious signs of human presence.

This is it. Max said.

Are you sure?

Positive.

They took off their shirts and flip-flops. Max was already wearing black swim trunks, and Chloe was in a blue bikini. She looked over the edge at the dark green water way down.

You've just got to do it. Don't stand around thinking about it. Max said.

How far is it? She asked

About seventy-five feet.

She sighed heavily.

Let's do it together. Max told her.

I need a minute.

Chloe took some deep breaths.

Alright, I'll go first.

Max took a running stance, breathed out hard a few times, and then ran toward the cliff's edge, jumped, and disappeared. She heard a splash and then the distant echo of him whooping in wild abandon, and strokes in the water as he made his way to shore. The last thing she wanted was to be still standing there when he climbed back up to the top. She ran and jumped.

Literally ten times in mid-air she said to herself, I should be hitting the water, I should be hitting the water, I should be hitting the water… Finally her feet slammed through the surface and she plunged deep into the green cold depths, and when her downward motion stopped she felt a thrill, and swam excitedly toward the top. She broke through to air and screamed in exhilaration. …But the second time she jumped, as soon as she thought, I should be— she splashed. …Time is relative. At the moment of death, after your whole life flashes before your eyes, your only thought will be, What was that?

* * * * *

She rented a black Volvo 850 station wagon and went to pick up Anika at her apartment in Denver late Saturday afternoon. There was an awkward moment when Anika answered the door. It seemed Anika half-expected Chloe to hug and kiss her when they first saw each other. That surprised Chloe — she didn't expect Anika to be so receptive so soon — but it boded well for later.

Chloe touched her arm and asked, Have you got everything?

Anika said yes and they went out to the car. Anika opened the passenger side door and found a single long-stemmed white rose, a card, and little box of three chocolate truffles on the seat. She picked them all up and got in excitedly.

Are these for me?

Yes.

She put the rose to her nose first, and inhaled.

Mmm. Thank you.

Then she opened the card and read.

It said, "I tried to find the perfect rose, but I realized I already had, when I found you." And it had a cute little drawing of Snoopy with a shy look on his face holding out a rose in one paw, with his other paw tucked behind his back.

She turned to Chloe and said, That's so sweet!

There was a folded 8 ½ x 11 sheet of paper with a poem printed on it inside the card. Anika unwrapped the truffles, took a bite of one, became absorbed in the rich flavor, and read the poem.

Memory is the echo
Of disappeared experience
The sweetness of truffles
When they're gone, the feeling

Remember delicate shell crumpling soft
Inside, dark spiced aromas and liquor
Drowning trifles in silky dreams
You don't want to end

And even if the mood doesn't break
It's easy to find takers, they won't linger long
But for the echo, how sad, and yet
Melancholy can be a requiem
For beauty

Who wrote that? Anika asked excitedly.
I did. Chloe said.
That's beautiful!
Thanks. What kind of music do you like?
...I've been into that new U2 CD lately.
Chloe pulled a CD out of her shoulder bag on
the console between them and put it in the player in
the dash. "A Beautiful Day" by U2 played, and
Anika cupped the flower in her hands and smelled it
intermittently as they drove.

They made the half-hour trip to Boulder and
drove up Flagstaff Mountain, rising 3000 feet in
less than a mile, right next to the towering red
Flatirons over Chautauqua Park, with a picturesque
view of the town beneath. She parked on an isolated
dirt path fifty yards past a little dirt pullout on the
side of Flagstaff Road, and they hiked a trail over
hard dry soil, powdery on top like red tempera, and
flagstone rocks like the surface of Mars — the red
contrasting the cover of green juniper, mountain
sage, prairie grass, and pine. Chloe held Anika's
hand to help her over some of the boulders on the
trail. When they got to a large secluded flat stone,
warm to the touch having absorbed the sun all day,
she took a blanket out of her shoulder bag and
spread it out, and they sat down, and looked out at

the town in evening autumn haze. She opened a
bottle of Chateau Neuf du Pape, got two crystal
glasses out of their wooden box, opened the wine
and poured. They clinked glasses and drank and
made small talk, listening to the wind in the pines,
till the light began to fade. As the first stars
twinkled, Chloe touched her hand and looked into
her eyes, and gently kissed her. Anika's firm lips
were luscious, but Chloe didn't linger.

We'd better get going before we can't see the
trail. Chloe said.

They packed up everything and headed back to
the car. How do you know this place so well? Anika
asked.

I went to school here.

…This is really nice, Chloe.

Thanks.

They neared the car as the sky was darkening,
sand and gravel creaking under their shoes as
crickets trilled in the quiet evening.

Time to change. Chloe said.

They got inside and Chloe undressed in her
seat; she was naked underneath. Anika got down to
her bra and panties, but before Chloe could put on
her dress, Anika touched her arm and Chloe looked
into her eyes. Surprisingly, Anika leaned towards
her, and kissed her on the mouth. Chloe held a
handful of Anika's baby fine hair, pulled her mouth
to hers, and they kissed with more intensity.

Chloe said, Let's get in back.

They climbed through the space between the
seats; the back ones already lowered, and Chloe
spread out the blanket on the carpeted bed.

Anika breathed long slow breaths. She put a
cold trembling hand between Chloe's thighs, looked

her in the eye, and said, Before we do this, can we get high?

Did you bring anything? Chloe asked.

I thought you might have.

I don't know if I did.

She rummaged through her shoulder bag and smiled when she felt slick plastic on her fingertips way down at the bottom. She pulled out the tiny clear plastic wrapper with tar-like brown goo inside and held it up.

All I've got is a little opium. Have you smoked before?

Anika said a little apprehensively, No... Do you smoke that?

Only occasionally... We could have sex all night on opium. She said.

Anika briefly closed her eyes, considering it.

Chloe reached over and gently touched her ass, and said, Is this my letter?

They both cracked up and belly laughed for several minutes.

Anika said, Okay.

Chloe stuck a new CD in the dash and The Sneaker Pimps "6 Underground" played; she took out a little piece of aluminum foil, a red plastic lighter, and a clear Bic pen from her bag; unwrapped the dark brown goo, swiped a smudge with the tip of the pen and smeared it in the middle of the foil. Then she bit the tip of the pen and pulled out the insides making a tube of the outside, held the foil with the opium in one hand and gave the lighter to Anika.

Light it and hold it right under it, moving it a little. She said.

Chloe put the tube to her lips and held the end right over the brown smudge. Anika flicked the lighter and held the flame under the foil, moving it back and forth under it. When the opium liquefied and started to bubble and smoke, she inhaled deeply and held the smoke in her lungs as long as she could, and finally blew a cloud. Chloe gave her the foil and the pen and Anika gave her the lighter.

Put the pen right over it and inhale when I tell you to, and hold it in. Chloe said.

She flicked the lighter and Anika repeated what Chloe did. As soon as Anika exhaled she flopped down on the blanket, head toward the hatchback.

How do you feel? Chloe asked.

She smiled and said, Oh my God…

The stars twinkled brighter and glimmered like underwater in dark blue euphoria as she lay down on the soft blanket next to Anika and lightly brushed her fingers over her baby soft skin. Anika wriggled out of her panties, sat up briefly and took off her bra, and lay down again. Chloe felt her firm plump breasts and her nipples, big and perfectly cylindrical, like thick soft pink pills. Then Chloe lay beside her head to toe, and they pleasured each other simultaneously.

* * * * *

They changed into their dresses, Anika brushed her hair, Chloe poured a little water from her bottle in her palm and smoothed that into hers, and drove to the Flagstaff House, only two minutes from where they parked. Although they were an hour late for their reservation they were seated immediately — it wasn't crowded inside because everyone wanted to sit outside on the terraces overlooking the city lights since it was so warm. Inside, the contrast between modern clean-lined wooden architecture and old rustic stone structures was interesting, and the huge plate glass windows gave a good view of the city in the valley below. From their candlelit table they could see the massive rough stone fireplace with a huge ornate brass disc over the uneven stone mantelpiece where brass candelabras stood on each side, with an antique rust encrusted lucky horseshoe in the middle.

The champagne was Taittinger from the famous painters collection — the bottle decorated with a black and white collage by Robert Rauschenberg — paired with a dozen Kumomoto oysters in a lime and Tanqueray gin drizzle. With ravioli of duck confit and pumpkin, they sipped glasses of deep purple Chateau Potelle Zinfandel, 1996, and stayed with that for the rest of the dinner. For Anika, the waiter brought chicken breast stuffed with goat cheese, wrapped in pancetta, with baby turnips and porcini mushroom risotto, and Chloe had bloody rare filet mignon with a pinot noir sauce, a gratin of gold and sweet potatoes, and seared rainbow chard. Anika scooped up fresh peach tart with vanilla bean ice cream for dessert, and fed a spoonful to Chloe; she offered a spoon of her chocolate mousse over almond cake with fresh raspberries to Anika, and they finished with thé forte — Ceylon tea with white jasmine flowers brewed in a Yi-Xing clay pot.

Let's write a poem together. Chloe said.

Anika was reluctant, I don't know. I used to try when I was in junior high, but then I got into other things. You know.

Maybe it's time to try again.

Anika looked uneasy, How long does it have to be?

It doesn't have to be long. I'll start; we'll trade off — I'll do a couple of lines, you do a couple.

The waiter brought over a sheet of paper and a fountain pen.

New beginnings all the time,
Life is fresh with my new love.

Strangers, but familiar in life,
Fit together like puzzle pieces.

Good wine and food paired,
Perhaps to know is to be with:
Shared experience.

I begin to know myself in a new way;
I see life's secrets in your eyes.

In your mirror my reflection is naked,
Raw, and ready for anything.

Chloe was pleasantly surprised. It wasn't Nobel Prize material, but Anika definitely stretched.

This is good. She said.

Thanks. Anika blushed.

You should do it more often.

…I think I was just inspired by the moment. She beamed into Chloe's eyes and touched her hand.

9

A Giant Bong for God

"We don't give ourselves to Nature, we try to correct it. We think there's good and evil in Nature and we're supposed to be on the side of good, so there's tension. But if you don't venerate Nature what else is there? Some figment of your imagination you put up in the clouds?"

— Chloe Pentangeli, The First Cycle

On their third date she went with Chip to Jax, his favorite seafood restaurant — fresh fish flown in daily. Karlsson's Gold vodka martinis with olives preceded Maine lobsters, because that's what the woman of his dreams would eat on his ideal third date. This time it was easy for Chloe to get him to come over to her place afterward, because in his mind she would naturally want to spend the night with him by then, she would trust him — like he was on a schedule — and he believed most women felt more comfortable about sex in their own house or apartment.

It made Chloe think though, these people who are obsessed with the future are also obsessed with the past, because what they really want is to create a future they can relive indefinitely in memory, and that's the past. Maybe to replace the past they didn't want to remember? Anything but the present…

In Chip' mind it was all a fait accompli at that point. According to his script, they would sleep together, they'd be a couple, share the same goals, she'd support his career, have a few babies, he'd make tons of money, the two of them would live happily ever after, and they'd grow old together, and God and Dad and all the other superegos would be proud and happy.

Kissing and undressing, they got naked into her bed. Chloe let him be on top because she knew he would feel emasculated if she rode him. She could tell he'd spent a lot of time alone wanking it because, although he was in great shape, he was done in under two minutes, and it wasn't that "I haven't had sex in a long time" kind of orgasm. Chip was self-absorbed, focusing only on his pleasure, completely inattentive to her. To his credit, though, because he was in such good shape, he was ready again pretty quickly. They were on their third time when she said she wanted to go down on him. He rolled over on his back, and she reached under the bed for her handcuffs, and locked one of his wrists to the gnarled wooden bedpost.

His eyes went wide in disbelieving shock, his mouth working open and closed like a goldfish on the carpet, unable to form any words. This was so far outside of his realm of possibilities the only sound that came out of his mouth was, Uhhhh...?

Chloe asked politely, Have you ever been tied up before?

Um... No...?

Do you want to try? It'll be fun.

Unlike a lot of women, many men prefer questions. It gave him the power of making the decision. And she knew he wouldn't back down from a challenge.

He smiled in a nervous play-along sort of way, and said, ...Okay. ...I guess. For a little while.

She put the other pair of cuffs on his other wrist — both arms now locked to the bedposts at the head of the bed — belted his ankles to the railing at the foot with thick leather straps, and blindfolded him with a silk scarf.

I'll be back.

She stood up.

He asked, Where are you going?

To the kitchen.

He wasn't satisfied with that answer but he let it go. There he was... flat on his back, spread eagle, strapped to the bed, ready for anything. Out of control. It was the best thing for him, really. A disruption in the smooth artificial stream of his life; meeting uncertainty face to face... He would have second thoughts. And that was the problem. His "first thought" wasn't even his first thought anymore. This was the ultimate, "Think Fast!" Except it was never about thinking... It's always been about not thinking. This would shake him out of the rote practiced reaction to every anticipated situation he'd been dreaming up for years, if only for a moment. But good for him, he never dreamt of this one.

Chloe...? She heard him calling plaintively from the bedroom like a lost little boy. She rolled in the service cart with all the equipment, and sat on the bed and touched his shoulder.

I'm right here. She said.

He heaved a relieved sigh, then sniffed the air and asked uneasily, Is that pot?

She said, Yeah. Do you smoke?

Not very often. He answered, sounding embarrassed.

Notice the smell? It doesn't stink like skunk. This is sativa, grown outdoors in sunshine and soil — organically — not in some artificial greenhouse under lights in sand. It won't make you sleepy. Here, breathe in. She said.

Chloe filled her mouth with smoke, put her face close to his, he parted his lips, pulled in air, and she puffed the smoke into his lungs. He held it in then exhaled a cloud.

When faced with a radically new experience, the knee-jerk response for a lot of people is to pull back and define themselves in opposition to the experience, as in "I don't usually do things like this." The smoke would counteract that, keeping things undefined, keeping him going with the flow, helping him lose track of time. To reacquaint him with his senses she put on Portishead, took the nose-shaped bottle of Salvador Dali perfume from the cart, lifted the top and held it close to his face.

That's nice. What is that?

He took several deep breaths.

She asked him, Do you like coffee?

I drink about ten cups a day. He said, and chuckled nervously.

She opened the jar of freshly ground dark roasted Ethiopian Yrgacheffe and held it towards him. It used to be the exclusive property of Emperor Haile Selaisse of Ethiopia, the birthplace of coffee, grown on his private plantation, and could only be obtained as a gift from the royal family, but now it's available in small quantities through a few exclusive importers. The aroma is like French Roast but richer and more complex.

He inhaled and said, Mmm... What kind of coffee is that?

She didn't answer. She didn't want to indulge the tendency to randomly label everything, to cut it off, limit it, put it in a box and kill it. She left it open and alive. 90% of communication is non-verbal.

They went on like that. Chloe had him smell wildflowers from the back yard, vanilla beans, fresh ripe cantaloupe, cinnamon sticks, some of Luis' Issey Miyake cologne. She had him taste seven different kinds of chocolate. They listened to Air, Hooverphonic, Cibo Mato, Morcheeba. She brushed him down with a loofa to wake up his skin — the soles of his feet; the palms of his hands; his ears. She rubbed tiger balm on some of his acupressure points. The blindfold was necessary to help him focus on his other senses — visual being the most relied upon, it tends to block out the others.

Chloe whispered, Pleasure and pain are two sides of the same coin, but let me know if it's too much. The safe word is demasiado.

She pushed a long skinny stainless steel rolling pin filled with scalding hot water over him, and he twitched and panted; she slipped it beneath his lower back.

That releases pent up sexual energy. Chloe said.

He gingerly settled onto it, and then she proceeded to lash him with the flagellum, the Roman whip with several straps dangling from the handle, but without the traditional metal pieces attached to the ends. Not too rough. But it had to sting a little. By then he was sweating and red and breathing hard. His body tensed up briefly, shook violently, and then relaxed.

He said, astounded, I just had an orgasm without coming…

Chloe mounted him and they made love one last time. Tears streamed out from under the blindfold as he arched his back and his whole body shook out of control like he was getting electroshock, and he yelled at the top of his lungs. As he

160

reached orgasm she had to hold on tight just to stay on top, otherwise he would have bucked her off.

* * * * *

On Monday at work he looked flustered, but for the first time he looked alive. Actually smiling at people. He brought Chloe breakfast — a Borgia and a cherry Danish — and he continued to bring her breakfast every day after.

I can help you with scanning if you want. That way you can focus on OCR and editing. He offered.

That's okay. But thanks.

You're welcome.

He stared at the floor awkwardly and his eyes glazed over.

I feel shaky, and unstable, and vulnerable, Chloe.

That's not so bad is it? At least you can feel your life.

I guess... Then he perked up, Where do you want to go for lunch? My treat. Anywhere you like.

Chloe sighed, I've got a lot of work I need to get done.

Oh... Okay. ...I just have two words for you, Chloe.

What?

Thank you.

Tears welled in his eyes and he hurried away. Chip offered to give her a ride home and to pick her up in the morning. He bought her perfume, a silk scarf, lingerie, boxes of imported chocolates, bottles of expensive wine, and even a riding crop he wanted her to use on him. Repeatedly she reminded him he didn't have to buy her anything. It made no difference. Chloe was really happy he'd had such a gigantic change of heart and that he'd rediscovered his generosity, but really…

* * * * *

The project was over. It was her last day. She fit the little Hibachi grill carefully into her shoulder bag; when she got to work she shoved it way under her desk, out of sight, and then followed everybody streaming like lab rats in the same direction through the maze of cubicles to the dining hall. Amy stood before the crowd with a microphone next to several buffet tables laden with desserts and soft drinks. Anika, Trent, Emerson, Chip and several others gazed at Chloe with deep love in their eyes.

Congratulations everybody. Amy said. All our paper files have been scanned, edited and formatted with Optical Character Recognition software, and uploaded onto the server. They're all electronic now, in a web accessible database on the company Intranet.

Everybody applauded politely.

Special thanks to Chloe Pentangeli, who did the lion's share of the work—

They all applaud again.

The executives and directors all agree we'd hire you again for any future project, Chloe. Great job.

People applaud a third time.

Everybody, help yourselves to cake and dessert. There's coffee, juice, milk—

They drown her out in their excitement as they hungrily converge on the buffet tables.

Chloe had been upfront as usual about sleeping with other people, so none of them had any illusions. She said goodbye to each of them. Chip wept openly, which was probably a good thing. He

162

hadn't cried in public since he was a boy, and Chloe held him as he shook with sobs. His façade had come down. Anika gave her a warm kiss and made her promise to come back to Denver. Because of their date Anika was thinking of going back to school to get her Masters in Creative Writing, or Literature.

Then Chloe slipped out quietly, took the elevator down to the third floor terrace, crossed past the outdoor tables and chairs, climbed over the railing separating the rooftop patio from the part of the structure that extended under the huge air-conditioning intake on the side of the main tower, set up the Hibachi under the giant grating, fired it up, and dumped three pounds of marijuana on the grill; she put it close enough so all the smoke flowed into the intake and the rushing air kept the fire stoked. The entire tall skinny building became a giant bong for God, smoke rising from the carbur-etor, filling the whole tube. She could almost make out His wispy white beard drifting in the sky as he wrapped his skinny pale lips around the rim and sucked.

Marijuana smoke poured from the AC vents into the dining hall where everyone was still enjoying dessert. Some people coughed, others laughed uncontrollably, Emerson talked incessantly, Anika fell asleep in one of the armchairs, Trent leaned over a trashcan and vomited, one woman cried, Amy sat hunkered down over a paper plate piled with cake and stuffed plastic forkfuls in her mouth ravenously.

* * * * *

The job was finally over and the leaves were starting to turn in the foothills, so she and Luis got in his Subaru Outback and drove up into the mountains.

This is like the official car of Boulder. Chloe said.

Everybody's starting families. Luis replied.

All the way up they got hints of what was coming, Cottonwood trees with a few yellow leaves, small groves of chartreuse aspens, not yet that deep rich Cadmium gold. It was a quiet drive up Boulder Canyon. Luis liked the silence, and drove without any music. It felt appropriate to Chloe and contemplative. Fall always seemed like a reckoning to her, maybe because her birthday was in the fall and she always tended to take stock of her life — maybe because of the approaching Autumnal Equinox: it's traditionally a time for celebration, reflection on the year past, planning for the winter, performing rituals for protection and security, all the way back to pagan times in Europe. She looked out at steep angled vermilion cliffs and saw a herd of bighorn sheep, and a little farther up they even saw a mountain lion on a rocky hillside. They went up through Nederland, passed it, and drove into the peaks and pine covered buttes beyond, found a park, and walked far away from everybody.

The sun was bright and pale, preparing for winter, and there was a dreamy cool breeze, and a cloudless blue sheet overhead like she'd only ever seen in Colorado in the fall. A roaring white stream tumbling over steep boulders cut through a shady pine stand padded with eons of fragrant fallen needles, and they made their way over the duff to a thick fallen tree that spanned the water... On the other side, she sniffed different pine trunks. Luis didn't believe her when she told him they had different scents, but he laughed when he tried for himself — some smelled like chocolate, some like butterscotch, and some like vanilla — the first time she'd seen him laugh in ages.

Finally, they walked over a rise away from the isolated trail and found a wide aspen grove in full color — trillions of golden leaves fluttering in the breeze among hundreds of thin white trunks, literally glowing. Fallen ones littered the path shimmering golden where they stopped and listened to the wind hissing through shining yellow, under sunlight so rich and clear it felt wet, and everything against deep cerulean blue above. They just breathed... The wind suddenly gusted, blasting leaves off of branches, and billions of tiny black shadows raced across the ground to meet them where they fell.

This is so powerful. He said.

Every aspen grove is a single creature. They're all connected at the roots. She responded. They're the largest living organisms on the planet. And they're dying out.

Luis took her hand and smiled sadly. They walked into the aspen grove. It was a surreal flickering golden labyrinth as the wind rushed through myriad leaves and shadows danced, the whole grove vibrating.

Deep in the middle he stopped and said, I want to make love with you. And he stared sadly at her with his deep brown eyes.

In that moment she couldn't say no to him. They undressed, lay on a dense bed of golden leaves, and he touched her smooth brown body, and kissed her softly everywhere. When they were finished they stayed entwined as their breathing got slower and slower, listening to the wind's undertone hushing through surrounding forests, blending with the distant sigh of water plashing over stones, male hummingbirds flitting hundreds of feet in the air, blacking out, wings whirring as they plummeted in death-defying mating rituals, coming to just before hitting the ground, and mounting the sky to try again.

Luis gently rolled onto his back; that woke her, and she gazed up at the world of blue and gold; white light and black shadows...

...Did you hear what I said? He asked.

I heard you. I love you too, Luis...

But?... He asked.

But it doesn't necessarily mean we have to be a couple. I'm not a normal person. You'd be disappointed if we tried to be monogamous. She said.

You don't know that. He offered.

Trust me, it wouldn't work.

She felt like she could have stayed there forever. The guest house was cozy, and Luis would do anything for her — she knew it — but the first thought that came to her mind was, Time to move on. A golden eagle soared west overhead and screeched... San Francisco...

Lemon

High over the east bay in the brilliant afternoon, the 777 soared over the orange bridge and the bulbous ochre headlands, banked steeply southwest giving a clear view of the city shining zinc white in the sun, past the long flesh-tone beach, out over the gray-blue ocean and back around, over the permanent green hills of the southern peninsula, dropping speed and altitude over the steely inlet, shaking as it fell, past the strange crimson and white salt flats with snaky canals curving through right next to the water, getting slower and lower, finally gliding just over the tops of metallic washboard waves cresting titanium white, in for a landing at SFO.

She stayed with Lily and Trevor in North Beach. There was a saying at CU that every family sends their most beautiful child to college in Boulder. It's actually stunning how many beautiful people there are in such a small town, and Trevor and Lily were prime examples. He could have stepped out of a Ralph Lauren ad, with his thick blond curls and dark blue eyes. Lily was LL Bean to the letter: strawberry blond dreads and blue-green eyes, always wearing rustic looking sweaters, with a crunchy granola attitude. There was another saying, that when you go to college in Boulder you "grow up" and move to San Francisco. It was where most of our college friends lived.

Lily was one of those people who thought all acoustic music was better than all electronic music, never stopping to think that all her Widespread Panic, Phish, and Dead CD's were just an amalgam-mation of digital bleeps. She ate so much granola freshman year she got an intestinal blockage and actually had to be hospitalized. She really thought if you smoke dope and like the Dead, wore hippie clothes and dreadlocks, that you had to eat only granola. She was a LUG in college — Lesbian Until Graduation — and smoked kilos and kilos of kine bud. But when she graduated Mommy and Daddy expected her to get serious and toe the family line. Either get real or get cut-off. …Trustafarians…

So, senior year she met Trevor. Now they were going through the typical post-college San Francisco straight routine. First you get a job and your own apartment in a "cool" neighborhood like North Beach, The Haight, or The Mission. Then you find a girlfriend or boyfriend if you don't already have one. Then you move in together in a "safe" neighborhood like Cole Valley, The Avenues, or The Marina. And then after a couple of years, you either break up and start over, or you get engaged and start looking for a house.

It was a cute little drama, except the players were too often so self-satisfied. Those couples who got together with the intention of staying together felt like they'd arrived. Especially the women. They were nesting, getting ready for the little chickies, and the last thing they wanted was to go back into the fray. They looked down their noses at single people, arched their eyebrows, and thought, Poor things... I know it's hard. ...But for the grace of God... They never dreamt that in 20 years at least 65% of them would be divorced and single again trying to deal with their children.

Lily and Trevor were like "The Truman Show". Except they were both Truman and the bad actors paid to permanently pull the wool over his eyes. Their own eyes. They had no desire to seriously engage the world, and no reason to ever question that. The wool... Fluffy and white... Still 93% of the student body at CU. They flocked into classrooms, chewing the dried hay scattered on checkerboard linoleum floors as the balding, sweaty, bleary-eyed professor lectured about psycho-biology, writing something on the chalk board about 4-methelene-dioxy-methamphetamine.

He turns to face the flock, So, based on your analysis of the two studies, which one seems more plausible? Does the data in the US Government study conclusively prove MDMA aggressively destroys brain tissue, permanently reducing serotonin levels by 80%, or is the German study more accurate, concluding MDMA doesn't destroy brain tissue at all, and only temporarily reduces serotonin by 3 to 4% for a few days? The Germans invented it, by the way...

...Silence. ...Blank expressions. ...Chewing. Endless chewing and swallowing. Yellow teeth, brown around the edges, with bits of hay stuck in between, and quivering cleft upper lips.

The professor says, Come on! This is something you should all be interested in! Ecstasy!? This is the number one party school in America!

Lemon

Horizontal pupils in gray-brown irises. Not
human. Not real. Like a picture in Time magazine
of a clone. You could shave all their hair off and
sell it. You could slaughter them and serve them up
as mutton, and still they'd come back in droves,
staring blankly, chewing, endlessly chewing.
Waiting for the poop that was their diploma.

At least Trevor convinced Lily to stay in North
Beach when they moved in together because he
liked the nightlife. She did what he wanted because
his family had more money than hers. We're talking
about the difference between tens of millions. He
was supposed to graduate from an Ivy League
school like his brother and sister, but got kicked out
of boarding school for smoking angel dust before he
even got close, and went a different route after that.
He watched B horror movies everyday, and
explained it away by saying, At least I know there's
somebody more "F-ed" up than I am.

They sipped expensive red wine and smoked
sin semilla. All natural. The acceptable drugs
according to the Trustafarian code. Late night after
work in the Mission by the BART station entrance,
there were always a couple of guys standing,
shifting nervously from foot to foot, saying, "Ses,
Ses, Ses", as people streamed by. At first Lily
thought they were saying, "Sex, Sex, Sex." And she
reflexively avoided them. But after seeing a couple
of exchanges, she realized they meant sin semilla —
which means "without seeds" in Spanish — but they
were mispronouncing it "Sensimillia", and
shortening it to "Sens" and then dropping the "n"
making it "Ses", which Lily was glad to buy. She
felt proud she remembered at least one thing from
Spanish class.

Occasionally she and Trevor would come home from their menial go-nowhere jobs they kept for appearances sake, eat some mushrooms, drink some red wine, smile at each other, and reflect on how awesome it all was, reciting the California script — Niiiiice... Right On... Yuuup... Watching the calendar peel, waiting for their parents to kick so they could finally inherit it all.

I may seem a little harsh on Lily and Trevor, but deep down they were really sweet and harmless. Something I wouldn't say about their families. If I grew up in a house where my father called professional basketball "Niggerball", or where everyone would do anything for money — lie, cheat, steal, anything short of kill — I'd probably turn Rasta or smoke some PCP and get kicked out of boarding school too.

They owned a four-bedroom flat at Union and Castle close to everything: Washington Square Park, where the old Chinese did Tai Chi every morning, Cafe Trieste where Coppola adapted Puzo's book to the screenplay for The Godfather — and the best coffee; The Savoy Tivoli where all the young European tourists went to drink beer and hang out — it must have been highlighted in their guide books. Good Italian restaurants, art galleries, City Lights Bookstore, Specs and Vesuvio — the original "Americana" bars where Kerouac drank; Tosca — the first Italian-American club in San Francisco; and Yuet Lee, the best Chinese seafood anywhere — steamed giant oysters on the half shell sprinkled with sea salt, red pepper flakes, drizzled with a sesame oil and rice wine vinaigrette; salt and black pepper squid with sliced jalapeños in black bean sauce with lime; live trout pulled fresh from a tank and grilled ten feet away, with scallions, lemongrass, and thyme.

* * * * *

Hector lived in the Mission. He was Chloe's best friend in the Art Department — she found him far more interesting than the dorky theoretical physics types. Peruvian by birth, he looked like an Inca with pin-straight jet black hair and mahogany skin; he came to the US as a teenager and got his citizenship, but still had a South American depth of soul. Her first day there Hector and Chloe went for breakfast at Ton Kiang out in the Richmond District — the best dim sum east of China.

Waitresses rolled around carts of freshly steamed dumplings stuffed with shrimp and snow peas, or with mushrooms and pork, or Chinese broccoli and crab meat, in stacked cylindrical bamboo baskets, and checked them off their ticket as they asked for them. Hector loved the deep-fried whole shrimp, and ate them headfirst, crunching them all the way down to the tip of the crispy tail. Chloe's favorite was sticky rice and spicy duck breast steamed in banana leaves. Two homemade hot sauces, one green and one red, were crushed fresh daily. They drank Tsing Tao beer, and chrysanthemum flower tea — absolutely nothing like it in the world — the whole dried flower expanding as it steeped in the teapot. For dessert they had almond cookies, mango custard, and sweet puffy rice buns with dark tamarind syrup in the center.

The bus took them all the way back to Fisherman's Wharf in North Beach, where they went walking. Chloe always liked to reacquaint

herself with San Francisco with her feet on the
ground. To her the city had a vivacious personality
like a beautiful woman — one of the few American
cities that did — and she liked to let her know she
appreciated her with sensual contact.

Fishy smelling sea lions basked on the docks of
Pier 39, barking awkwardly. Crooked old wooden
stairs on the east side of Telegraph Hill lead them
through lush foliage, like the country in the city,
past bungalows with wooden decks overlooking the
bay, up to Coit Tower's observation floor at the top
where they looked out onto North Beach.
Continuing west to Russian Hill they passed
through George Sterling Park on the plateau, and
read the plaque with an excerpt from his poem "The
Cool, Gray City of Love":

> Tho' the dark be cold and blind,
> Yet her sea-fog's touch is kind,
> And her mightier caress
> Is joy and the pain thereof;
> And great is thy tenderness,
> O cool, grey city of love.

Turning north, down past Ghirardelli out onto
the spiral jetty that cut through the rough bay, they
looked back at the city towering over gray water, as
idle fishermen lazily tossed their hooks; and gulls
wandered, scavenging for dropped pieces of bait;
couples meandered, searching for a connection; and
sailboats drifted crisscross over the chop. On North
Point Street in a cramped little Chinese-run conven-
ience store they got a couple of twenty-two ounce
Carlsberg's in paper bags and crossed through Fort
Point Park past all the old dismantled gun emplace-
ments looking out over the channel, and then
walked through the tunnel of trees to the center of

the wide open field and sat down by the giant knotty centuries-old juniper tree, smack in the middle of the park, and watched people play Frisbee around them with the Marina and the orange bridge in the background. They'd been walking for a couple of hours, not saying much. They never felt compelled to talk, but Chloe wanted to catch up.

So. She asked him. What's new with you?

…I finally got a job at MoMA.

Congratulations!

Thanks… And we found this cheap gigantic Victorian in the Mission. We lucked out, really. We've got this crazy old hippie landlord who charges us practically nothing. He's perpetually remodeling the upstairs, but rarely shows up to work on it, so we've pretty much got the whole place to ourselves.

That's great.

I've been up there a couple of times. It's painted all white with clear plastic drop cloths everywhere, and fifteen different skylights that leak every time it rains, and weird little alcoves and angles and changing levels, like he was on acid or something when he designed it, or he's making it up as he goes.

Hector described the downstairs as one wide open space with hardwood floors and a big salvaged stainless steel professional gas stove, refrigerator, and double sink; and a tall counter separating the kitchen area from the rest of the living room, with barstools on one side. At the far end of the spacious living room were two bedrooms, and on the opposite side past the kitchen was a bathroom with a claw-foot tub, and an office with a futon for guests, about 2000 square feet altogether. Someone nicknamed it Crumbling Gardens because one entire wall of the living room was French doors that led out to a wide brick patio the length of the house where the landlord installed a big crumbling stone circular water fountain, surrounded by a ten-foot-tall chain-link fence with datura plants growing all over it so nobody could see in. Their parties were legendary. Once they went to the warehouse store a few bocks away and got cases of Czech beer for ten dollars apiece, charged two bucks a can, hired a DJ, and took some Ecstasy. About two hundred people showed up, and Olivia wound up dancing-in-place to the beat with her hands clasped in prayer, unable to speak, staring up at the blue light bulb they screwed into the ceiling socket in the living room, having a spiritual experience. It didn't affect Hector like that. He manned the bar at the kitchen counter all night and made a killing. He had a good business head. Although he did say he felt waves of pleasure washing over him as people danced all night till the sun rose. Maybe his everyday state of mind was already like being high on Ecstasy.

It was getting towards sunset, so they walked up to Van Ness. Hector caught a bus south to the Mission, and Chloe took the cable car back to Trevor and Lily's, catching one going east on Jackson, and another going north on Mason to Union. As the trolley crested Nob Hill heading toward North Beach — the cool wet breeze rushing past, the spiking Transamerica building iconic, and the Bay Bridge in perfect golden light — feeling sort of elevated above it all, Chloe suddenly felt a deep sadness.

This is all Samsara. She thought. No matter how beautiful, it's all suffering. Even the President of the United States, supposedly the most powerful man in the world, is still a victim to the monster we're collectively creating. He may be able to fire the CEO of a major corporation but he's still not free. Every moment of his life is determined by dealing with his circumstances, this so called reality. Even he can't do whatever he wants. Chloe looked back toward the west and watched the heavy fog bank roll in low over the water and swallow the legs of the Golden Gate Bridge as the sun set. She called me — the only person she thought could understand — and told me how she was feeling as she rode the cable car home.

Don't let Samsara get you down. Was all I could think of saying.

She got back to Trevor and Lily's and they ordered some delivery from Indian Oven, passed around a joint, and dug into saffron rice with hot mango pickle and crushed papadam mixed in. The saag was authentic, made with mustard greens as well as spinach, and the red tandoori chicken had a light smoky flavor; lamb skewers were expertly roasted too, with just the right amount of garlic and lemon; and the ginger shrimp with bell peppers was the perfect combination of sweet and spicy. Tearing pieces of naan glistening with ghee, they scooped up the food the traditional way, and followed it down with Kingfishers.

It was the time of year when the moon rode the hills as it dove into the fog, and after dinner they watched from the roof as the big beaming orb dropped from the clouds, slinked behind black silhouettes of Nob Hill towers and distant tree covered crests of the Presidio, skirting the ragged dark edges, plunging between tips of the twin bridge spires, down into the shining mist that now buried everything west of Fort Point.

iGeneration

* * * * *

Chloe and Hector went to Dalva, Hector's
favorite bar in the Mission with the best jukebox in
the city — "The Endless Night" by Suba, "This
Strange Effect" from Hooverphonic, Photek's
"DNA", Peace Orchestra — always the coolest
tunes. Bar seats were all taken as usual, but there
were plenty of empty tables — the sign of a really
good bartender — so they sat at a table.

What are you reading these days? Chloe asked.
Have you heard of the Arhuaco?
No.
They live on Sierra Nevada de Santa Marta, a
mountain in Columbia that rises from sea level
directly to 18,000 feet, with glaciers at the top, the
highest coastal mountain on the planet. They
believe in a primordial creator, not as a being, but as
a force, and they call it "The Mother". Their whole
society is led by priests called Mamas. ...I know,
it's weird. Mamas and mother. But you can't be a
priest till you study for eighteen years, most of it
spent in a cave in complete darkness, until you
develop the conviction it's your responsibility to
keep the entire universe in balance, which of course
is whacked right now. Glaciers at the summit are
melting. Once they're gone there's no bringing those
back.

A lot of people see the primordial force as
feminine. Chloe said.

Well, humans get in touch with it by what they
call Se — Creativity — which is sort of paired with
what they call Aluna, human thought and Imagination. We're constantly creating the world we live in,
both literally and figuratively.

177

I know what you mean, but give me an example.

To them the universe has nine layers but we can only see one.

That's like String Theory. She responded.

A child is in the womb for nine months, and their main temple has nine levels... A hill could be a house, or the mountain they live on could be the entire universe. Or your body could be the mountain, the hairs on your body the trees, and your blood the rivers and streams... Thoughts are clouds or stars and the empty sky behind is Mind. And they think every living creature is your teacher because everything reflects everything else.

Like Samantabhadra's Net... Chloe said. How else would all these different cultures all over the world get the same ideas?

What made me think about you when I was reading it was that they see the universe as spun on a spindle — it's woven, and we're all woven into the fabric too.

Like tantra. Chloe said. The warp and the weave.

They move to different places to harvest all their different crops so they have villages all over the place, but they only live in any one of them for a few months at a time. And all their moving around — they call it weaving. I thought that was kind of like what you're doing.

...I guess it is. Chloe said.

But they believe their weaving lays down a protective cloth over the earth, so they can create balance.

I feel like I'm doing the same thing. She responded.

A couple of people left the bar and Hector and Chloe quickly took their seats. As they settled on the barstools, Hector saw a girl walk in, and perked up.

Lemon... He said.

He used that expression for whenever he noticed he stopped thinking, like when you first bite into a slice of lemon, and there's only that experience — no thoughts. Always watching for spaces between his thoughts. Chloe wasn't sure it was such a good thing that he felt compelled to label the gap, which naturally brought him out of it, but at least he was being mindful.

That's Charlotte. The one I told you was touching me last week.

Hector was in love with his girlfriend Olivia, so a beautiful girl touching him in his favorite bar didn't mean that much, but she did make his thoughts stop. Charlotte sat at a table with another beautiful blond, and a couple of older white guys with white hair. Something strange was going on because it looked like one of the older guys was trying to lift up Charlotte's friend's shirt and show her breasts to the bar, and she was fighting him off as best she could. It didn't look violent, it definitely looked playful, but rough playful.

They drank and listened to the spacey tracks from the jukebox. Then Charlotte came over and touched Hector on the back.

Hi, Hector.

Hector lit up again. She was gorgeous, with long blond hair, big breasts, and a thin athletic figure.

Hey, Charlotte. He said. This is my friend Chloe, visiting from Colorado.

Hello, Chloe. And she put her other hand on Chloe's back. What are you two up to tonight?

Hanging out. Hector said.

Taking in the sights?

He chuckled, Yeah...

Chloe noticed she had a slight English accent, but suppressed, and she asked, Are you from England?

Good ear. I'm from Devon. She said.

Sounds like you've almost lost your accent.

She responded in a very British accent, But I can put it on whenever I like.

I've been to Devon. Chloe said. Exmouth, and Bath. There was this great pub in Taunton where I drank cider with the owner, Cubby.

Oh, you've got to say it like *Taunton*... Say it.

Chloe said, *Taunton*. In an English accent.

Very Good! You sound absolutely British when you say it that way.

She rubbed her hands on their backs. Chloe looked at her eyes and her pupils were gigantic.

So what do you do, Charlotte? Chloe asked.

I do a lot of things. I'm going to The Bahamas next week. I'm a personal trainer, and I'm going to spend a few months down there. It's an exchange program. ...My sister and I are cooks as well; we're going to cater a topless party in Los Angeles when I come back...

Chloe saw Charlotte had something in her hand the whole time — a g-string with the same black and white checkered pattern chef's pants usually have.

She said, I got these for her.

And she held them up with both hands so they could see.

They make these things so skimpy these days. They barely cover anything.

Charlotte grinned deviously and pretended to daintily dab something from Hector's mouth with the thong.

Hector looked confused, and said, I thought you were a chemistry professor at State?

I am... She said. Assistant Professor. I never found that 50-thousand-dollar-a-year teaching job I dreamt of, and I couldn't afford the $3000-a-month mortgage on my flat, so I branched out.

They didn't have anything to say to that.

She asked, What do you do Chloe?

I studied theoretical physics; right now I'm traveling around temping.

You still have to get your PhD. She said.

Exactly.

Well, tick, tock. ...I'm going to get back to my sister. Good to meet you Chloe.

She kissed Chloe on the cheek.

Bye, Hector.

She kissed him fully on the lips, and walked away.

Chloe and Hector looked at each other with raised eyebrows.

He said, Whoa...

A girl's gotta do what she's gotta do. Chloe responded.

* * * * *

San Francisco is the most sex-obsessed city in the world. Everybody defines life itself by sexuality: Queer, Straight, Bi, Gender Queer, F to M, M to F, Butch, Fem, D/S, B & D, S & M, Bull, Cow, Pig, Monkey, etc. The City of Moonlight.

Lemon

Last time I was there I met a bartender who supplemented her income dancing at peepshows, watching guys masturbate on the glass between them every night.

I asked her, What do you think of men?

She said, I think they're all pigs, present company excepted.

Waitresses in five-star restaurants moonlight as high-priced prostitutes. Women writers pay the bills doing phone sex; male writers as street whores. Medical school students earn their way through as strippers. Performance artists of all kinds make a living in sex massage. And law students moonlight in all-night clubs with glory holes. All of them defend themselves with the same argument: "It's actually really empowering; people only bad mouth it because I'm financially freer than most of them", etc. Defiantly damaged. Most of them I just want to give a hug and tell them, "It's going to be alright", even though I know they would most likely say, Ew, get off me.

* * * * *

Charlotte came back over with a tiny box-shaped handbag covered in fuzzy faux black-and-white cowhide. She opened it up and handed them two cards.

I hope this isn't too forward. She said. I'll be there after eight and I'd like you two to come.

They both looked at the cards. They read, The Merry-Go-Round, Admit One Free. It was one of the premier strip clubs in San Francisco... Chloe glanced at the handbag.

Charlotte noticed, and said, Oh, that's my fuzzy little box... because I don't have one anymore.

Hector asked, Because you have to wax?

No, shaving's best. You just have to go the right direction. Ta ta. And she sauntered back to her table.

Hector took a sip of his drink, and sighed, and arched his eyebrows, then looked at Chloe, and asked, Well... are we going to do this?

Chloe said, Why not? I'd sleep with her.

* * * * *

They called it the Merry-Go-Round because the outside of the central circular stage rotated slowly like the baggage claim carousel at the airport. Strippers rode around on little animal-shaped figures, each with a slot for a dildo on the saddle they could use if they wanted as they slowly circled the stage. All of them were drop-dead gorgeous, and in great shape. This was San Francisco. The Ivy League of strip clubs. There was serious competition. Charlotte's stage name was Lollipop because a little bag of suckers dangled from a cord around her waist. You can probably imagine why. She didn't put them in her mouth.

On the four surrounding stages strippers pole-danced: jumping up, spinning, and hanging upside-down from the shiny brass poles, sliding down to the black lacquered stages, waiting for their turn on the merry-go-round in the center.

Chloe laughed briefly, and said, It's laid out like a mandala.

Oh yeah… Hector replied.

They sat at a tiny round table away from the main stage and got some drinks.

God... My normal life is at about volume 2. Dalva is at about 5. This is like cranking it to 10! He said. I'm going to go play some pool.

He got up and went to the pool room.

Chloe watched Charlotte dancing on a side stage after some other girl took her place on the merry-go-round. She jumped up, clung to the pole with only her legs, spun slowly down, slid gently to the floor and undulated her torso on the glistening black stage under black light; draped her legs over some guy's shoulders, and gyrated her pelvis in front of his face.

When she was done dancing, she came over and abruptly sat on Chloe's lap, Hey there.

Hi, Charlotte.

We're going to give you the royal treatment tonight. She said.

Oh really?

I'm really glad I met you despite all this, really... She said.

Me too. Chloe responded, a little taken aback.

She wrapped her arms around Chloe's shoulders and draped her blond hair on Chloe's face and said, You look so yummy. I bet you have a whole bevy of young paramours.

She answered, A few.

I want to give you a private dance — you and Hector.

Alright. I have to find him first.

I'll be looking for you.

She kissed Chloe on the mouth and strode away in her skimpy silver stripper's outfit, briefly glanced over her shoulder with a smile, and winked, her hips swaying, wearing towering clear plastic platform heels each filled with water and a live guppy.

Chloe was feeling a little hungry so she ordered some French fries and went to the pool room to find Hector — a plate in one hand and a martini glass in the other. As she got to the swinging door a pretty stripper in a leopard print bikini with short dark hair and light brown eyes arrived at the same time, noticed Chloe's hands were full and held the door open for her.

Thanks. Chloe said.

She smiled and said, Mmm... grabbed a few French fries, and grinned mischievously. They went inside.

Have some more.

She took some more while chewing the others, and said, Thanks. I'm so hungry!

Take all you want. Chloe offered.

She grabbed a handful and sat on one of the black leather sofas where the strippers came to rest between dances. Chloe found Hector at one of the pool tables. He seemed distracted when she told him Charlotte said she really wanted to give them a private dance.

You could get a private dance from any of them. He said.

I think a dance from her would be different tonight. Chloe replied.

Whatever...

A stripper and a guy were talking, sitting at the opposite end of the long black leather sofa where the girl she bumped into at the door was sitting, with a lot of space between them. Chloe sat next to the girl who took her French fries. She had three tattoos of tigers on her body.

Cat Woman... Chloe said.

That's my name. Cat.

Chloe.

What are you drinking? Cat asked.

Chopin with a twist.

Do you like lemon drops? Let's do a shot!

Okay.

The waitress was nearby and Chloe waved to her and ordered two lemon drops. She brought them pretty quickly.

Cheers! Cat said.

They clinked shot glasses, knocked them back, and bit into sugar covered lemon wedges.

Cat smiled, Mmm…

Her pupils were huge just like Charlotte's.

Then the blond who was with Charlotte at Dalva — "her sister" — came in and abruptly sat on Chloe's lap. No intro.

Hello…? Chloe said.

You have the most beautiful hair. "Her sister" said.

Her pupils were huge too.

She ran her fingers through Chloe's loose caramel curls, Mmm... She turned to Cat, Feel her hair. It's so soft.

Then they were both running their fingers through Chloe's hair, and ooh-ing and ah-ing.

Finally Chloe said, Alright… And gently removed their hands from her head.

I saw you at Dalva. The one on her lap said.

I saw you too. Chloe replied. You're Charlotte's sister?

I'm Brandy.

Chloe.

She wondered why Charlotte's sister gave her stripper name… or even stranger, maybe it wasn't.

Then Brandy leaned over to Cat and said, I love your new haircut. And stroked her short dark bob.

It looks really nice. Chloe chimed in.

Cat smiled, Thanks.

Then Brandy sighed, leaned back on Chloe and relaxed and watched people playing pool as "How Soon Is Now?" by the Smiths blared from the speakers. Chloe didn't want Cat to feel left out, so she touched her hand, and Cat wound her fingers through Chloe's, scooted close, leaned her head on Chloe's shoulder and sighed too.

Charlotte peeked her head through the door and smiled, then disappeared. Hector glanced at Chloe with two women draped all over her and let out a short jealous laugh. Then the DJ said something Chloe didn't catch, and both girls stirred. Brandy got up and walked out of the room like a robot.

Cat leaned close, and said, Come watch me dance.

She walked to the stage in the pool/smoking room and Chloe followed.

She sat at the edge of the stage and watched her strip. Cat did this thing with her breasts, flexing each of her pectorals individually, making each firm plump breast wobble separately.

I thought only guys could do that. Chloe said.

Cat smiled hungrily.

When her time was up, she got down on her hands and knees at the edge of the stage, put her hands on Chloe's shoulders, leaned close, sucked Chloe's earlobe into her hot mouth and briefly bit it. Then she got off the stage grinned and strode out of the room. Chloe went back and sat on the couch to finish her drink.

The stripper who'd been at the far end of the couch talking to a guy the whole time looked at Chloe cynically and said, What's *your* deal?

I don't know. Chloe said. Sometimes the stars are just right, I guess... Karma.

Lemon

The stripper shook her head in disbelief, and continued her conversation with the guy next to her. Chloe got up to go to the ladies room, and on the way she ran into Charlotte going the opposite way.

Are you ready for that dance? It's only forty for three songs.

Alright. In a few minutes.

I'll wait for you on the other side.

Okay.

* * * * *

Chloe went over to the other side of the club and Charlotte was standing there with a smile. She grabbed her hand and led her to one of the private booths with high padded walls so only the security cameras on the ceiling could see what was going on inside. She sat down and Charlotte started dancing in front of her as the next song played. She took off her bikini top and her g-string then leaned close to her ear and said, You're not supposed to touch me, there're cameras, but I want you to touch me. Put your hands on me.

Chloe asked, Won't you get in trouble?

Not if it looks like I'm fighting you off. Put your hands on me.

So she touched her and Charlotte made feeble feigned attempts to remove her hands from her body. Charlotte kissed her mouth, and put her breasts on Chloe's face, and rubbed every part of her naked shaved body all over Chloe. The third song ended and she put back on her bikini top and g-string, and they walked back toward the other side hand in hand. She said, For eighty we can get a private room. We can do anything you want in there. I've got toys.

Chloe smiled and said, I want to check on Hector.

Charlotte hugged her and briefly kissed her and said, I am really glad I met you, Chloe, aside from all this, really.

Me too. She said.

Wait... Charlotte opened her fuzzy little box and gave Chloe her business card. She said, This is against all stripper rules, but that's my real number. Call me.

It read, Dr. Charlotte Tanner Ph.D., Assistant Professor, Chemistry Department, San Francisco State University.

Chloe went back to the other side and told Hector what went down, and showed him the card, and Hector practically lost it.

He slammed the pool cue on the table and said, I can't believe you! You've got the scent, or something!

I tried to tell you.

He stood there slowly shaking his head for a while, then he looked at his watch and said, Let's get out of here.

Okay.

As they left, Charlotte was doing a solo dance in the center of the main stage as the merry-go-round swirled around her. The DJ announced Lollipop was the stripper who'd made the most money for that portion of the night, so two of the other strippers slowly poured champagne from the bottle into her mouth as she tilted her head back and let it dribble down all over her slender naked curves, and then she opened her fuzzy little box and dumped flocks of paper money all over herself, twenty dollar bills sticking to her breasts, her torso and her thighs, as paper money fluttered to the floor. Chloe had to laugh.

The Inquisition

Would it kill us if we laughed?
Kicked a pile of dead leaves, scattered ourselves
Flower petals to the wind from the demigods of rose
On virgin snow field, under a cloudless dusky sky,
Jumped off a cliff into red light traffic,
Alone together exposed?

— Chloe Pentangeli, Collected Poems

The company was a dot-com called OneLife. Really Californian. It was an online forum where people found energy healers, herbalists, homeopaths, yoga instructors, etc. The only job available. The agency rep said Chloe was lucky to get any work at all with 9/11 and the Dot-Com Crash — nobody was hiring temps. There were forty people in line ahead of her for this assignment but they gave it to Chloe because she was their biggest earner, i.e. they could charge the most for her services based on what she'd made before.

That's what the Mafia calls a capodecina who regularly brings in a lot of cash for the family — "a big earner". Chloe said. I have some distant cousins on my stepdad's side who're mobbed-up. Temp agencies are kind of like Mafia families. They definitely take advantage of other companies' misfortunes like wise guys do. If somebody quits and the company needs somebody right away — like a mark who needs a loan to cover a gambling debt — the company calls up the temp agency rep, who's basically like a mob shylock, and the agency rep either tries to sell the company on the temp who would cost the company the most, or tries to talk up the agency's per hour percentage for the other temps' services. It usually ends up costing the company at least twice what they would pay a regular employee in the short run, but minus benefits, overtime, and other costs, in the long run it costs them less than a permanent employee. So the mark gets his loan at an exorbitant interest rate, he pays off his debt, and the loan shark makes out with a lot of "vig" or "juice" over time.

But temps aren't like "buttons", i.e. "soldiers", or "made men", as one might think. She explained. They're like "associates" — "almost-theres" — people who work for the wise guys, but who haven't been sworn in as members of The Family yet. Some agency reps start out as "associates" and get "straightened out", becoming part of the agency, but not too many, because the agency doesn't "open the books" to new members very often. And the temp agency operates with something like Omerta, the code of silence upheld by members of the borgata.

All temps are told not do discuss how much they get paid with any other temp, on the current job or on any previous job, and the agency reps won't talk about any temp with another temp, or about any job other than the one they want the temp to take. They don't want you doing anything "off the record", without the knowledge or approval of the Family. It's obvious why. They don't want a temp that gets paid $15/hr. freaking out when he meets me, who gets $25/hr. for the same work. And in this particular instance, they didn't want the other temps to know I got the only job available, at a company they may have been way more qualified to work for.

And just like in the Mafia, a person could get "knocked down", demoted in rank, so to speak, if they were found out to be a "snitch" — someone who violated Omerta — or if they didn't take a job the agency rep wanted them to take. There aren't any real ranks, but a temp can get passed over for future jobs, or get offered less and less pay, or get all the most difficult jobs — like being placed at Pandora sweating in a hot cubicle deciphering Cocteau Twins lyrics — if they were known to be "loose lipped". As it turned out, a kindergartner could have done what I was doing at OneLife.

* * * * *

It was almost October, and the gloom in the heavy gray air was palpable. She rode BART from San Francisco through the dark tunnel under the bay, and through mist and drizzle over raised tracks, to the office building in Emeryville, right next to the water in the East Bay. The year before, it was like a fashion show every day on the train. Cars were always standing room only, and people sported brand new square-toed shoes and shiny microfiber windbreakers in early-60's-reminiscent fashion mag outfits, with skinny glasses, and little silver razor scooters. They made a big show of talking on their cell phones about nothing in particular, like how soon they thought the train would get to their stops, and other mindless drivel. And they ostentatiously checked their email on hand-helds, or pinged messages to their friends on the train, looking around with smug gleeful grins.

Now there were open seats everywhere. Tens of thousands were fired or laid off or were simply left without a job. The ones who still sported the

"Dot-Com Look" were reserved and self-conscious now. They didn't want to appear to be so full of themselves, and sat quietly with heads stooped to PDA's, checking out the over 400 barely-used Porsche Boxters — the official car of the dot-com boom — suddenly for sale locally on eBay. At least now people could get good service at restaurants again. Most of the dot-com crash victims went back to waiting tables.

OneLife's CEO was a longtime yoga practition-er, a skinny white New Ager, who sat on a dark blue meditation cushion on a maroon Persian rug with his legs folded in lotus posture, with soft sitar music playing, his laptop on the carpet in front of him, and didn't have any furniture in his office. Executives from other companies thought he was a pathetic clown. There were even articles in The Wall Street Journal making fun of him. Chloe sat awkwardly on one of the two other cushions facing Dave.

It's not a big deal. He said. I make a point of meeting every new hire. We're glad to have you with us, Chloe.

Thank you.

We'll start you out in the stockroom. Marcie will show you.

Marcie stood in the open doorway. She was skinny and pale and wore her hair in that super-cool SF retro style, dyed jet black, pin-straight down to her shoulders, with blunt cut bangs across her forehead — a punk rock Wednesday Addams into recycling.

She smiled and said, Hi. And mooned over Chloe with seductive eyes.

They walked together through a maze of hundreds of cubicles taking up an entire floor of the ten-story building.

Do you smell that? Marcie asked.

Chloe didn't smell anything unusual, and asked, What?

That's the reek of fear. Marcie said. This whole section is customer service, fielding complaints from everyone who logs onto the website. Not a good sign. Anyone could get fired any day. ... They did an internal study because profits are down for two years now, and found out employees are five times more likely to send an email than pick up the phone and call the customers. It's all getting too impersonal.

We'll adapt to it. Chloe responded. There's always been some technological change some stick-in-the-mud says will ruin us, but none of them have so far.

* * * * *

It would take time. Employees were increase-ingly distracted by the Web, which most people were surfing all day, missing deadlines, failing to meet quotas. Cyberloafing. The sense of being a team was evaporating because there was less and less social bonding between employees, absorbed in the technology, paying less and less attention to the people around them. They held meetings and trainings where workers were urged to engage with others personally because it was better for the company, but nobody was complying, as if they were ashamed of themselves, afraid to let anyone know them, for fear of being judged, as if they were criminals guilty of breaking laws imposed by the culture they knew they could never uphold.

"iGeneration" harkens back to the label given the 1970's — "The Me Generation" — but there's a major difference. The Me Generation implies "it's all me" or "it's all about me", which, although self-centered, indicates a degree of cutting through duality, dropping the walls that separate self and other, which was somewhat true of the spirit of the time, everybody jumping into bed with each other and whatnot. iGeneration, on the other hand, also true to the current zeitgeist, maintains a sense of duality. There's confidence that with all the new information "I define the world" — which can be true and beneficial — yet in defining the world a tendency also develops to conceive of "*my* world" as opposed to "*the* world", which only reinforces duality and separation. That's why a teenager can take his parents' gun to school and murder his classmates and teachers without remorse.

It doesn't have to be bad, though, as Chloe said. She was among the first wave of digital natives. The university got their first computer lab in 1983 and because her stepdad was a professor she had full access to it at age nine. She taught herself how to use a Mac and when the Internet came along she felt like it was invented for her. And it never did anything but enhance her life because her experience with it was self-directed — she felt free to turn it off whenever she liked. She never felt addicted or compelled.

* * * * *

In the stockroom Chloe stared at row after row of gray steel shelves filled sloppily with big torn up cardboard boxes overflowing with thousands of crumpled t-shirts of different colors all with the company logo.

Dave wants them folded and organized by color and size. ...At least you can listen to the radio back here.

I can't stand all those commercials. Chloe replied.

Chloe sat silently at a folding table and one by one took boxes off the shelves, emptied them, sorted the shirts separating them by size and color, folded them, broke down the boxes, and placed the neat stacks of t-shirts on the shelves with a label for each pile.

After a while she sang "Wave of Mutilation" by the Pixies under her breath.

"Cease to resist giving my goodbye.
Drive my car into the ocean. You
think I'm dead but I sail away, on a
wave of mutilation, wave of mutilation,
wave of mutilation...
Wa-a-a-ave... Wa-a-a-ave...

I've kissed mermaids, rode the el niño,
walked the sand with the crustaceans,
could find my way to Mariana, on a
wave of mutilation, wave of mutilation,
wave of mutilation...
Wa-a-a-ave... Wa-a-a-ave..."

* * * * *

OneLife was overfunded by some venture capitalist firm, like a lot of dot-coms, and there was this creeping sense it could all collapse any day, like hundreds of others. Everybody felt it. The air was thick with the stench of anxiety that anybody could lose their job at any moment. So what did they do? Everyday droves of OneLife employees streamed down the promontory on foot and in cars to Trader Vic's out by the waterfront for happy hour as soon as the clock struck five.

Walking with Marcie on the sandy Marina Park Pathway lined with ice plant next to narrow Powell Street, Chloe observed the steady procession of people and cars and said, All we need is a hearse in front and a police escort.

Marcie laughed at the joke a little too eagerly. They sat inside the crowded tiki bar sipping water as the bartender made the giant Mai-Tai-for-two Marcie ordered, pouring crushed ice, Kraken rum, curaçao, fresh squeezed lemon juice, and grenadine over sliced ripe pineapple muddled in orgeat syrup in a quart-sized glass goblet with a little paper umbrella and two straws, taking in the view of the San Francisco skyline across the bay through tall plate glass windows. Marcie couldn't handle her liquor and started getting loopy pretty quickly.

Dave... Can you believe him? What a poser! Just because you do yoga and meditate doesn't mean you have to throw it in everybody's face! There's nothing wrong with it, but he could at least have some chairs in his office for people who can't bend their knee behind their head!

...He is sort of forcing the issue. Chloe responded.

I'm going to a party Saturday night. Will you be my guest?

Taken aback, Chloe asked, You mean like a date?

Well, yeah...

Against her better judgment, Chloe said,
Okay…
So can we say we're sort of a casual couple?
Chloe suddenly understood she may have
blundered into a minefield.
Let's wait and see about that. She squirmed.

* * * * *

OneLife had a big quiet room where anybody
could go when they were on break. People could
meditate in there, or take a nap on one of the futons
if they wanted. They offered free acupuncture for
all employees at lunchtime once a week. The pretty
Chinese girl stuck needles in Chloe's ears and left
them there for about ten minutes, and she felt perky
afterward. Dave himself gave free yoga classes after
work three days a week in the health club downstairs, and people came to work with their rolled up
yoga mats under their arms and bags full of work-
out clothes, even Chloe. It was a good opportunity
for her to get to know her co-workers in a casual
setting…
After she finished folding t-shirts, they had her
doing random things like arrange brightly colored
soft cubes for people to sit on in the lobby, or set up
a Japanese stone fountain and bamboo trees with the
interior decorator. One day Dave even had Chloe
calling around to find a place to donate his old bed
because he'd just bought a giant futon. The strange
thing is not a single place in the entire bay area
would accept a donated bed.
Finally, Chloe asked one second hand store,
You accept all kinds of other furniture, why won't
you accept a bed?

The guy said, We don't know what went on in there.

Puritanical America.

After getting to know people in the office, Chloe started asking each one out for a quick drink after work. Americans already have a reputation for TMI when they get drunk, but Californians are the worst. Chloe was shocked by the things they told her. Their stories broke her heart.

Eva, the receptionist, grew up in Monterrey. She was really pretty in the conventional sense; modeled for a couple of Macy's catalogs. Not supermodel material but beautiful with big green eyes an aquiline nose and long dark ringlets. Her dad left her mom when she was two, and her mom, a clerk at a grocery store, had a string of loser boyfriends. It's hard to repeat the story of how they were left alone with her when her mom was at work, and they sexually abused her, the first time when she was only seven. She stumbled around the apartment afterward, leaving bloody handprints on the white walls and on the beige phone as she tried to call her mom at the store.

Now she was completely in her head. Always lost in thoughts. Who wouldn't be? Who'd want to remember that? In any spare moment she perched behind her desk reading some thick book like Proust's "Remembrance of Things Past", or something obscure like Lermontov's "A Hero of Our Time". She sat bolt upright in her chair as she answered the phones, her spine so straight she had to get it Rolfed. But by the day after she got it put back into the natural shallow S-curve, it had already straightened up into the telephone pole again. She called it carrying her sword.

Laura was originally from California, but grew up in Idaho. Her father illegally poached elk horns, shooting the animals, hacking the antlers from their dead skulls, and leaving their carcasses to rot. He used to come home drunk, filthy, smelly and hairy from weeks of slaughter in the woods, the back of the old blue Ford pickup piled high with bloody antlers he sold for hundreds apiece to Asian buyers who ground them up and used them in aphrodisiacs. She froze and cowered in her bed when she heard his heavy boots crunching the ice and dead leaves in the driveway. He stumbled into her bedroom and put a pistol to her head and had his way with her while her mother whimpered, bit her fingernails, and prayed the rosary in the next room, but said and did nothing.

By thirteen she decided she wanted to be a prostitute and went around to the local college apartments knocking on doors with garish make-up on, dressed how she thought a prostitute would dress, in a blue sequined miniskirt and a red and white polka dot bikini top. One day she knocked on the wrong door. They were some drunken frat boys doing Internet porn. They made a fortune on her. Now she was terrified of sex, but she was taking testosterone and Avlimil and kava-kava to help her get over it. Increases libido, enhances sexual enjoyment, balances hormones, relaxes you, etc. She wanted to get over her past, have sex again, and enjoy it. And yet she dressed Plain Jane in a California outdoorsy sort of way, her mousy hair cut blunt above the shoulders in that "mom in training" look — long enough to be attractive to men, short enough so baby can't grab it.

She went to a Native American shaman once who looked at the palm of her hand and told her,

You have no personality. She asked him what he meant; he reached out and grabbed her breast, and she froze. He squeezed her nipple under her t-shirt and rolled it between his thick rough fingers and she did nothing. He withdrew his hand and said, See?

Several others were terrified of sex because of abusive past experiences — most of whom did it anyway without truly enjoying it, to please their partners — but none who remembered it as clearly as Eva and Laura. Most partially or completely blocked it out, saying that they think something went on but they couldn't remember exactly. This is the sex sickness that results from the backlash against Puritanical thinking.

* * * * *

Chloe couldn't sleep. She wrapped herself in her comforter, brewed a cup of chamomile tea, opened the French doors at the back of Lily and Trevor's apartment and gazed down at the city night from the balcony way up on Union Hill. Thousands of lights in windows meant lots of people were still awake. A tiny reserve of car traffic still whispered through the streets.

So many people were out there suffering daily because of their sexuality alone, and there was no way she could help them all, not by herself. She couldn't even help the people at OneLife by herself. She especially needed help with the women. It wouldn't be meaningful enough if she gave them orgasms. She needed a man to do it. The next day Chloe called Max, said she had a temporary job for him; it would pay well, Trevor and Lily would let him stay with them, and she would buy his round-trip plane ticket. She'd pay him out of pocket this time, but right then she realized she'd have to start her own temp agency eventually.

He asked her, Are you making me an offer I can't refuse?

* * * * *

At the corner table in Mario's Bohemian Cigar Store, Max and Chloe sipped Irish coffee, sharing a tiramisu, overlooking the foggy intersection of Union & Columbus and Washington Square Park. It had an old world feel, and they didn't actually sell cigars — only beer, wine, coffee, focaccia sand- wiches, pizza, and desserts. The tiramisu had an excellent balance of flavors. Marsala wine shined through without being too fumy like of some tiramisu that substitutes rum. The espresso taste was rich and satisfying. The chocolaty flavor was bright, the lady fingers weren't soggy, the mascarpone and Chantilly layers were delicious and light, and it was perfectly balanced with a mellow sip of Irish coffee. Chloe explained to Max what she was doing, and what she wanted him to do.

You just have to give them orgasms. She said. You don't have to say anything in particular. I'll take care of that beforehand.

A wispy smile spread on his face as she instructed him. This was a little out there, even for Chloe, but it didn't completely surprise him. After first inviting Eva for a drink one-on-one, Chloe then asked her to go out with her and Max, and then Max asked her on a date. He took her to the Museum of Modern Art after work one Thursday when they stay open late, to see an exhibition of Bay Area Figurative Art. As they meandered through the exhibit talking quietly, getting to know each other, she revealed that Chloe had told her his full name, Massimiliano, and she looked up the history of it. Massimiliano was the Italian version of the German name Maximilian which came from the Roman name Maximus which means The Greatest. In the 15th century the Holy Roman Emperor Frederick III gave the name to his son and eventual heir. In his case it was a blend of the names of the Roman generals Fabius Maximus and Cornelius Scipio Aemilianus, who Frederick admired.

Max took a deep breath, exhaled, and reserved judgment. So she was a little in her head… He would have to get her back into her body. They gazed at Manuel Neri's "Untitled (Nude Model with Bischoff Painting)" for a long time without speaking.

He asked, What do you see?

…It's like the world is stripped down to its basic elements: form, muted color, all the noisy cultural details silenced; only the haunting presence of human beings, in some undefined place. It's how I think a Buddhist monk would see the world after a long retreat. She responded.

They looked at the mysterious portraits by Nathan Oliveira, awash in gray Northern California light. She asked him what his impression was.

They look like ghosts — half-here, temporary, stopping for a little while, passing through. He answered.

Finally, they came to the glowing complex compositions of James Weeks that loosely articu-lated his subjects' experiences in seascapes, land-scapes, and cityscapes of San Francisco. Max gently took her hand without taking his eyes off the paintings.

It looks like he wants to have it all. She said.

On the ferry over to her place in Sausalito, it was dark and windy on the upper deck, and from the middle of the bay, away from the city lights, they could see all the stars, and the arm of the Milky Way splattered across the black. Nobody else was up there. They were alone as they cruised past Alcatraz and she lay back on the bench, arms raised, hands behind her head — the universal sign of surrender — dark ringlets tousled by the breeze, one knee up, and her sheer floral patterned dress undulating, the other leg stretched across his lap.

I don't know why I feel so comfortable with you. She said. I feel like I've known you before.

He lay down on top of her and kissed her. Her back arched like the spine of an open book, and they made love right there. All sounds faded to silence except her self-stifled cries as she reached orgasm. She told him she felt like they were merging with the stars and the fathomless black all around them, her sighs resonating to the ends of space. Max didn't want to stop, but they were nearing the lights of Sausalito, and it was getting cold, so he let himself go.

She said, I've never had an orgasm the first time I made love before…

The ferry landed in Sausalito and they walked a short distance from the docks to the community of houseboats where hundreds of vessels clustered against the shore, moored to a maze of floating piers. Inside, it didn't look like a boat at all — the wide living room had high ceilings and walls of smooth polished redwood, a free-standing black metal fireplace facing a worn brown leather sofa and two armchairs; a white fleece rug on hardwood floors in front of it. Farther in were a wooden dining room table and chairs that matched the walls, and behind that the stylish kitchen and bathroom and a stairway leading to the bedroom and studio upstairs. The only downside for Max was the constant motion, however slight, but he supposed a person would get used to that.

Nice place.

It's my boyfriend's.

Where's he?

Down in Costa Rica for a month. We're taking a break.

Domesticity… Max opined.

That sounds a little cynical.

Well, if it was working, you wouldn't be taking a break, would you?

Do you know how to start a fire? She asked.

Does a one-legged duck swim in a circle? He replied.

She chuckled.

He made a fire and Eva made a simple dinner — stir-fried broccoli, onions, carrots, and tofu, seasoned with fresh garlic, black sesame seeds, chopped ginger, soy sauce, and cilantro, over brown rice. She gave him a bottle of Bonterra Organic Pinot Gris to open and they sipped as she cooked.

When was your last relationship? She asked.

Not since college. Seven years ago.

Have you ever been in love?

That gave Max pause.

Does puppy love count? I thought I was totally in love when I was sixteen.

What happened?

He sighed, She was strange… or maybe not strange enough. She was the most beautiful girl in high school, like Grace Kelly, and one of the most popular — not because she tried to be; people just gravitated towards her because she was beautiful.

How did you meet her?

On the first day of school I saw her in the bleachers at orientation in the gym in the middle of 800 other people, and I walked right up to her, sat down next to her, and introduced myself. I was the new kid, because we moved and I switched schools halfway through, so people were curious about me. She liked me too, but she had a boyfriend. We talked in the hallway between classes, or at parties — she even invited me over to her house to hang out and listen to music and go cross-country skiing — but she was always dating the quarterback of the football team, or the captain of the wrestling team, and she just wanted to be friends with me.

How did that make you feel?

It was frustrating, of course. One time she asked me to come over and her dad answered the door and told me she was up in her room. I walked into her room and she was lying in bed in a rainbow-striped tank top with a hand down her pink shorts, masturbating. She froze, nonchalantly removed her hand, and said, Hi. As if she hadn't been doing anything at all. Can you imagine? Sixteen-years-old? Hormones raging?

What did you do?

I kissed her. She was completely into it and we made out for a long time. She let me touch her breasts but she wouldn't let me put my hand down her pants. After a while I got irritated. How could she masturbate when she knew I was coming over, how could she kiss me like that, let me touch her breasts, and then without a second thought go over to her boyfriend's house that night, who by that time she admitted was dumb as a bag of hammers?

Did you stop being friends?

I graduated a few months later and didn't see her that summer. In the fall I went to CU but she came to visit me in Boulder once — she was a year behind me — and we made out again, despite she still had a boyfriend; and she still wouldn't have sex with me.

Did that make you angry?

I stopped talking to her.

Was that the last you saw of her?

No... She ended up coming to CU too, but I wouldn't call her, and I didn't see her on campus for years. There were 25,000 other students; if you don't have the same major... I saw graffiti about her in one of the men's restrooms. She was still that popular. January senior year she was at a party off-campus and the girl I was with noticed how I was looking at her, and said, You're totally in love with her! And got up and left. I didn't talk to her but she looked me in the eye, and smiled.

Do you think she wanted to talk to you?

I don't know... I was over it. A few months later, I finally did bump into her on campus and she invited me to go on a hike in the Flatirons, but when it came time to meet her, I found something else to do. That night, she called and asked why I didn't show, and I made some excuse.

What happened after that?

Well, when it was almost graduation, despite me blowing her off, she invited me to be her date at her graduation party at her grandparents' house by the creek in Boulder — I took a year off to travel so we ended up graduating the same year — but I turned her down. It was too little too late, and I never saw her again.

Do you think she wanted to marry you?

Maybe... I heard she did end up getting married about a year later to some professional skier. I was way too young for that anyway.

How about now?

Some people aren't the marrying type. I'm an artist. Life's a gamble for me. Will people get what I'm saying?

They ate dinner sitting on the white sheepskin in front of the fire, leaning back against the sofa.

What about you? What's your story?

Uh-oh, now you're onto me. She said. That's my talent — I get people to talk about themselves so I don't have to reveal anything. They used to call me "The Inquisition" in high school.

He thought for a few seconds, and said, You don't have to settle for a guy you don't like just to get all of this. He looked around at the beautiful houseboat. If you don't take risks, you stagnate. Trust your gut. He said.

I grew up poor. She replied. I can't go through that again.

They made love once more on the floor next to their empty plates and wine glasses. She liked making love a little buzzed and on a full stomach. It was work for him, but he managed. She felt like she could really let go in the privacy of her home, and shouted at the top of her lungs when she came, letting it all out — the tension of all her circumstances, past and present. She fell asleep immediately afterward, right on the rug, with her arm across his chest and her head on his shoulder. He lay there awake on his back.

12

Violated

*"Everyone is necessary — from the person you love the most
to the one you absolutely despise — even you. [laughter]
Without one the other wouldn't exist. We're interdependent."*

— Chloe Pentangeli, Selected Talks on The First Cycle

    Marcie was kind of a political activist rebel.
"Kind of" because she went to demonstrations, and
she dressed unconventionally, but she would never
do anything that would really make an impact. She
did, however, buy some lethal bacteria once online,
imagining she'd use it in a daring terrorist act, but it
was only collecting dust in a jar in her closet.
Basically, her rebel attitude was a lifestyle choice.
Because there wasn't any dress code at OneLife,
she wore things like tight red plaid straight-leg
pants, or short Catholic school tartan skirts, combat
boots, and wife-beaters, or sleeveless t-shirts, and
never a bra. Her shirts all had political sayings, like
"Question Authority", or "Peace is Patriotic", one
even said, "Vote Republican: God wants 99% to be
poor, dumb, sick, and afraid." Showing off her
blond hairy armpits. She actually had "Liberal"
tattooed on her left shoulder.
    On the scale of the world's most ridiculous
ideas, trying to define yourself as either liberal or
conservative weighed in pretty close to the top for
Chloe. Conservatives fixate on a fantasy "Leave it
to Beaver" past where there were rules everyone
adhered to unquestioningly, without any comp-
licated messes like racial diversity, or abortion

rights, or immigration, or climate change, or foreign policy, or freedom of expression. Life could be perfect if we all just shut up and follow the rules — to paraphrase a certain Austrian army corporal. Liberals, on the other hand, fixate on an ideal "John Lennon" future that may never come: "Imagine" no countries, no war, no religion, no pollution, no possessions, no greed or hunger, a brotherhood of man... It's a good dream to aspire to, but not at the expense of ignoring the conflicts of the present, and forgetting the urgency for relevant positive change. Conservatives typically say the goal of an election is to win; Liberals too often say, lamely, elections are "the greatest expression of the democratic process". Wah, wah... Yet, at the end of the day, liberal's who get held up at gunpoint become conservatives; and conservatives who have near-death experiences become liberals. How pointless is that? And we're stuck here spinning our wheels.

* * * * *

Marcie took Chloe to a party in an old ornate Victorian house out on 26th and New Van Ness, where there were lots of earnest, artsy, multi-cultural people, vintage furnishings, and huge potted plants in low lamplight. They played world music, drank Mexican beer, smoked ganja, danced, and had conversations about poets, political artists, and movements, but nothing really out of the ordinary. Another bunch of do-nothings...

One guy was talking about how sexually liberated they are in France compared to here. "I don't speak French well enough to understand everything on the national news, but it was hilarious to see the anchorman wearing a hat with a big silver penis erected on it as a joke. Someone on the level of Brian Williams. No big deal."

Another person said he was sick of the US and wanted to move to Belize, when someone asked him, Do you actually have the balls to move to a foreign country and leave everything familiar behind? Do you know how racially diverse Belize is? *You'll* be the minority. They understand English but they speak Creole. Are you ready to learn a foreign language and speak it everyday? Are you aware that nothing works all the time like it does here? The power cuts off intermittently, the sewers stop flowing and have to be dredged, they don't put trash in plastic bags and they don't always pick it up when they say they will; it floods every year in hurricane season, roads wash out and are pocked with potholes; they repave them at a rate of a mile a month. Most of the food you eat here isn't even available; people will never really open up to you because you're foreign, and they don't trust Americans. Plus, it's brutally hot almost all year long and not everyplace has air conditioning. You think you can handle that?

A woman spoke to the danger of nuclear weapons. "What happens if a hydrogen bomb falls into the hands of terrorists, or if a psychotic leader takes control of a nuclear power? We're actually in more danger now than in the Cold War."

The ocean crossing iGeneration faces is wider than ever previously — coastlines morphing; earth quaking with more intensity; glaciers liquefying, rushing in torrents, polar ice caps cracking, now mobile, plunging in mountains to the waves; sea levels surging world-wide, hurricanes and tsunamis raging wilder with climate change. The shore we left is barely recognizable, a ghost of itself; we don't know where we're heading, and we've never fathomed the mystery and complexity of the depths that have borne us to now. Once again the world has altered irreversibly.

* * * * *

When it was winding down, Marcie invited Chloe over to her place for a drink. Her apartment on 21st and Valencia was another beautiful Victorian, with the entrance on the second floor because of the hill — the entrance for the neighbors underneath was on the side, down an old wooden stairway. In the large remodeled kitchen with huge picture windows at the back of the house overlooking an acacia tree lit by the dusk-to-dawn floodlight in the courtyard between buildings, Marcie poured shots of Hornitos tequila under soft track lighting at the gray marble island. The more they drank the crazier and more belligerent Marcie got. She probably had a chemical imbalance and would've been better off never touching the stuff.

She yanked on her own hair and to Chloe's surprise, it came off. It was a wig, and she had a blond buzz-cut underneath. She threw her arms around Chloe and sloppily kissed her on the mouth.

I want you right now. She said.

Chloe rarely felt this way — she was uncomfortable, and felt a little taken advantage of. She couldn't remember the last time anybody treated her like that. Charlotte was a little forward, but a Girl Scout compared to Marcie. Because of her good looks alone, most people who approached Chloe were usually at least a little intimidated, but combined with her intelligence, the response she was most used to from prospective paramours was abject fear. Marcie had no fear. She had no regard of any kind for anyone but herself.

Chloe said lamely, I think I'm going to head home.

Marcie glared at her, and shouted, What? How dare you come home with me after a party I invited you to, kiss me, and then just walk out! I can't believe this! What are you, a cop? You have no right!

She tried to hit Chloe with a couple of flailing girly hits, but having taken Muay Thai classes, Chloe covered up in time. Then Marcie turned, swung her arm in disgust, knocked the bottle of tequila off the counter, smashing it on the tiled kitchen floor; took a few steps away, stooped her head, folded her arms, and cried.

Marcie…

She looked up with big sad teary eyes, and said, I'm sorry. It's just that you're the first person I've liked in… I don't know how long.

Marcie came back over to Chloe, threw her arms around her, and buried her face in the crook of her neck. I'm sorry. She said again, and sobbed.

Chloe felt warm tears soaking into her collar, It's okay. Chloe replied.

Marcie sniffed and looked up at her hopefully with a red wet face, I can't wait to see Dave's face when I tell him we're going out. He's had a crush on you ever since you started.

Chloe tried not to cringe. She knew Marcie was one of the few that needed her help the most, but the prospect was not appealing.

* * * * *

The next Friday she went to happy hour with Max, Eva, and Laura at Aztlan in the Mission. Cut sheet copper palm trees arched over the bar where they sipped margaritas, eating chips and guacamole while they waited for a table in the deafeningly busy restaurant. Waiters made the guacamole right in front of them with fresh avocados at the peak of ripeness, none too hard or soft, added chopped red onions, a squeeze of lime, salt, and some cilantro. The chips were homemade too, fresh corn tortillas cut into sixths and deep fried. And the margaritas were luscious — Corazon tequila reposado, fresh squeezed pink grapefruit juice, Triple Sec, Cointreau, and lime.

She's been going around the office telling everybody we're dating. She even told Dave the CEO we were going out! Chloe said.

She cares more what people think than about your actual feelings for each other. Max commented.

I don't have feelings for her!

She thinks you do. You got yourself into a twister.

Thanks.

Be ruthless and break it off.

I'm not even close to finishing the job.

Sometimes you have to cut your losses. He said. And glanced over his shoulder at Eva and Laura noticing someone leave the seat next to Laura. ...Are we still greenlit?

I'm not giving up yet. Chloe said.

* * * * *

Violated

Laura said to Eva, I'm sick of being afraid. I want to be okay with having sex again. I used to love it.

Pretend you're someone else. If it's too weird or scary, just pretend it's not you having sex.

Laura sipped her drink.

Max stood next to them, Hey Eva.

Max, this is Laura.

They both said hi, and beamed at each other. There was an instant attraction.

I'm going to take off. Eva said. Have fun.

She briefly hugged Laura, whispered in her ear, Fuck him! And abruptly left, partially because she was a little jealous — although she had no place to be, since her boyfriend was back — and partially because she hoped Laura would sleep with Max and finally enjoy herself.

Max felt like Laura was ready.

Let's get a drink somewhere not so frenzied. He said.

We can go to my grandmother's restaurant. She responded.

They sauntered down Valencia Street toward downtown behind a mariachi trio in white cowboy hats, dressed in white leather charro suits, and vaquero boots, carrying a guitar, an accordion, and a trumpet as the sky rapidly darkened.

The taxi dropped them off on the northeast corner of Leavenworth and Union as darkness fell, and they walked to the front door of the white corner building under a sign that read "Top of the Hill". All the lights were off.

It's closed. Max said.

I have the key.

Laura fished in her pocket, unlocked it and they went inside. They crossed the eerie emptiness

216

between tables with white tablecloths and bentwood chairs over black and white checkerboard linoleum floors through a swinging door into the kitchen. In back, she didn't want to turn on the lights because they had a view of the glowing city and bay through the picture windows. She got them a couple of bottles of beer out of the cooler and they gazed out over the dark misty water as they sipped. Just then a foghorn blew and they heard the distant clang of a buoy bell. Max took her in his arms and kissed her. Immediately she melted. Her lips seemed to fit his perfectly; her intention was absolutely clear but not the least bit forceful. It was by far the most seductive kiss he'd ever felt. She had to know how to let a man know he was wanted with just her mouth. It was a matter of life and death for her.

He undressed her and as he did she kept repeating, I want you to fuck me so hard...

He undressed too, and laid her tall thin body prone on the long stainless steel prep table, took a gallon jug of olive oil, dumped it on her and rubbed it all over, including her rear entrance.

That feels good. She said.

Then he climbed on the table and entered her from behind, his hands on the backs of hers, their fingers intertwined, squishing oil. Soon she started laughing and crying at the same time.

He asked, Are you okay?

Yeah. She said. I haven't enjoyed sex in so long. That was the first orgasm I've had in... I can't remember.

Then she held him, slowly running her hands up and down his body, and they writhed languorously on the slick table like eels kissing, and watched flickering lights on the black bay. The fog had cleared.

Violated

* * * * *

Lots of people in San Francisco get snooty about the neighborhoods they'll go out in. Lily only wanted the rock & roll lifestyle of the Upper Haight. Trevor only liked North Beach and the post-college meat market of the Triangle. Some people only went out in the Mission and SOMA. Others wouldn't leave the Richmond and the Avenues. A few preferred Oakland and the East Bay. Everyone was desperate to define their world. But parties were definitely the exception. If there was some-thing at somebody's apartment or house then everybody showed up no matter where.

Chloe invited Lily and Trevor, and Lily invited Caroline, because she wanted Max to hook up with her. Lily always secretly had a crush on Max, and now she wanted him to join her and Trevor in their Truman Show. That was her safe way of showing Max she liked him without jeopardizing her relationship with Trevor. They let Max drive their BMW M5 sedan to the party, which they immedi-ately regretted, as he sped through the streets ignoring all speed limits and traffic signs, tires squealing around corners, the back end fishtailing, even catching air over a couple of hills. A car pulled out right as they approached Marcie's apartment house in the lower Haight, and Max swerved into the empty place, and slammed on the brakes.

Rock star... Chloe commented.

Lily and Trevor chuckled nervously and pretended they weren't rattled as they got out.

Caroline was another one of our college friends, part of the conservative minority in San Francisco. She came to the city to establish a career, find a husband, and start a family, and she pined away for her dream, going through boyfriend after boyfriend, month after month, getting more and more devastated by each breakup. Max felt like telling her, You picked the wrong city, kid.

She saw her future all around the bay area. Bitter women in their forties who were finally making the kind of money they'd always dreamed of, who gathered in gaggles at each others' homes and condos they all owned — where they each lived alone. They honked and quacked and hissed about how they just couldn't meet any decent straight men — either because they didn't have the time because of work, or because the ones they met only wanted to sleep with them, or because they were getting too old, or because San Francisco was too queer, or whatever.

In their softer moments they'd toy with the idea of "lesbianism". One might even take a girlfriend for a while, all the others in the group salivating every passing week for the gossip. But eventually she'd realize she wasn't queer, and everyone would hang their heads and sigh, as if they hadn't the foggiest notion it would never work out in the first place. They weren't being honest with themselves. Then they'd all swallow their anti-depressants, double up on sessions at the gym, and bury themselves in work again, and try to renew their faith in an impossible dream.

Caroline had long curly brown hair, warm almond-shaped brown eyes, fair skin, and a calm way about her. She was the girl next door, the one that was supposed to happen for Max, according to Lily. They slept together a few times freshman year, and all her girlfriends thought they should get married. She did too. But Max had no interest, back then or now. He never bought into the tacit agenda most college girls have to find a husband and make babies. The MRS Degree. He saw it right away. He felt it, like a ghost lurking behind their smiles and their wily bright eyes, and understood their overtures for friendship, or even just sex, as an extremely subtle but relentless effort to furtively usher him toward the altar and the maternity ward.

Max chatted with Chloe on the couch in the dark living room under the multi-colored Christmas lights Marcie kept burning all year, as Gilberto Gil played on the stereo, and Marcie seethed. They looked stunning side-by-side — Michelangelo's David and a dark Bo Derek — and it showed that they liked each other too, although, as ever, they were just friends. But together they had a glow everybody noticed. It wasn't a big part of her character, but if she were honest, Caroline would have to admit she was jealous of Chloe.

To get Max's attention off of Chloe, Lily asked him, You used to go out with Caroline at CU, didn't you?

I wouldn't say we went out... He responded.

How did you first meet? Lily pressed.

He sighed, and said to Caroline, You tell the story.

No, you can. Caroline replied. Trying to keep the dream alive...

We were freshmen and I went to a party one night and they were playing Bauhaus, Sisters of Mercy, The Birthday Party — all dark 80's stuff — and everybody was wearing all-black except her. She had on jeans and a white t-shirt. She stood out. So I went over and talked to her... It was one of those things... I saw her.

Caroline practically purred. Nothing sounded as good to her as those three words coming out of a man's mouth — "I saw her". Except the other three words. It made her think, though, I'm different from all the rest to him, I'm special, unique. He get's me, he's paying attention, he understands, and so many other men don't have a clue.

We went out for a year after that. Caroline added proudly.

We weren't really going out. He reiterated.

Caroline pretended she didn't hear him.

Chloe went to the kitchen and got a beer from the refrigerator, and Marcie followed her, picked up a "handle" of tequila from the counter, opened it, and started swigging straight from the jug.

You know what I think when I look at him? I know he's your ex-boyfriend and everything, but I think he's a cad and a womanizer, and he has no respect for women!

He's not my ex-boyfriend.

Well, it's disgusting how he's coming on to you and Caroline at the same time.

We're just friends.

I can't believe you're doing this right in front of me! She said. Letting a man hit on you in my house! At my party! I never should've brought you home with me! I never should have let you kiss me! Get out! Right now! Get out!

Chloe gently took her hand and said, Marcie... Let's talk about this. Tell me what's bothering you.

Chloe thought men could learn from this, so she explained it to me. Never try to solve a woman's problem, or you become her problem. It's like defusing a bomb. Be patient. Don't argue. Don't jump to conclusions. Don't react. Don't try to explain yourself. And never ever try to reason with her, because when she's emotionally upset, reason doesn't come into it. Most importantly, don't take anything she says personally.

She said, When a woman is emotionally upset, she says things most men tend to take literally. Men are usually looking for answers — information. But you're barking up the wrong tree. In a woman's mind, emotional expression is a form of bonding. Anything she says in a highly emotional state is for affect. It's meant to make you feel the same way she does, creating a bond. Women are like David Lynch movies. Chloe said. We're expressionistic. Lynch puts together images that affect you, make you feel a certain way, because those images affected him, and they express the emotions he has in relation to the information he's working with. It doesn't really help to analyze.

You could say most women aren't looking for solutions, we're looking for problems. She continued. To us there's absolutely nothing wrong with a problem. You'd feel the same way if you bled once a month. To solve a problem is to destroy life. That may sound strange to a man, but for example, we all have the problem of trying to survive. If you solve that problem once and for all — i.e. eliminate the problem — then you're dead. To women, life is a group of important problems, and without problems there's no life. Even if you have all the money in the world, you still have to eat to survive, so eating is one of life's necessary problems, and will continue to be until the moment of death. But if you're in relatively good circumstances, that's a good thing, because think of all the different kinds of food you can eat. So men's constant quest for solutions to problems seems pointless to us. The whole world would be better off if we could all admit problems are part of life instead of grasping for a fantasy world that's problem-free.

In the living room, Caroline took Chloe's place on the couch next to Max.

You should come over to my place and tell me about New York. She said. It's only a few blocks from here.

They could hear Marcie screaming at Chloe in the kitchen, which was killing the vibe of the whole party.

He said, Okay.

Everybody left or was leaving by then. Trevor and Lily took a taxi home.

Marcie ranted and Chloe listened, nodding her head, saying, Mmm-Hmm... I didn't know you felt that way... I can see why that would be hard for you... It's important for me to be able to talk to Max, though. I know how frustrating that must be, but that's how I feel, and I don't think that's going to change. But I want you to know it's really important to me that you're happy too...

Marcie stopped abruptly and smiled, Really? Of course.

And suddenly happy tears welled in her eyes, and she quickly wiped them away. She threw her arms around Chloe and giggled, not knowing what to say, and kissed her with her hot wet face. Chloe thought she'd probably have to sleep with only Marcie at OneLife for the rest of the time she was there. It was pretty obvious she needed it.

Max and Caroline stepped into the kitchen briefly.

I'm going to walk Caroline home. Are you okay?

Yeah, I'm fine. She said. Don't go back to Lily and Trevor's without me. I'll leave the door unlocked.

* * * * *

Walking through the fog over to her place a few blocks away on Dolores Street, the fine mist filling the air made luminous rainbow ellipses around streetlights. It was too late for any traffic. After climbing the stairs to her front door, and crossing through the living room, they sipped red wine in her spacious dining room sitting at the oak table on hardwood floors under a small crystal chandelier surrounded by floor to ceiling wrought iron wine racks like a cage. Caroline worked for a wine distributor and had cases of bottles from everywhere. She looked at him with sad eyes, like a bird with clipped wings, as he told her about New York, about his latest graphic design projects, and how three of his paintings were accepted to a group show at the Mary Boone Gallery in SoHo, and that he went to a rave at the top of the Chrysler building — the party promoter knew one of the security guards.

He finished his story, there was a lull, and then she blurted out, I want to be with you, Max!

As if she hadn't listened to a word he said.

I know I'm not cool or intellectual like Chloe or your other friends, but I love you! I've loved you ever since freshman year! ...I want to get married and have kids.

And she cried quietly. He sighed, and didn't know what to say.

You have to say something! What do you want? Do you want to do me right here? Right now on the table? She quickly took off her jeans and panties. What? She said. I feel like you could just walk out the door and I'll never see you again. She started to sniffle, and said, I feel so stupid for loving you, but I'll do anything… Anything you want...

He stood up, and said, I'm going to take off. I've got your number. Take care.

He kissed her on the cheek and left her standing there half-naked.

* * * * *

Chloe waited in the kitchen, sipping a beer, leaning back next to her purse and a big glass jar of utensils on the counter. Marcie appeared wearing a florescent blue bob wig, an aqua blue satin lace-up bustier, crotchless black fishnet hose, thigh-high black patent leather high-heel boots, and a mischievous smile.

What do you think? She asked.

Sexy. Chloe replied.

Marcie wrapped her arms around her and kissed her wildly with a gone look in her eyes. She was drunk already and acting crazy.

Marcie said, Let's have sex right here.

…Okay. Bend over on the recycling bin.

She bent and put her hands on the edges of the blue plastic bin full of empty brown beer bottles. Max walked in and was a little surprised by the scene but dismissed his impulse to speak and rolled with it. Marcie was taken aback to see Max but by then she was lost in the moment, the room swirling drunkenly around her. Chloe took the strap-on out of her purse and grabbed a spatula with a thick rubber handle out of the jar of utensils from the counter.

Take him in your mouth. Chloe said.

Max unzipped, Marcie held onto the edge of the recycling bin with one hand and Max with the other, and Chloe entered her from behind with the strap-on and the spatula handle — Triple Penetration — gripping the black laces of her bustier on her lower back with one hand, the empty beer bottles jingling every time Chloe thrust.

Marcie made muffled sobs as she came multiple orgasms but when it was done, she was indignant. She wiped her mouth with the back of her hand, turned to Chloe and said, What the hell do you think I am, some kind of whore?

Chloe was shocked, and said, No…

Marcie stormed off to her bedroom and slammed the door. Max and Chloe looked at each other quizzically.

I honestly didn't think she'd have a problem with that. Chloe said.

Well, you got that one wrong.

Then Marcie burst back in with a jar of water and threw it in Chloe's face.

Get out before I call the police! Get out of here!

* * * * *

The following Monday, Chloe sat at her desk and Dave immediately approached and said, Will you come to my office?

She followed him to his office with everyone tracking them with their eyes. Chloe felt her face get hot and her stomach turn cold; her sinuses cleared and sweat dripped from her armpits. Marcie sat cross-legged on one of the two cushions facing Dave's cushion, her face red and her eyes dark and sunken.

Take a seat. He said, and gestured toward the other cushion next to Marcie. Chloe sat cross-legged too, and Dave took his seat behind his laptop, and spoke haltingly.

Chloe… Marcie has… made a complaint that… you forced her to… give fellatio to a man… and I wanted to… give you a chance to… respond.

Chloe sighed, I didn't force her.

You made me do it! Marcie said.

I didn't make you. You could have said no. And it was outside of work. Chloe responded, and looked at Dave.

Now Dave sighed, I understand that.

According to her, we're dating. Chloe added.

She told me… but I can't have this kind of antipathy in the office. You can go back to your desks.

Before Chloe even got to her desk her cell rang and it was the temp agency telling her she would no longer be working at OneLife because of sexual harassment, and to get off the premises immediately.

…Alright. …Okay, I get it.

She gathered her things and left without a word to anyone.

Right after work Marcie went to the Mission Police Station at 17th and Valencia, sat in an office on the second floor next to one of the tall narrow windows under small Romanesque arches looking out over 17th Street, and reported to a uniformed female cop, who bore a strange resemblance to Marcie, "she'd been forced by Chloe to have oral sex with Max".

* * * * *

227

That night the woman cop showed up at Lily
and Trevor's. Lily answered the buzzer.

Who is it?

It's the police. The voice said over the
intercom. I'd like to speak with Chloe Pentangeli.

Lily glared fearfully over her shoulder and
buzzed her in. Chloe stood in the entranceway
holding the door open while the female cop stood in
the hall. Trevor and Lily sat on the couch
eavesdropping as the TV showed a horror movie
with the volume muted.

She claims she was forced by you to have oral
sex with a man named Max. The cop said.

I didn't force her. How can you force someone
to do that? I asked her to do it and she did.

I thought as much.

It confused Chloe that the cop was acting like
the whole thing was a big waste of time, but
strangely, before she left she took the spatula out of
a large Ziploc bag and handed it to Chloe.

Oh, she asked me to return this to you.

Chloe didn't know what to do but take it, and
noticed the cop was wearing protective black
surgical gloves. When the cop left, Trevor and
Lily's eyes went wide and they immediately took
big bong hits. Chloe ran to the kitchen holding the
spatula like a piece of feces, buried it at the bottom
of the kitchen trash, ran to the bathroom, jumped in
the shower and scrubbed herself from head to toe
under scalding water. Afterward she sat at the
dining table in her thick white terrycloth bathrobe
with a towel around her hair, sipping a steaming cup
of chamomile tea. Max sat with her nipping a
tumbler of Wild Turkey.

I still feel violated. She said. It's so wrong to
have a cop in her dark uniform and combat boots,

with a gun and a radio, with all the ugly unruly energy of the street, standing in my "home", even though I'm only a guest.

Max laid a hand on her shoulder, and said, You'll be okay…

She got up and wandered toward the French doors at the back, softly crying.

What the hell am I doing? Am I insane?

Max went to her and put his arms around her. You're not insane.

Am I even making a difference? Is it true nothing really matters?

It matters to you. He replied. That's all that counts. At least you're doing something.

I need to slow down. I need to step back. She sighed deeply, sniffed, wiped her eyes with the back of her wrist, hugged him, and looked into his eyes. Thanks. She said, and kissed him warmly but briefly.

Lily and Trevor both raised their eyebrows again when they saw the kiss, and both immediately took another big bong hit.

I need a break. Chloe said. I need to take some time off and figure out what's next.

You deserve it. He said. You've been working hard. It's like you have two jobs.

She let out a short breathy laugh, and glanced at him with an appreciative smile.

13

Half an Ox: Her Second Epiphany

"There's no necessity the human race should survive. Every living thing comes to death. The light we're an expression of is beginningless and endless. The present moment is only a flash on the surface of the waters of eternity."

— Chloe Pentangeli, Selected Talks on The Second Cycle

Chloe got her hair braided back into corn rows and she and Max went to the Asian Art Museum with Lily and Trevor. Lily liked art more from the standpoint of an accessory than something necessary — something to match the sofa, as they say — but at least she liked it. Trevor went because Lily insisted. They saw paintings of couples in sexual positions illustrating the Kama Sutra, rough stone Ghandarvan sculptures of Buddha that made everything feel old; bronze multi-armed Tibetan wrathful deities with ritual weapons, fangs and claws, and strings of severed human heads dangling from cords around their waists.

There was a special show of Chinese ink and brush paintings from the time around the Boxer Rebellion when opium smoking was rampant — the drugs dumped on the Chinese market by the British to bury the xenophobic sentiment sweeping the country, like when the US government poured crack into American streets in the 1980's to snuff backlash against Reaganism. Remember that?

One painting particularly struck Chloe. It was a view as if seen from up in a tree, like the painter was waiting for a flood, with large leaves and flowers in the foreground, partially obscuring a secluded country house with intricate lattice work, which in turn obscured tall dark peaks in the far background. Pretty radical for Chinese ink and brush. It reminded her of the Zen koan about an ox seen through a window from inside a house but it's half-obscured by the window frame and the wall. Where's the other half?

Then they walked through Golden Gate Park to the Japanese Tea Garden for rice crackers, almond cookies and tea, and sat at one of the wooden tables under a wooden-roofed canopy right next to the Tea House. The young Asian waitresses shuffled around slowly, dragging their flip-flops, with utterly bored expressions, and grudgingly took customers orders, rolling their eyes and sighing as they carried the orders from the tea house to the tables.

Lily said, See? They have no concept of customer service in their culture. They might as well be delivering mail!

Max responded, They probably don't make good tips selling tea and crackers, Lily...

After tea they split up — Max with Trevor, and Lily with Chloe — walking down sandy paths through the gardens, over arched bridges with little streams running beneath them, and across round stepping stones in lotus-covered ponds with big orange koi in the dark water.

Lily asked, So what's going on between you and Max?

...I don't know. Chloe said.

Well it's obviously something from the way you kissed him.

Chloe cringed remembering the cop.

We've always been just friends. We never slept together.

That's probably a good thing. Most women drop their thongs the second they look at Max. Maybe he's starting to appreciate that about you. Lily said. How do you feel about him?

Chloe sighed, I'm not in love with him. I mean, I love Max, but I love lots of people — you, Xavier, James, Hector, Olivia…

Maybe he's the one who can really understand you. Lily said. You don't have to be in love. That always wears off anyway. I've never been in love with Trevor but we make a good couple. You should tell him you love him. If he doesn't feel the same you'll still be friends.

It's not like that. Chloe insisted.

Lily and Chloe came across a small bonsai garden, with tiny trees, rocks, and a flow of white sand representing a landscape with a river running through it, as if seen from fifty feet above. She thought of the koan with the ox again and suddenly it hit her like the sun bursting from her skin. The other half is Mind.

Do you see that? She asked Lily excitedly. The river, the noise of water, the movement — what brings it to life is Imagination! That's the Third Eye.

Lily had no idea what Chloe was talking about, Oh, yeah…

She had her second epiphany. She stood there entranced watching dark shadows of low fast-moving clouds and tall swaying eucalyptus trees dance against the beige back wall of the tea house, listening to the hiss of the stiff leaves bristling in the cool ocean breeze; breathing their pungent scent.

* * * * *

She asked them to drop her off on the Upper Haight, and Max said he wanted to go too. He wanted to do something touristy while he was in San Francisco because he'd be shunned out of town by his artsy friends in New York if he did anything like that there. Right on the corner of Haight and Ashbury they walked toward the park through the throng streaming past bars, restaurants, and clothing stores. She felt like something had changed. Like the ground shifted after the whole Marcie debacle. Why should it be her job to single-handedly save the world? Sure, it's good to do something helpful, but really… She needed to have some fun too.

Let's get a drink. Chloe said.

In Aub Zam Zam Chet Baker was singing "Let's Get Lost" on the jukebox filled with only classic jazz. It was dark and tiny with a couple of tables and a small sitting room off to the side of the wide semicircular bar. Moorish arches decorated every doorway, and a mural behind the bar depicted a mounted Persian prince, and a kneeling princess by a stream, her chestnut horse not far, and two white rabbits in the woods behind her. Opposite the bar framed black and white photos of the place dating back to 1941 hung on the red walls, showing all the celebrities who'd been there. Max put some money on the countertop, Chloe ordered her favorite Chopin with a twist, and Max had the house martini of Boord's gin and a splash of Boissiere vermouth they'd been serving since World War II.

I feel like dancing. I want to completely let go. Chloe said.

A shaved-headed dude sitting next to her in baggy black jeans and a black t-shirt, with tribal tats, a nose ring and a goatee, stooped to the bar over a pint of ale, pricked up his ears, and put a glossy cardstock flyer next to her drink. It read "Off World", and had a digitally rendered kaleidoscopic design of a shining blue butterfly in outer space whose wings were each the face of a beautiful woman, and there was a telephone number.

Thanks. She said.

Max asked him, Do you know a bakery where we can get some rolls?

The dude looked him up and down, and said, Show me some ID.

Do I look like a cop? Max responded.

This is Haight Street, dude. For all you know I'm a cop.

Max unzipped his pants and discretely exposed himself for a second.

The dude said, Let's go outside.

In the alley behind Zam Zam, he pulled two big Ziploc baggies out of his pockets — one filled with pink pills, and the other filled with yellow pills.

I've got red apple and green apple. Red apple's more touchy feely; green apple is more speedy.

Is it E? Max asked.

This is Foxy. It's like E, but without all the bullshit. You won't get hot or thirsty, and it's more psychedelic.

How much?

Twenty a hit.

Max handed him $80, Two of each.

The dude opened the baggies, handed Max the pills, smiled, and said, Later, dude.

He ghosted down the alley.

* * * * *

FADE TO:

ROAD TRIP MONTAGE:

A) In Zam Zam, Chloe dials the number on the flyer and gets the secret map point. "One More Time" by Daft Punk PLAYS.

B) At Lily and Trevor's, on the day of the party, Chloe and Max pack a cooler full of ice, drinks, and food.

C) Chloe and Max speed north in her rented white Nissan Z over the Golden Gate Bridge.

D) In a parking lot in downtown San Anselmo, Chloe gives the party promoter $30 and gets two maps to the party.

INT. CHLOE'S RENTAL CAR - DAY

Max takes his turn driving; Chloe SINGS along to "One More Time" and bounces lightly in her seat with the map to the party open in her lap as they speed through golden hilly countryside.

She briefly touches Max's thigh as she grooves to the MUSIC, which surprises him -- she's never been so affectionate.

                    MAX
        Foxy?

                    CHLOE
        Sure.

He pulls a small Ziploc baggie out of his pocket.

                    MAX
        Red Apple or Green Apple?

She takes one of the yellow pills.

                    CHLOE
          Save Red for later.

She puts the pill on her tongue and puts
the other yellow pill on his tongue,
turns and looks out the window.

POV CHLOE, the fabled caramel hills of
Northern California streak past in a
blur.

                    XAVIER (VO)
          He told her about how he lost
          his virginity at age thirteen
          with a sixteen-year-old in
          the back of her Volvo station
          wagon parked in a citrus
          grove, inhaling the intoxi-
          cating scent of orange
          blossoms. She told him about
          Candy.

EXT. ROAD - EVENING

Chloe's white Z stops at a metal cattle
gate on a rural two-lane highway and she
shows their maps to an attendant to get
in.

                    XAVIER (VO)
          Maybe it was the drugs… In
          any case they connected like
          they never had in all their
          years.

EXT. DIRT PARKING LOT - EVENING

The white Z parks amid hundreds of cars,
the trunk opens, and Max and Chloe get
out. They gaze up at darkening redwoods
towering on hills around them as night
falls.

                    XAVIER (VO)
          They were blazing high by the
          time they got there, and so
          was everybody else.

EXT. REDWOODS - NIGHTFALL

Max and Chloe lug the cooler, a blanket,
and a few bags down a dirt path marked by
a string of flashing rainbow colored
Christmas lights, Max illuminating the
way with his pocket light.

                    XAVIER (VO)
          It wasn't one of those
          commercial raves like
          "Tomorrowland". The viral
          corporate world will co-opt
          anything.

EXT. MEADOW - NIGHT

In an open meadow with more Christmas
lights strung up in the trees, a DJ at a
booth PLAYS spacey down-tempo on a low
stage, getting warmed up. Chloe and Max
lay down the blanket, set the cooler on
top and sit with it as the drugs come on
hard.

                    XAVIER (VO)
          There weren't any restaurant
          chains hired to setup fast-
          food booths, or sporting
          goods companies contracted to
          furnish tents for campers.

FOREST RAVE MONTAGE:

A) Hundreds of people stream in from the
parking lot and dance immediately, arms
and legs leaving light trails.

Half an Ox: Her Second Epiphany

> XAVIER (VO)
> It wasn't just another frothy
> frat party where everybody
> gets wasted and cheers when
> the DJ says "it's all about
> being one with everybody"--

B) Two guys wearing ogre masks walk
around on six-foot-tall stilts. Women
dressed as wood nymphs and lace-winged
fairies flit here and there. Elves,
witches, and wizards mill through the
crowd.

> XAVIER (VO)
> And as soon as it's over and
> the drugs wear off they go
> back to being numbed-out
> narrow-minded pigs.

C) Pan appears with goat legs and a giant
phallus; a pudgy little Cupid with
feathery white wings, a tiny golden bow
and quiver of golden balsa wood arrows
runs around shooting people.

> XAVIER (VO)
> At least the intention of
> "Off-World" was to have an
> open mind and to reconnect
> with Nature.

D) Bacchus sits on a huge throne of
twisted branches drinking from a big
jeweled golden cup wearing a crown of
laurel leaves, eating bunches of grapes.

EXT. MEADOW - NIGHT

People dressed in all-black set up
tripods with digital video cameras all
over the meadow. Max and Chloe sip
electrolyte water.

                    MAX
        There's going to be a
        webcast.

                    CHLOE
        We'll be metaphorically
        dismembered -- beamed all
        over the world.

                    MAX
        Most people focus more on the
        video they shoot than the
        real thing right in front of
        them.

                    CHLOE
        Let's hope they take some
        time to dance too.

A DRYAD, (22), covered in leaves, with
dirt smeared on her face, briefly leans
close.

                    DRYAD
        You can't escape the tyranny
        of the DNA! You may think you
        can outsmart it. Ha! Where do
        you think the smarts come
        from? But you can still
        evolve on the Planet of the
        Apes. Time to evolve!

She disappears.

                    MAX
        Don't you think they're
        acting out a bit for the
        cameras?

                    CHLOE
        Well, we're all "on the
        spot". This is my movie. The
                    (MORE)

                    CHLOE (CONT'D)
mystery is how you got in it.
I'm the actor, I'm the
camera, the cameraman, the
director, I'm the audience,
and I'm the world outside the
theater -- I am the Mind.

                    MAX
I guarantee you 99% of them
don't take it that far.

                    CHLOE
Mass exposure can either make
the wall between self and
other drop, and the world
becomes a stage in the
Shakespearean sense -- which
is Enlightenment -- beyond
the scope of the performance;
or it can solidify subject
and object into narcissism
and solipsism, where Mind's
every movement becomes
amplified as self-important.

                    MAX
Terminal self-absorption...
Like people who roll out of
bed and blog about their
dreams every morning.

                    CHLOE
It's up to each one of us.
The imperative dilemma for
iGeneration, more than any
other in history, is "Choose
Personal Evolution or Choose
Spiritual Death".

                                FADE TO:

              * * * * *

                    240

Greedy un-evolved zombies who sit smugly in their seats of power would do well to consider that 99% of the world *is* evolving. For centuries the majority has been unable to see through the blanket of misinformation that lulls us to sleep, accepting the shackles that keep 1% in control. Even if a few were able to see what's true, they've often been unwilling to act for fear they be ostracized by the blinded and lose their place in society, or be stomped out by those in power.

But the blanket the golden minority has been weaving for centuries has begun to unravel irreversibly. No longer is the truth simply too much information for 99% to even fathom. A generation is growing that not only can process it all, but can see reality in its totality and act on it. iGeneration will inexorably multiply until by sheer numbers alone we can't be bought off to perpetuate the lie. A few naysayers and critics are easy for 1% to dismiss, but when hundreds of millions see clearly, find alternatives and solutions to the problem, and take action, sovereignties will crumble and the people will rise. Prophetic examples abound on the Internet. Censorship can only work for so long — it's becoming clear in China. Best to accept what is and move forward with the tide than be drowned by it. 1/99 will become 50/50, aka. 1.

* * * * *

Eyes glistening, Chloe got up and pulled Max toward one of the smart bars off to one side. A black gender queer bartender in a Chanel suit poured them some herbal cocktails and they sipped. She asked their names and chatted them up; said her name was CoCo.

Half an Ox: Her Second Epiphany

I only have three words for you, Max, honey.
Prada, Prada, Prada. And Chloe, dear. Please don't
take this the wrong way, but there is only one Bo
Derek. And, honey, you ain't it. Read.

Chloe said, That's mean.

All I'm saying is both of you are too beautiful
not to be fabulous. What else is life for? And part of
being fabulous is being the real you... but accent-
uating. CoCo noticed their giant black pupils and
said, Okay, why aren't you two dancing?

* * * * *

The DJ spun mid tempo IDM. Chloe looked
over the crowd. A few large fires burned in stone-
ringed pits on the outskirts, about twenty people
sitting or standing around each, the light of the
blaze making silhouettes of them. One by one they
tossed their plastic lighters into the flames, absorbed
in the present moment, making intermittent loud
pops, tripping out on the sound, like dropping coins
in a wishing well listening for the plop. Chloe
flowed warmly up against Max, surprising him
again, and beamed into his eyes. He took her in his
arms and kissed her, tongues sliding and twisting
over each other's, pushing and pulling in and out of
each other's mouths.

Then, like a vision, they saw two beautiful girls
walking toward them in slow motion, hips swaying.
One was dark with a round afro, in an aqua blue
tube top, white leather hot pants, and white go-go
boots. The other was fair with blond pony tails on
the sides of her head, licking a big round rainbow-
spiral lollipop, wearing saddle shoes, white knee-
socks, a pleated plaid mini-skirt, and a white short
sleeved blouse with a rounded collar; the shirt tails

tied in a knot exposing her slender midriff. Both were grinning, ear-to-ear, surrounded by a swirling swarm of tiny twinkling rainbow-colored spheres, like a trillion little Tinkerbells. Chloe recognized them: their faces were each one of the wings of the butterfly on the flyer.

The black one said, Max?

He said, Yeah?

The white one said, I'm Poppy — like the flower.

And I'm Bridget.

Max looked at Poppy and said, Nice outfit.

It's kind of slutty, I know. She replied.

Bridget said, You're Chloe?

Yeah.

CoCo said she'd be really pissed if she doesn't see both of you dancing.

Poppy added, She wants us to make sure you two have a good time.

They stared at both of them as if from outer space. Poppy hooked Chloe's arm. Bridget hooked Max's. Max hooked Chloe's. And without another word they all walked arm-in-arm-in-arm-in-arm-in-arm-in-arm into the dancing throng — boundaries of bodies undulating fuzzy, in sync with everybody's all around vibrating — here and there not so clear.

* * * * *

EXT. MEADOW - NIGHT

The DJ BLASTS up-tempo Psytrance. Chloe and Max get on one of several black wooden platforms near a black plywood dance floor. A winged fairy puffs baby powder onto the flat surfaces making them

243

slippery so people can better move their
feet.

EXT. MEADOW - NIGHT

Max holds Chloe's hips, and she drapes
her arms over his shoulders; Bridget and
Poppy spoon each of them and they all
pulse to the POUNDING BEAT like amoebas.

                    CHLOE (VO)
          We dance to heal... We may take
          medicine... Native Americans
          say to mend the tribe. We
          dance to clear the way, the
          vibration resonates with
          unstructured Mind; one wave
          crashing is all waves
          crashing, turning mountains
          to beaches, the rhythm of the
          waves, of the rolling beat,
          of endless-beginningless
          Awareness, the expanding
          collapsing multiverse, of
          golden slippers treading
          silent stars, arcing
          eternity.

EXT. MEADOW - NIGHT

Max pulls Chloe closer and they kiss,
skipping fingertips down each other's
spine as rainbow lights flash, and the
hot Psytrance POUNDS to a crescendo.

EXT. MEADOW - NIGHT

Chloe and Max sit next to the cooler --
salty, sweaty, and exhausted. Bridget and
Poppy join them. He takes out four
bottles of electrolyte water, and they
guzzle them down.

MAX
Red apple?

CHLOE
Okay.

He pulls out the baggie with the two pink
pills and gives her one. They put them on
their tongues and gaze into each other's
eyes.

EXT. MEADOW - NIGHT

Chloe, Max, Bridget, and Poppy lay on a
soft patch of grass and watch multi-
layered psychedelic video projected onto
a giant screen strung up between
redwoods. Two VJs at laptops in a booth
edit it live, in real time.

MAX
It's like "Infinity and
Beyond" at the end of "2001"
non-stop… but richer.

CHLOE
They must have written the
code for the program
themselves.

MAX
It's a whole new art form.

* * * * *

I did a cutup of two paragraphs describing them
watching the video, blind-selecting words and
fragments, and minimally edited it for flow;
surprisingly this is what came up:

Abandoned, rapidly flower. A woman's sweaty and
exhausted watery stars fade into the brightening

blue, strung up between redwood trees. They
watched video projected of Kubrick's "2001", a
litter of psychedelic kittens, and plurred nonstop.
Chloe and Max touched, skipping fingers up and
down, all superimposed, or wallpapered Victorian
houses, Russian soldiers on mountains, leaving
behind a trail of shimmering rainbow dust to
beaches, each other's psychedelic pumping human
heart, undulating fuzzy, in sync with rhythm of the
waves, of the rolling beat, of endless bodies. His
fingertips down her smooth long neck, over plump
breasts, her long torso on parade; Poppy and
Bridget a multi-verse of golden new art forms —
live street, and the text their spines as they must
have written the code for stroking each other and
Beyond. At the end everybody's adding them up,
adding new screens lightly over his eyebrows, and
followed the curvy ridges of his ear, then down his
jaw line to his Adam's apple, and over his chest. It
was like Infinity, the Mars Lander rolling on Off-
World, slowly against silent stars, filling the whole.
Chloe draped her arms with little Pinkie sitting next
to the cooler, Max powder puffing it on down,
backing plump breasts of soft grass in the meadow
shoulders. Poppy and Bridget spooned the beat of
the music: a whole. The images were boundaries of
bodies, their feet better. They kissed again, rainbow
slowing them down a cobblestone, abstract and
colorized, in Red Square rotating, pyramidal forms
of four-20 real time layering with unstructured
Mind.

* * * * *

EXT. MEADOW - NIGHT

Poppy and Bridget writhe slowly against
Max and Chloe's backs, pleasuring
themselves with little BUZZING pinkie-
sized vibrators as light from the video
flickers over them.

                    POPPY
          Plur…

                    BRIDGET
          Yeah…

                    MAX
          What's that?

                    BRIDGET
          "Peace, Love, Unity,
          Respect".

                    CHLOE
          …Let's go to the hot springs
          and watch the sunrise.

                    MAX
          Good idea.

EXT. FOREST - NIGHT

Max's pocket light illuminates a dark
footpath through the underbrush of the
river valley; Chloe's map shows the way
as they hike to the man-made cave at the
source of the hot springs.

                    XAVIER (VO)
          Native Americans 600 years
          ago piled up boulders to make
          a steam cave at the source,
          and two collecting pools, one
          cooler than the other because
          it mixes with the river.

INT. MAN-MADE CAVE - NIGHT

Max and Chloe sit naked over the scalding
spring and build up a sweat.

                    XAVIER (VO)
          The water stank because it
          had a lot of sulfur in it, as
          well as a lot of other
          minerals, but Bridget and
          Poppy said it was
          therapeutic; they came there
          whenever they felt sick and
          were instantly cured.

EXT. RIVER BANK - NIGHT

Chloe and Max run naked out of the cave,
follow the hot rivulet to a cold eddy
pool on the river bank, and jump in
WHOOPING and HOLLERING.

                    XAVIER (VO)
          They also built a cold pool
          in a river eddy to temper the
          heat. If all we knew was what
          they taught us in school
          before college, we'd think
          they were incapable of
          anything more complex than a
          teepee.

They climb into the warmer of the two hot
pools.

EXT. HOT POOL - NIGHT

Max and Chloe sit in a hot pool listening
to the faint DANCE BEAT from the redwood
meadow ECHO through the river valley.
Chloe watches bubbles rise.

                    CHLOE
     Do you ever think all life's
     experiences are like
     temporary bubbles in water,
     separate perfectly formed
     events in a singular medium?
     There's no hierarchy. One
     bubble isn't more important
     than another. I'm here in the
     water now, and when I leave,
     this bubble will pop, and
     then there will be the bubble
     of walking barefoot over cold
     ground, then the bubble of
     being inside the car.

Max doesn't comment.

                    CHLOE (CONT'D)
     The potential for a bubble to
     begin is Creation, and being
     in a bubble is the Expression
     of Creation, and the capacity
     of a bubble to end is
     Destruction. Hindus made gods
     out of those: Brahma the
     Creator, Vishnu the
     Preserver, and Shiva the
     Destroyer. They're every
     moment of our lives. I can
     remember past bubbles or
     foresee future bubbles, but
     then they become new bubbles
     -- the bubble I'm in. So,
     really there's always only
     one bubble, but the one
     bubble is also infinite
     bubbles. I guess the idea is
     to get out of a bubble
     completely.

Max heaves a SIGH.

                    MAX
          You really went out there…
          I'm getting hot.

He moves to the cooler of the two hot
pools, and she follows.

EXT. HOT POOL - NIGHT

Chloe straddles him and they kiss, and
she nuzzles her wet head into his neck.
Her breathing becomes heavy and slow, and
she reaches underwater and puts him
inside her.

EXT. RIVER BANK - NIGHT

The sun peeks over the horizon as she
reaches orgasm, her CRIES REVERBERATING
down the river valley.

EXT. RIVER BANK - NIGHT

She sits quietly next to Max in the
steaming water.

                   CHLOE
          Do you think we could ever be
          together?

He's quietly astounded she would even ask
that question, and casually shrugs it
off.

                    MAX
          …You know me. If all's fair
          in love and war, I'm a
          blitzkrieg kind of guy. …I've
          got to get back to New York
          anyway.

                   CHLOE
          I know…

He briefly kisses her wet mouth and gets
out. She follows. THE FRAME STICKS, IT
BUBBLES AND BURNS OUT; THE SCREEN FLASHES
TO BLAZING WHITE. Pop.

* * * * *

A few days later, it felt like just desserts when
Chloe found out OneLife folded. The venture
capitalist firm that was overfunding it called an
emergency meeting and decided they couldn't stand
another day of unprofitability. They demanded full
payment on their loan and Dave had to liquidate the
company.

She could picture everyone in shock, cleaning
out their desks in a haze of anxiety, and imagined
Marcie in the bathroom crying, her sobs echoing
between metal stalls, against cold white tiles,
porcelain sinks and steel plumbing. She imagined
her dragging the heels of her combat boots over the
fuzzy carpet in the lobby, snapping static — her
head hung low with a confused look on her red
ragged face, and the elevator doors closing over it,
once and for all.

14

Bardo

"Shedding defenses — transition between
Being revolted and wanting completion.
Breathing the power to throw off the end —
Reference points dying — the need to begin."

— Chloe Pentangeli, Collected Poems

Chloe called James in Old Town Alexandria. She asked him if she could stay at his place for a while and of course he agreed. She felt safe with James. He reminded her of her dad, and she needed that because, honestly, she felt jilted by Max. James wasn't outright queer, but she suspected he was closet. As far as she knew he'd only had one girlfriend his whole life, and that was only for about six months — or maybe he preferred to be alone — not everyone has to have a partner. She took the next red-eye to DC and got to Alexandria at 8:30 am. It was a three story colonial brick walkup right on Union Street close to the Potomac and all the shops and restaurants on King Street. James answered the door in his boxers with ashy dry patches on his black skin and a nappy short afro, looking sleepy, carrying a big .44 revolver. We used to call him Rusty because his skin was always so dry.

Sorry if I woke you. Chloe said.

No, I was up. Couldn't sleep... How are you?

They wrapped their arms around each other in the sunny foyer, the gun still in one of his hands.

Good. Did you think I was a burglar? Chloe asked.

James looked confused, then realized Chloe was talking about the gun, Oh... no. I was just carrying it around. Here, feel it.

He handed her the .44 and she hefted the cannon from hand to hand.

Substantial... She said.

It was loaded. Chloe handed it back.

You want some steak and eggs? James asked.
Sure.

He shuffled over the hardwood floors into the kitchen, and rattled around the pots and pans.

James shouted from the kitchen, Sorry about the mess — the maid's coming tomorrow. Make yourself at home. Watch some MMA.

Chloe sat on the sofa in front of the giant screen TV which was muted, turned up the volume a little, and watched some Brazilian guys beat each other bloody. She cringed, picked up the remote, flipped through the channels till she found the guide, clicked on some queer porn and watched that.

James quartered fingerling red potatoes, brushed them with olive oil, and baked them on a sheet with fresh rosemary and whole peeled garlic cloves, seared two filet mignons in a pan of butter, cracked black pepper, sea salt, and scrambled some eggs with chopped chives.

He didn't have to work. His dad paid for everything. He was one of the few people we knew who really meant it when he said, "the maid's coming tomorrow". To his credit he did paint for his own pleasure, even though most of his canvases were pretty morose. He had one he called "The Man on the Corner" that Chloe liked. It was a black man in a gray suit holding a briefcase with a thousand-mile stare standing on the corner of an empty city intersection, with a gray building behind him. It looked like a depressive Francesco Clemente. But at least he was creative. He set the food and his gun on the antique dining room table and Chloe joined him.

Why do you have that thing? The gun... Chloe asked.

I always carry it. I sleep with it under my pillow.

Why?

For protection... In case somebody breaks in...

Would you really shoot someone if they broke in?

Hell yeah. I wouldn't necessarily try to kill them. ...It's also for... in case I can't take it anymore.

James studied philosophy at CU, got really into the existentialists and took it all on a pretty nihilistic bent. Chloe believed at least Sartre wasn't actually a nihilist — if you read him properly — but Western Philosophy was still a bunch of crap to her. Of all the westerners she thought Nietzsche made the most sense. He saw nihilism as the logical end point of all Western philosophy because we imagine a truer or better world beyond appearances, and when we fail to reach that true world we become hopeless, and so we imagine ourselves to be guilty or punished by some higher power outside ourselves. Christianity solidifies that notion, suggesting we're permanently guilty in a hopelessly corrupt world beyond our control with the only thing to look forward to an imaginary afterlife. For Nietzsche the only solution is to let go of our fantasy of a true world, and have the courage to live in this world as it is, here and now.

They settled on the sofa, she pressed mute and they caught up with each other while gay porn flashed on the giant screen across the room. James didn't seem to mind. She figured he needed a tune up anyway.

* * * * *

After a long nap, when it was dinnertime, Chloe suggested they get Ethiopian food. They took his maroon Alfa Romeo Spider to Adams Morgan, a neighborhood on the north side of DC that was an ethnic stew of immigrants from South and Central America, the Caribbean, the Middle East, Africa, Asia, and European expats, with good restaurants and cafés, and a good nightclub where they played danceable world music. There was the Pakistani laundry, the Sikh-run corner store, and kids of all races played soccer in the street. Jews and Arabs shopped in the health food market; the old French woman with the apricot tree in her back yard gave jars of jam to the gangbangers in puffy down jackets and baggy pants as they walked by; and the dark fat Haitian lady played mother to everybody who passed her front steps, saying, How you doin' baby? You take care, now...

Roasted lamb and tomatoes, chicken with green peas and potatoes simmered in cumin, cinnamon spiced eggplant and garbanzos, and spinach with roasted garlic cloves were served on giant brass plates with spongy flat bread instead of silverware, and they scooped up handfuls. Chloe wanted him to eat with his hands; get back to basics — out of the head, into the body — back to the senses. And he seemed to lighten up a little.

Bardo

James wanted to impress Chloe and drove to a bar in Arlington called Bardo — "the in between" — for a digestif. It was in a "Googie" space-age style former car dealership built in the 1950's, and there was an old black Cadillac with giant fins stuck halfway through a glass wall next to the front entrance. The former car showroom was gigantic, and packed with hundreds of people, and there were paintings of nude figures all over the walls and up onto the 30-foot ceilings — consciousnesses on their trip between death and rebirth. Apparently somebody in Washington had some soul. It figured they ran a bar. There were hundreds of beers on tap, including Chang — real Tibetan barley beer. He wanted to impress her, and he did.

Back in Alexandria they took a walk by the water, the lights of the city glimmering on the rolling black Potomac. James stopped to buy a pack of cigarettes at the lone all-night newsstand, and there was a line. A Muslim woman wearing a black hijab — only her beautiful face and hands visible — was near the front of the line, and when she got to the clerk he decided to do the PC thing and start up a conversation with her. There was a lot of anti-Arab sentiment in Washington, but the clerk didn't say a word to anyone else.

She asked for a magazine, and he spread a fake smile on his pink face, and asked, Where are you from?

She obviously wasn't in the mood, and replied flatly, Abu Dhabi.

He didn't understand, and asked her again, No, I'm asking where you're from. What country do you come from?

She said it again, Abu Dhabi.

He wasn't getting it, and kept on... I'm sorry, I'm just wondering what part of Arabia you were born in. Where were you born?

She got angry, and shouted, Abu Dhabi! Abu Dhabi! Abu Dhabi! And she stormed off without buying anything.

He raised his eyebrows and shrugged his shoulders, and grinned... Jeez! Touchy!

Chloe thought Political Correctness was no more than another version of conservatism. Be nice to everybody whether you mean it or not. Don't just be yourself. Whitewash.

She said, It's the perfect ideology for cattle who grin obsequiously through the fence at their neighbors, never really making contact, chewing their cud, shuffling obediently down the chute after a fattening life of conspicuous consumption, never questioning themselves, never questioning anything, with American flags waving in front of them, all the way to the final nail in the head — Bang! — X's over the eyes, a toothy grin, stiff legs pointed skyward; hamburgers for everybody. The American cash cows... Wall Street loves us. So does the IRS... and all the oil and car companies... and the national banks. In fact, every big corporation loves us while they work so vigorously in cahoots with the government to take away our rights while we feed and snooze and numb ourselves. There's nothing closer to being a cow on growth hormones than living life PC and on Prozac.

They walked on.

Let's find a party. Chloe said.

This isn't like San Francisco, or New York. James bellyached. Everything shuts down at two, or even earlier.

Chloe said, Shhhh… If you want to find a party, listen.

He kept his mouth shut, and Chloe heard a faint beat coming from down the street. It was a doumbek. In that moment she understood why they called it a doumbek, because that's exactly how it sounds — doumbek-doumbek... do-doumbek-doumbek...

At a stairway on King Street leading to a basement where the sound was coming from, Chloe noticed the door at the bottom of the stairs was slightly ajar.

That's probably a private party. James said.

So? Chloe shrugged. That's probably all there is this time of night.

They walked into an Iraqi wedding reception, everyone dressed in white, sitting around tables with white table cloths in a dimly lit room with white stucco walls and pointed Moorish arches, and white Christmas lights hung everywhere giving the place an otherworldly glow, and they watched two young slender belly dancers with long brown hair swirl around in sheer skimpy outfits and glittering bangles in the middle of the floor. A man at one of the tables finally noticed them standing by the door and hurried over.

I'm sorry, this is a private party.

Chloe said, We just want a couple of drinks. The bars are closed, and we heard the music... Please... We'll pay you.

The man smiled at them, glanced at the belly dancers, and said, Okay, come with me. He led them away from the crowd and the dancers to a vacant bar where they sat on tall stools as he went around to the other side.

James said, I'll buy. Vodka on the rocks?

Okay.

The guy set two giant pint glasses with a few ice cubes in each on the bar and proceeded to fill them to the rim with Absolut vodka. They raised their eyebrows as he poured. He charged them only five dollars apiece, James gave him a ten dollar tip, and they turned to watch the belly dancers.

Seventy more, and this would be Muslim Paradise. James said.

You'd probably need a few extra. Chloe responded. They don't look like virgins to me.

It felt like they stepped through a wormhole straight to Mesopotamia three hundred years ago. Everybody was relaxed and warm, minding their own business. The dancers twirled in the middle of the floor, hands over their heads gracefully wiggling smooth hips to the doumbek. They finished their drinks and Chloe went to the restroom. When she came out, James stood at the door with his hands in his jacket pockets and a devious look on his face.

Time to go. He said.

Up on the sidewalk he carefully pulled two giant pint glasses of vodka with a few ice cubes floating in them out of his jacket pockets.

You asshole. Chloe said.

He grinned and handed her one. I gave him a big tip. He replied.

They sauntered down the empty street sipping.

* * * * *

At James' house, Chloe found "The Crying Game" on pay-per-view and a bottle of Mescal on the kitchen counter among several others, set it on the coffee table in front of James like a challenge, leaned back on the black leather sofa and ordered the movie. James got a cutting board, a lime, some salt, and two shot glasses from the kitchen, and set them on the coffee table too. Chloe muted the TV, cranked The Pixies on the stereo, sliced the lime, and poured them each a shot. Right away, after downing it, James started complaining again.

They don't even sell this stuff in Alexandria. I had to go all the way to downtown DC to find this.

Chloe started singing the lyrics.

Stuck here out of gas...
Out here on the Gaza Strip.
I'm driving too fast...
Two, three... Let's ride a ti-re
down Riv' Euphrates
Let's ride a ti-re down...

Dead Sea make your thoughts?
Washed up from the salty whine.
Dead Sea make a joke?
Two, three... Let's ride a ti-re
down Riv' Euphrates
Let's ride a ti-re down...

Go with the flow. Chloe said. That's what he's saying. Let loose.

James looked at her blankly, and responded, I don't know how anymore.

Okay, we're going to drink this whole thing, shot for shot, and split the worm at the bottom. She said.

That made James chuckle, but Chloe was serious.

Why?

To show you you're not stuck. And we're going to listen to only the Pixies tonight. Not for uniformity but because they rock!

He chuckled again.

Who understands when Frank Black sings "Wave of Mutilation" what he's really saying is Wave of New Relation? She said, and filled their empty shot glasses. Ready?

They licked salt off the backs of their hands, knocked them down, bit a slice of lime, and went on like that as the room swirled around them and the Pixies blasted...

How many poets does it take to screw in a light bulb? She asked. Three. One to hold the light bulb and the other two to drink till the room spins.

He chuckled again, despite himself.

Ten shots each, and a lot of Pixies songs later, they got down to the worm. It was that electric kind of drunk you only get with good tequila or mescal where you don't feel tired, and there's a strange kind of clarity. Swaying, Chloe put the worm on the cutting board, chopped it in half, and dropped one part in her eleventh shot and the other in James'. They raised their shot glasses and knocked them back. Chloe swallowed the whole thing right away, worm and all. James tipped his shot glass back and held the Mescal in his mouth, his eyes bugging.

Swallow it. She told him. He tried but couldn't. Swallow it! She said again.

James grimaced. Chloe could practically see the half-worm bobbing in a mouthful of Mescal tickling the roof of his mouth. James tried to swallow again, but then projectile vomited on the coffee table and floor.

They cleaned up his mess, collapsed on the sofa right next to each other with their clothes still on, and sank into the black fuzz of dreamless drunken sleep — nowhereland.

* * * * *

A few days later James took her to the National Gallery. It was billed as the best show the museum ever put on — The European Modern Masters. "Wheatfield with Crows" was on loan from the Van Gogh Museum in Amsterdam. The dark, forbidding sky, the golden wheat field, the indecision of three paths going in different directions and the black crows overhead like signs of foreboding, or death.

He committed suicide the same month he painted that. James said.

Gauguin's triptych "Where Do We Come From, What Are We, Where Are We Going?" depicted sensual architectural figures of golden naked Tahitian women in quotidian activities, against a blue mountain with lush foliage, and a gray stone sculpture of a deity. Several paintings by Cezanne of Mont Sainte-Victoire, his unattainable goal, his truer better world, showed blocks of color that he used to achieve what he called Flat-Depth. And Picasso stole from all of them, taking Van Gogh's daring to break from tradition, Gauguin's architectural figures and muted colors and primitivism, and Cezanne's flat-depth, eventually creating Cubism — much less colorful, but a synthesis nonetheless. They stared at one of Picasso's early cubist paintings, "Portrait of a Woman with a Guitar".

He saw the order the so-called primitives found in nature and made it modern by turning it around and showing the order we impose on nature... like a warning... James said.

A warning of what? She asked.

The dehumanization of industrialization... Just like the Internet and all the information technology today.

* * * * *

In the guest bedroom, Chloe sat on a cushion on the floor with her legs crossed and attempted to meditate, but fidgeted and sighed and scratched her head restlessly. James came in with an overnight envelope.

Sorry to disturb you. This just came from your mom.

Chloe opened it and pulled out a letter from Paris.

Stephan... She said.

Who's Stephan?

The only one I could really say was my boyfriend at CU.

She opened the letter and read a few lines.

He got married...

Why would he be telling you that?

Such a guy... It means he still has feelings for me.

She suddenly turned pale.

Weird... I feel like I'm coming down with a cold or something. She said.

Her head throbbed and she felt dizzy. She tossed the letter and went to lie down. That was unreal for her. Chloe never got sick. Never even felt sick. She had her body fine tuned. The second she started to feel even a little bit strange physically, she'd do one of six things. She'd either eat, sleep, drink a lot of water, use the toilet, do some deep breathing, or have sex, and invariably whatever it was would go away. But not this time. She tried the first five and nothing changed. She couldn't understand it. She lay in bed shaking and sweating with a fever. Something was really wrong with her. She tried to sleep but stayed half-awake all night obsessively thinking of Stephan.

She thought, Maybe I'm in the Bardo — halfway between two parts of my life. Maybe all of life is a Bardo between conception and death, or every moment is the Bardo in between its birth and its cessation. Like a bubble.

15

Epiphany #3: Paris

"It's possible to bring Nature to its highest fulfillment in humankind through a relationship with a lover if both partners see the light of eternity shining through the other.

— Chloe Pentangeli, from the introduction to The Third Cycle

He was the TA for her History of Modern Art class — one of her electives. On the first day the professor already asserted that all of Modern Art was an outgrowth of the Symbolist movement, citing Gauguin's quote, "Soyez Symboliste". Guess what was going to be on the final? At the break between the slides and lecture, Stephan came outside to smoke with everybody else. He stared at Chloe with burning brown eyes, in his dark gray tweed jacket, and lit up a Gauloise. He looked like Jean-Pierre Léaud in "Masculin Féminin".

He said very simply and matter-of-factly, You're beautiful.

That got Chloe's attention. She was used to men telling her she was beautiful, but it was usually so cloying — charged with emotion and expectation — it was a turn-off. But not the way he said it.

She asked him, Why are French cigarettes so short compared to American ones?

He responded, Perhaps because we like short intense bursts of pleasure. When the break was over and everybody else went inside, he winked at her and said, I'd like to come over for dinner sometime…

A few nights later she invited him over and made pasta.

You can tell a lot about a person sexually by the way they cook and by the way they drive. He said.

Oh yeah?

Her stepdad taught her how to make perfect pasta sauce every time. She put extra virgin olive oil in the saucepan over low heat, chopped a large white onion and let it simmer till it was translucent; chopped an entire head of garlic and let it cook with the onion for about thirty seconds to dehydrate, then poured in a 16 oz. can of crushed tomatoes, and a cup of red wine.

Alcohol brings out the flavor of any vegetable. The longer you let the sauce simmer the better it tastes. Her stepdad said.

She fried some Italian sausage with fennel seeds, and boiled some fresh tortellini with spinach inside, and when it was all ready she combined the three, adding salt, a few bay leaves, some red pepper flakes, fresh basil, and dried oregano leaves.

Stephan tasted it and smiled, Mmm, it's really good. You didn't time the pasta, but you kept testing it to see if it was ready, and you made the sauce to taste, without measuring or using a recipe.

Does that mean you want to sleep with me? Chloe teased.

We'll see. He said, coyly.

Then they went to watch "Breathless" at the cheap university theater. He watched old foreign films over and over again — "Hiroshima Mon Amour", "Aguirre: the Wrath of God", Jacques Tati's "Mon Oncle", "Last Tango in Paris" — and liked old American Films too — "The Apartment" with Jack Lemon, "Paris Blues" with Sidney Poitier;

Richard Burton and Elizabeth Taylor in "Who's Afraid of Virginia Woolf?"...

After the movie they went back to his apartment on Sixth and Aurora near the mountains. He'd painted the living room grass green, the kitchen canary yellow, the bathroom periwinkle blue, the study brick red, and the bedroom off-white. On the Persian rug in his bedroom they talked about the movie, drank screwdrivers, and made charcoal drawings on 18 x 24 sheets. Vodka and orange juice was the only thing he'd drink after a certain hour. With no ice. It seemed he thought orange juice was somehow special. He did a portrait of her and she did a portrait of him. Then they tore off each other's clothes and made love right on the carpet like their bodies were on fire.

In many ways he was her match, maybe even more than Max. She always had at least five guys interested in her at any given time, and he always had several girlfriends at once. They agreed on an open relationship and he talked about it as the difference between desire and passion, and drew a diagram of it. Very French to diagram it. Desire was an arrow leading from one point to another.

Grasping, possessive, fixated. He said.

Passion was a single point with multiple arrows radiating out around it in curved lines like hurricane winds, without a single reference point outside itself. He was a tornado of lucid passion for everything. But it didn't last... Every storm blows itself out...

* * * * *

After a few months of "going out" with Stephan, Chloe ran into Alison at The Harp, an Irish pub right off the Pearl Street Mall. She was in their History of Modern Art class and was from New Hampshire, thin with sharp pretty features, and pin straight shoulder-length mousy hair, smart and well-dressed in a preppy conservative way.

How's Stephan in bed? Alison asked.

He doesn't last the longest, or do it the most times, but he's got incredible finesse; it's intense. The savoir faire, he would call it. He's so into it, it makes me into it.

I'm so in love with him. Let's go over to his place.

I'll call him. Chloe offered.

Let's surprise him.

* * * * *

They all lounged on his bed under floor-to-ceiling built-in bookshelves and drank Bordeaux in candlelight as Jacques Brel played. Alison pulled a book from his shelf.

You've got Anaïs Nin.

She leafed through and found a passage.

Here's one about a ménage à trois.

Read it. Chloe said.

I won't bore you, but the gist is that there was no jealousy between them.

She set the book down, put her hand on Stephan's chest, pushing his back to the bed, kissed him on the mouth, and repeated, "There was no jealousy between them".

Stephan grabbed Chloe's hand urgently and pulled her toward him; Alison withdrew and Chloe and Stephan kissed. Then Chloe and Alison — somehow in sync — got up on their knees, leaned over him, and they kissed. Alison's lips were soft, and hot, and dry. She unbuttoned Chloe's blouse and they all made love. Afterward, Alison dressed quickly and left, smiling like the cat that got the cream and couldn't stop licking itself. Stephan lay on the bed staring into space.

He sat up and said, The only reason that happened is because she wanted me, you wanted her, and I wanted you…

…I thought you wanted an open relationship. Chloe said.

He smiled grimly and slowly shook his head.

Shortly afterward Stephan stopped seeing his other girlfriends. He only wanted Chloe. They went to a party together and all he did was follow her around saying nothing, standing next to her like a giant stuffed animal. If she went to the kitchen to get a drink, he came to the kitchen with her. If she went outside to get some fresh air, he came too.

Finally she said, What do you want from me?

He said, I want to be with you.

But what do you want? She asked.

I want you to need me. He said.

Chloe responded, That's exactly what I don't want from anybody!

At the end of the month he graduated. He was going back to France and asked if she would come see him; gave her an open invitation. She said, Okay. Without really thinking about it. And he disappeared.

* * * * *

Chloe woke up and she still felt dead. She thought she needed to have sex with somebody. She considered James, but rejected the idea. She didn't know how he would react and didn't want to ruin their friendship. She thought about all the men she'd slept with, but the only one she really wanted now was Stephan. Maybe she was in love with him back in college but didn't realize it. She wondered if possibly she'd had the chance of a lifetime with him and blew it. Perhaps Stephan really was her soul-mate. She looked it up — physical chemistry produces passion, intellectual chemistry produces interest, emotional chemistry produces affection, and spiritual chemistry produces love. She used to think everything was just a chemical reaction, and she had all of those with him.

But then again she doubted herself, Maybe I'm going insane. Why would I suddenly want to be with only him?

Finally, she got online and booked a ticket on the next available flight to Paris...

* * * * *

Charles De Gaulle Airport was like the set of "Blade Runner". Thousands of faces bobbing in crowds, and moving urgently with the shuffle of rushed footsteps, many pale and smooth, some swarthy and sun-weathered, others black and furrowed like virgin earth. Africans, Asians, Arabs, Aborigines, Arameans, and Europeans, swirling around like bubble universes, popping in, popping out; the din of fifty languages spoken simultan-eously; the indistinct metallic female French voice over the PA; flashing red neon numbers; blurry fluorescent blue letters, and white lighted signs. Out of the corner of her eye she caught some para-medics quickly wheeling away a woman that looked a little like her on a gurney.

270

Space Age moving walkways soared at
crisscross angles to different levels through the
pillbox shaped terminal under the cylindrical sky-lit
hole, infused with the smell of jet fuel and cigarettes
and the dank ferment of the bar. It must have been
the pride of Western Civilization at one time. Now,
some moving walkways were roped-off due to
malfunction, and automatic sliding glass doors were
stuck open. The concrete and glass structure —
stained, dusty, and old — still groaned on, but was
well into decay.

Chloe stopped to have a beer. En pression. A
"1664" in a curvaceous glass. The first sip was
golden coolness. Just what she needed after the long
flight.

Her illness had left her. Right after take off, she
overdosed on Vitamin C, turmeric (the most
powerful natural anti-inflammatory), Cold Snap (the
strongest herbal wellness formula), melatonin, and
some other vitamins and supplements, and slept the
whole way. She believed dosages on supplement
labels were arbitrary, there to protect the
manufacturers in case you had a bad reaction. And
it worked, she woke up cured. Or was it because she
was going to see Stephan? She sighed and watched
all the displaced travelers lugging baggage around,
possessed with plans and memories, reading the
directions with urgent looks to get where they
wanted. The clear autumn sun beamed through giant
plate glass windows, glinting off brass rails at the
bar and the cool sweating glass of golden beer in
her hand, bubbles rising. She finished it and walked
on. Bubbles break, rainbows fade, days end in night,
like tinkling wind chimes settling into silence.

After baggage claim, she called Stephan and he
told her which trains to take to get to his apartment.

At the airport station, the RER rolled in quietly —
rubber tires on metal rails — and she barely noticed
when the giant high-speed train arrived. The
French... She transferred to the Metro and got off at
Kleber in the sixteenth arrondissement, walked a
few blocks to Stephan's apartment, rang the bell,
and he buzzed her in. She pushed open the old thick
geometrically carved wooden door and climbed the
spiral staircase up to the top, panting with the
weight of her bag. The door opened and there he
stood — fiery brown eyes and silky dark brown
hair.

He smiled nervously, Did you find your way
alright?

Your directions were clear.

She felt like leaving right then. What the hell
am I doing here? She thought.

He kissed her briefly and said, It's good to see
you, Chloe.

Their eyes met for a moment. Chloe suddenly
felt embarrassed.

Then he smiled warmly and said, Come in. She
followed him inside and set down her bags. His
wife Chantal stood in the entrance hall on the
hardwood floor, hands behind her back, also with a
nervous smile.

This is Chantal.

Chloe...

Good to meet you, Chloe. Stephan has told me
so much about you.

She extended her hand in the French manner
and Chloe shook it. Chloe liked Chantal right off.
That surprised her. Not because she expected not to
like her, and she wasn't expecting to like her either,
not particularly, but she had the notion Chantal
might not like *her*, given her relationship with

Stephan. But there wasn't a hint of malice in Chantal.

Chantal reached for her bags, I'll get these out of your way. And she disappeared.

Chloe looked at Stephan and said, Congratulations.

Thanks... He replied.

She was also surprised to realize she was genuinely happy for him. She didn't expect that.

He seemed to understand, and took her hand, Let's have a drink.

They walked through the apartment filled with pieces from his father's modern art collection — large painterly geometric abstractions on off-white walls and a few small stone and bronze minimalist sculptures on tables and small pedestals.

I was a little worried when you said you were coming, but now I see I didn't have to. Stephan said.

She sat at the kitchen table.

He put his hand on her shoulder, I promise if you ever get married I'll come to see you too.

She felt a lump in her throat.

Wine? Coffee? Vodka and orange juice?

A screwdriver. She replied.

He went to the counter and brought back two drinks, and sat down. He raised his glass, A la tien. She raised hers too, touched his, and they both drank.

Chantal approached the table, Well, I'll leave you two alone. We're glad to have you, Chloe.

Thanks.

Chantal left and Chloe finished her drink and Stephan took her glass.

I'll get you another one. He went to the refrigerator.

She thought of that Jimi Hendrix song, "Castles Made of Sand". He came back with a full glass.

So, is there anything special you want to do while you're here?

I can't really think right now.

We can figure it out later. Do you want a shower, or to lie down?

Not yet. She sipped her drink. How did you meet Chantal?

He sighed and leaned back in his chair, She came into the gallery one day and we had a conversation. Then she kept coming back everyday for two weeks, and I asked her out.

Does she collect art?

She only likes to look at it. She teaches handicapped children.

Chloe couldn't believe it.

I never pictured you with someone like that. She said.

Neither did I. He laughed; then he got serious and looked her in the eye; leaned forward in his chair, and put his hand on hers, You know, Chloe... you may be the one for me, but she's the one I can live with...

She felt like a gutted fish, an empty shell discarded on the sand of some desolate beach.

Does she know you? She asked.

...She lets me be who I am.

He stared at a painting on an unframed circular canvas hanging on the wall that looked like a semi-abstract version of the Wheel of Life, and his eyes glowed.

That painter there... we had a weekend together. Look at her brushstrokes... I got her a residency in an artist's community in Provence. He

274

returned his eyes to Chloe, Chantal understands me. She takes me back when I go away.

Are you sure you're not just taking the easy way out? She asked.

I'm going to be thirty, Chloe. I want to start a family.

If she'd been a gutted fish before, now the skeleton was ripped out. A formless lump of flesh left to drift away and dissolve in the tide. She didn't feel much like drinking anymore, but she finished her glass and asked for another one. Stephan brought it back from the counter. She pulled out a cigarette and offered him one.

No, thanks. I quit smoking. He said quickly. Chantal doesn't like it. ...I almost had a nervous breakdown doing it. One day I put my fist through that window. He pointed at a small windowpane in the kitchen. We can go out on the roof.

Through French doors, out onto the roof deck, The City of Lights blazed under a black sky. She lit an organic American Spirit and stared at the illuminated Eiffel Tower, its triangular shape like a diamond studded path in one point perspective leading into the void.

She remembered the party in Boulder where they were bored with all the people, and sat in the corner drinking vodka and orange juice, and he talked passionately about some artist — Atlan — getting all worked up, when he suddenly stopped and stared intensely into nothing, and trembled. She asked him what was wrong and he said, "I feel this power..." He got up and strode straight toward a sliding glass door, smashed right through it, and stood outside on the deck under the falling snow. Of course people freaked out and crowded around him, but he didn't have a scratch, and just stared up at the big snowflakes drifting silently down under a street lamp. They left the party and he took off running through the snow, because he liked the way the speed felt when he got drunk. When they got to his apartment he immediately wrote a poem, and said he felt like the night was pouring out on the page in black ink.

You look tired. He said.

She flicked her cigarette, exhaled, and watched it sail over the edge of the roof into nothing. They went inside. He showed her the spare bedroom and she collapsed.

She didn't know how long she slept. When she woke up it was still dark. She stared at the streak of light on the ceiling coming from the streetlight outside through a tiny part in the curtains, and remembered what he said about love one winter night at his apartment in Boulder, smoking Celtiques over a bottle of Bordeaux.

Love is like getting drunk. The first few times you're fixated on the feeling, but after a few more times the novelty of intoxication wears off. Then you learn to appreciate the subtleties, like a good bottle of wine. He smiled and said, I like lots of different kinds of wine. But sometimes I want a glass of water.

Just then the door opened slowly and Stephan came in silently on bare feet and crawled naked into bed with her, and held her face in his hands.

I've missed you. He said. He kissed her softly. She responded warmly at first; he wrapped is arms around her firm smooth body, and stroked her slender familiar curves; she ran her fingers through his hair, but then she froze. Something about the situation repulsed her.

He pulled away and whispered, What's the matter? I want you...

She said quietly, You only want to have your way. You don't feel the same as I do.

He didn't know how to respond at first.

Then he said, What was I supposed to think? You showing up here out of the blue…

I shouldn't have come. She answered.

He sighed heavily, and lay next to her staring at the ceiling.

I waited for you, Chloe... As long as I could...

Her body shook with silent sobs and warm tears streamed down her face onto her shoulder turning cold. After a few moments she sniffed and wiped her face with the sheet and sighed. She lay there hot next to him, and breathed heavily through her mouth like a little girl, her full lips glistening in the pale light from the streetlamp outside.

Finally, she took a deep breath, kissed his mouth briefly, and said, Good night, Stephan.

He left.

* * * * *

Chloe got a room at the Hotel Papillon. What else could she do? Light streamed through the glass doors of the entrance behind her as she checked in at the front desk and the concierge handed her a key card.

In her room, as soon as she tipped the bellhop and he left, she stripped off her clothes and flopped on the bed. At "Off World" Bridget said, "$E = mc^2$ — emotions equal mind control squared". Square like the old hippie saying. She was lusting after someone she couldn't have, she was angry because she couldn't have him, she was ignoring the fact having him wouldn't make everything better, she was jealous somebody else had him and she didn't, and her pride made her feel like she deserved him, which all made her fear she would never get what he had to offer. Emotion's all boil down to fear — fear of how open-ended we really are. Negative emotions are the Mind's feces: why would anyone want to hold onto them?

She knew what to do. Or rather what not to do. She unpacked everything and made herself as much at home as possible; sat in a comfortable chair and relaxed.

Don't do anything. She said to herself. Just watch your thoughts like boats floating down a river. Don't resist. Don't react. Don't retain.

At first her thoughts went by like jet boats, then fast cigarette boats, then motorboats, then skiffs with little outboards, then row boats, and after a few hours her thoughts slowed to the crawl of inflated inner tubes drifting downstream, and she could watch them appear, float by, and disappear, and for a short time her thoughts stopped completely and there was only the wide clear inexorable river, and then that disappeared…

* * * * *

My phone rang at four o'clock in the morning and by reflex I answered.

She said, It's Chloe... I'm in Paris... I need you, Xavier.

What?

I want you to come here. She said.

I was confused.

Why?

She sighed heavily and said, I used to say trying to be your partner's best friend is a mistake. But I was wrong. In the end if you're not best friends then all you've got is drama and game playing. Drama is fake by nature, and in a game there's always a loser.

I was bowled over... I never heard Chloe admit she was wrong.

You had another epiphany? I asked.

I guess so. She responded. You've been there for me ever since we met, Xavier. I know you think I'm beautiful, and I never told you, but I've always been attracted to you too.

Thanks. I said, waiting for the other shoe to drop.

Attraction isn't everything, but without it, it won't last.

What won't last?

I feel like we could be a couple. She replied.

I dropped the phone, and quickly picked it up.

Hello? She said.

I'm still here.

I thought, Now, this is bordering on surreal. Chloe? The one who believed all romantic relationships were dead end sidetracks?

I know you want to be with me. She continued. I'm not blind. And of all the people I know, you're the one I want. I don't want to change you.

My heart pounded. My ears tingled icy hot, and my head felt like it was expanding and dissolving. I almost asked her, Are you really high right now? But I held back.

The only way for anyone to be happy is to make someone else happy. She said. And I want that to be you. If we're happy then the whole world is happy because we contain the entire universe.

Can you explain that? I said, trying to keep up on two-and-a-half hours sleep.

A fetus looks like a fish at first, then an animal with a tail and four legs, and then it loses the tail, and two legs become arms, and finally it looks human. All of evolution is within us. So if you're happy then everyone who's preceded you and everyone around you is happy too. Every little kid understands that instinctually. When your parents are happy, you're happy. But we forget when we get old. ...Don't come if you can't take the same attitude. I want us to be equals.

I didn't know how to respond. It felt like one of those windows that once it closed would never open again.

Hello?

I'm here. I said. ...I'll be there in two days.

* * * * *

The night I arrived we went out for Beaujolais Nouveau, to an old dark bar in the twentieth arrondissement packed with hundreds of people, filled with the acrid woody smell of black tobacco and musty oak wine barrels.

This is the one night the French admit they're drinking just to get drunk. She said. The rest of the time it's always supposedly only for the taste, even if a person drinks four liters of wine a day, which is an awful lot of "wine tasting".

That's like saying, I really only like the smell of cocaine. I commented.

The building was ancient — jagged mud brick walls, exposed rough beams on the ceiling, tables made of thick worn planks, and tall narrow windows in weathered frames on rusty iron hinges with mottled bleary glass looking out on a lumpy cobblestone street glowing pink under graven cast iron lampposts. In the noisy crowd, the red fruity wine served in earthen cups and pitchers felt prickly to the tongue.

Chloe said, It's piquant. The wine is so new it still has some bubbles from the fermentation. She asked me, How do you feel?

Like I've stepped into a parallel universe.

She smiled, briefly kissed my cheek, and sipped her wine. Was this the same Chloe I'd known all these years?

We walked slowly back to the hotel along the bank of the Seine, under arched stone bridges, dark blue in the night, glistening in the icy air. A noisy riverboat tour passed, jammed with tourists, spotlights glaring off the façades of buildings on both sides; waves created by the boat's wake lapping against the stone quay. We crossed Pont Alexandre III with the gold-leafed sculptures of winged horses near Hotel des Invalides over to Place de la Concorde, and stood under the towering Obelisk of Luxor — the grandfather of all monuments, the oldest one in Paris — in the center

of the elliptical island in the middle of the huge
intersection waiting for the light to change.

Chloe turned to me and said, Kiss me.

As the lights of moving cars swirled around us
in a glimmering black whirlpool, we kissed. I was
breathless and dizzy, and she was too.

Do you feel that? She asked.

Of course I do. I said.

Our barriers are dropping. She said. "I am" is
disappearing.

The light changed and we walked toward the
hotel.

"I am" is the beginning of separation. She
continued. "I am" in opposition to "the world". And
then the random labeling. "I am happy". "I am sad".
"I am confused". Like that black and white etching
my stepdad had of an old bearded white guy with
his hand raised in a dramatic gesture supposed to
represent God the Father that said "I am who am."
"I am" expresses all our false hopes and fears.

If there's no me, then what's left? I asked.

The whole world is left. You're not separate
from it. She answered. The world is our mother. She
supports us physically, emotionally, intellectually,
spiritually.

She stopped abruptly, looked intensely into my
eyes and said, You're the face of the world for me.
I'll be the same for you. …Kill your Father, fuck
your Mother.

She kissed me wildly, and I joined her in
complete abandon.

* * * * *

It stands to reason that the ancient Oedipus
myth has come to be portrayed as a tragedy. It is sad

to watch our conventional world view crushed by
the weight of the truth; it could be as calamitous as
murdering your father or having sex with your
mother; and the gravity of the disappearance of the
world we accept as real could well be dramatized as
striking oneself blind out of grief and guilt. But it
wasn't always portrayed as tragic. Oedipus is a
metaphor for the heroic path — the first human to
correctly answer the riddle of the Sphinx, a demon
superior to human beings, with the head of a woman
to symbolize the highest intelligence, the body of a
lion to represent super-human strength, and the
wings of a bird to show her ability to commune with
the gods above. The Sphinx's riddle asks, What
creature speaks in one voice and walks on four legs
in the morning, two throughout the day, and three as
night falls? By answering, Man, Oedipus expresses
his understanding that Time is relative. A baby
crawls on all fours, an adult stands on two feet, and
an elder walks with the aid of a cane — they're all
the same creature whose voice remains the same in
the expanded present, establishing that yesterday
and tomorrow only ever happen today. Blinding
oneself can also be seen as a metaphor for elimi-
nating "I am" — the personal perspective. It
becomes "There is", which acknowledges the
mystery and the miracle of phenomena; it takes
effort, and surrender to what Life brings. Let's not
forget that after expressing this truth, Oedipus finds
refuge in a sacred wilderness, cared for by his
children, and protected by King Theseus, the
founder of Athens, where he develops the super-
natural power to bring success to those who accept
him, and suffering to those who turn him away, and
is recognized as a hero in Thebes, the city from

which he was once exiled. That acceptance can be seen as becoming one with the world.

* * * * *

At the hotel we made love like trance dancers, building trust, playing, testing, becoming familiar, finding the secret pleasure centers; then intuitively giving each other what we need; finally losing ourselves completely in each other, sometimes moving slowly, sometimes quickly in synch, repeatedly reaching peaks of passionate release, and then flowing back down to stillness, to start again. We moved from room to room beginning in the shower, then on the tile floor; into the kitchenette on top of the stove, out to the bedroom up against the plate glass windows as the metro passed on raised tracks, the conductor blasting the horn; on to the silk Persian carpet, and finally the divan.

We weren't trying to set any records, we were beatifying the world, to set apart each moment after that kiss in Place de la Concorde from everything that came before, so now in all new circumstances we could recall these first days and nights together and remind ourselves that we each are the face of the world for the other, and relate with every new situation as such.

For a week we never left the room, and ordered room service whenever we got hungry. When we finally did start going out, we rolled out of bed at four in the afternoon, bundled up for the cold, bought vintage black leather jackets and gloves, trim black helmets and old aviator goggles at a flea market, rented a Vespa and sped around Paris — Chloe's arms wrapped around me — taking in all the sights: the steep stairs of Rue Foyatier in Mont-

martre at sunset with the glowing peach domes of
Sacré Coeur looming behind; billions of brilliant
white Christmas lights streaking past in the night on
our way to the glittering golden statues and
towering pillars of Place du Trocadéro; the flower
market exploding at dawn with the full spectrum of
color under greenhouse-like pavilions in Place
Lépine.

One might expect a treatise about food coming
on, this being Paris and all, but we usually ate
dinner at neighborhood bistros, ordered the plate du
jour which was cheap as any fast food and infinitely
better — made from locally farmed produce and
animals — and drank the table wine — the same
price as Coke. At the hospice back in Cambridge
where Chloe volunteered they were getting
complaints about the food, so they started serving
wine with dinner, and the complaints disappeared.

The Puritanical take was that the patients were
no longer "present", and they stopped complaining
about the food because they simply couldn't tell
how bad it tasted anymore since they had alcohol.
Meanwhile, on planet earth, all over Europe people
drink locally made high quality generic table wine
that complements the food. You can pay three times
as much in the US and still not get the same quality
or taste. And bread was always free.

She explained, Europeans are actually
emotional about bread. To them it separates men
from savages; it represents civilization, so no self-
respecting man, woman, or child should have to
endure a meal without it. It makes sense in terms of
survival. Chloe continued. All your brain really
needs is sugar-water; that's what wine is. And good
bread gives your body enough protein to survive.
My stepdad is first generation Italian and breakfast

for him every morning as a kid was yesterday's bread broken up with red wine his mom drizzled over it. She said. You could probably live your whole life on bread and wine. Jesus was onto something.

After dinner, our favorite bar before going out was "Hall 1900" in Beaubourg. Of course there were hundreds if not thousands to choose from in Paris, but 1900 was relaxed, and it reminded us of Manet's painting "A bar at the Folies-Bergère" with brass rails, turn-of-the-century-style furnishings, and the giant gilt-framed mirror behind the bartender. The first time we went she served us each a Kir Royale — champagne and crème de cassis — and a saucer of mild green olives, without asking what we wanted, so that became our first drink every time we went.

Then we'd go dancing till four in the morning, sometimes to Techno at a club, or to Samba at a Brazilian bar, or even "Rock & Roll" at "une cave" — a former wine cellar with vaulted stone ceilings. The French still like couples-dancing to 1950's oldies. When we got back to the hotel we swam naked in the warm glass-covered rooftop pool and watched the sunrise silhouetting the Eiffel Tower. We rarely spoke by that time. We didn't have to. A look into each other's eyes was enough to communicate anything.

People stared as we strode through the lobby like rare snow leopards with a sphere of white flames around us — the atmosphere heavy and charged, thick as electric Jell-o. But they always had wispy smiles. Everyone on the hotel staff was friendly, and they frequently told us we were their favorite guests, that it was an honor to have us stay.

We were blazing binary stars at the center of a universe.

One day, we went to the top of the Eiffel Tower. It was December, and cold, so hardly anybody was up there. Chloe leaned back against the railing with the stone city glowing dreamily white behind her under a creamy winter sky. She opened her pale ankle-length alpaca coat, and beneath her heavy turtleneck all she wore were maroon thigh-high stockings, a garter belt, and fur-lined boots. I opened my camelhair overcoat, she enfolded me in hers and we kissed, our bodies vibrating and tingling as we merged, electrified. I faded into her, and the city behind her, comingling with everything.

16

The Resurrection of Candy

"In deep dreamless sleep there is consciousness but of no object. Deep sleep holds all that is future because the future can come from nowhere else but the psyche. We can reach the same mind through trance."

— Chloe Pentangeli, Trance Dancer

Chloe wanted to stay in Paris. She still had lots saved up from temping, not having to pay rent, or a car payment, or health insurance, etc. for almost two years, but it was never hard for her to make money — she was charmed. One time, only to try it, she stood outside in Place Georges Pompidou with the other buskers and sang songs from the Cole Porter Song Book she'd memorized from volunteering at the hospice, and she made more money in an hour than I did in a whole day of work.

Open-air flea markets like the one where we bought our jackets and goggles were all over Paris on various days, and Chloe realized she was sitting on a goldmine. It was impossible to find second-hand goods of the same quality and quantity in the US. She started a business on eBay and within days she was shipping all over the world making a killing. She found us a big one bedroom top floor apartment in the 16th arrondissement that used to be an artist's studio, with a huge bank of north-facing panes, and filled it with beautiful second-hand furniture and framed paintings, a round mirror, thick old tapestries, and tons of clothes in folded stacks and hung on rolling garment racks ready to sell. The angled ceiling made it feel like a harem tent at night in low lamp light, and in the day, in the light from north-facing windows, it looked like a scene out of a Vermeer.

While I was at work Chloe spent her free time in café's and museums. Camille Claudel was her favorite sculptor and she spent hours at Musée Rodin mesmerized by the glowing masterpieces. She fell in love with Odilon Redon's bizarre floral paintings at the Musée d'Orsay. In Le Marais she went to the Jewish Museum and thought of her mother, fascinated by their collection of golden wedding rings. They were part of her ancestry. The guide said the wedding ring symbolizes God's ultimate purpose for creation, the union of man and woman, the union of God and His people, and also of Israel and the Torah. Chloe thought that was a little narrow minded but she couldn't take her eyes off the rings.

Her favorite café was hidden away down a little alley off of Rue de Lutèce on Isle de la Cité — Café Cardinale — definitely not in the tourist guide-books. It was quaint with powder blue walls hung with horizontal oval-shaped mirrors, with a stainless steel espresso bar — nothing spectacular — and floor-to-ceiling glass doors and windows that looked out onto the narrow cobblestone lane with granite slab sidewalks where she watched the red and brown fallen leaves blow by, reading Anaïs Nin. The view splintered kaleidoscopic by all the reflective surfaces whenever a patron opened the front door. It fascinated her that Paris was full of mirrors, inside and out — on stone pillars and storefronts, in shops, restaurants, and galleries — indulging the visual sense.

One night we went to see the annual parade of students from L'Ecole Des Beaux Arts through the streets of Saint Germain. There were loud horns and shouting as hordes of students sang and danced in wild costumes under the streetlights, a lot of them half-naked in the cold, passing bottles around, stumbling over each other to the beat of several drums. A large group passed silently, dressed as skeletons — black body suits with white bones painted on them, wearing skull masks, or faces painted like skulls — arms and feet moving in unison. I glanced at Chloe and saw she was wiping away a tear.

What's wrong?

I don't know. I always cry at parades. It seems so tragic and beautiful at the same time. I feel like it has something to do with a lot of people all dressed the same, moving together, doing the same things, like they're not individuals.

* * * * *

Her stepdad's brother, Enrico, owned an art gallery in St. Germain and hired me. I started at the gallery warehouse in a northwestern suburb — working my way up — first painting the concrete warehouse floor with marine paint, then transporting artworks in a van from the crammed storage closets at the gallery in St. Germain to the warehouse, and finally cataloging and organizing all the works. The suburbs of Paris were like any other suburbs. The buildings were shorter, and newer, and cheaper, and the level of sophistication dropped the farther out you got.

On my way to work, walking to the Metro, I watched the manual laborers all dressed in blue cotton jackets and pants standing at the bar, smoking, and drinking glasses of red wine before they started their jobs. In the train, administrators wore their khaki blazers, managers wore dark blue suits, and women of all levels wore smart Macintoshes belted at the waist. Everyone fit into their little slot, and I felt like I was starting to fit into one too.

About a month into it I finally got to install my first show at the gallery. I got off the Metro at Pont Neuf and walked a few blocks across the Seine to Saint Germain, down the little street by the river, Rue du Pont de Lodi. The buildings on the block all had crumbling ancient facades and recently renovated interiors. Nam June Paik was putting on a memorial installation to Joseph Beuys. The Art World heavies. It was a sunny day, but freezing cold. Paik showed up in $2 flip-flops and white cotton socks in the dead of winter; black polyester pants unzipped showing his navy and white polka dot boxers, an untucked white shirt buttoned up the wrong way under an expensive dark blue designer jacket, with a pale yellow sweater tied around his neck like a scarf, the body of the sweater draped sloppily over one shoulder. His hair a mess of different lengths stood on end with stiff gel, and he wore designer sunglasses — ever so artfully disheveled. A Post-Modern fop. An Art Star.

Beuys was one of those conceptual artists whose name alone would encompass whole nights of conversation at Art Department parties Max or Hector invited me to. I remember all the scarvy graduate students blathering away about one artist or another, or one theory or another, and then the conversation reaching its course. In the heady silence that settled on the room, someone would say, Joseph Beuys... And everyone would nod in agreement and affirm the truth, finally repeating the name, Joseph Beuys... I always expected to hear people snapping their fingers like beatniks.

I'd seen some of his work, little scribblings with pencil, some larger pieces about his theory that the tyrannical roots of Western culture came from Asia — Mongolia, or somewhere near Korea — as if the west wouldn't be tyrannical without them. There was a small painting of his trademark wide-brimmed felt fedora with flames coming off of it in the gallery on permanent display. He even did one exhibit in Berlin that was just a dirty claw foot bathtub in the middle of a clean white room. And guess what happened? One night the German cleaning lady scoured it, illustrating his point.

Jacques, a Chinese-Parisian who graduated from L'Ecole des Beaux Arts about a decade before-hand, was the other junior preparator, and we attached big heavy 1950's wooden TV cabinets gutted of all the insides to the walls at various heights and angles with screws and brackets, and put strobe lights behind the empty screens. We mounted several tiny TV monitors onto a giant loose canvas screen print of rows of small tele-visions with static, like they were popping out of the painting, screwed to the wall right through the canvas with drill guns. The tiny TVs each showed a closed-circuit video camera view of a little clock swinging on a pendulum — watching time. There was a video projected onto a giant screen showing a black-and-white loop of Joseph Beuys doing a piano performance with Nam June Paik, the music playing over speakers throughout the gallery.

Paik leaned under the lid of the grand piano and loosened the strings with pliers as Bueys played,

creating deep eerie Gothic sounds. In the middle of
the gallery floor, Paik placed a life-size concrete
replica of Joseph Beuys' signature fedora with the
top blown out in zigzag lines, like a cartoon
explosion, surrounded by hundreds of Japanese
transformer dolls placed in a circle around the hat,
watching it, or standing vigil — a robot audience.
The lights in the gallery were turned way down.
With the strobe lights flashing in the dark room, and
the eerie music playing, it wasn't bad. Sort of an
easy score though. Like a Post-Modern haunted
house.

Suddenly Paik decided he wanted more dolls
surrounding the hat in the middle of the room, and
wanted someone in charge to take him to the toy
store. I didn't know where the toy store was.

Paik asked me, Who is in charge here?

Mauro is the head preparator. I said. He'll be
here in a couple of hours. He works a half-day
today.

I want someone now! Paik shouted.

He paced around the gallery, his face radiating
heat.

He screamed, Where is Mauro?

He stormed over to the receptionist, and
screamed again, Where is Mauro?

The receptionist, Beatrice, stammered.

Paik screamed, Mauro is fired! He is fired!

Then he stomped out the front door. I called
Mauro to tell him what was going on, and he rushed
in to work.

Once Mauro got there he smoothed the whole
thing out. Paik came back, and Mauro spoke to him
charmingly. Mauro Panari. Sounds like a Formula
One driver, and he looked like one too, with thin
dark chiseled features. But he was a sculptor about

my age, trying to start a career in Paris. He went
with Paik to the department store where Mauro's
English girlfriend Elle worked; they came back with
hundreds more little robot-like dolls already out of
the boxes, and Paik dumped them out of a white
plastic bag in a sloppy ring around the concrete hat,
knocking over the ones that were standing, and that
was it. The installation was "perfect".

By that time Enrico showed up too, Chloe's
step-uncle. He looked like a giant baby — balding,
and pudgy, with a constant grin on his face. He
seemed like he was never quite all there, and always
slightly amused by everything. Maybe he was just
shy. He made sure Paik wasn't still upset. Paik acted
like nothing happened, went back to his hotel, and
Enrico took us all out to lunch.

At the noisy crowded restaurant around the
corner, Beatrice, a seasoned Parisian, fumed — her
voice gruff from decades of harsh cigarettes.

She growled at Mauro, Il est *en* star! Il a besoin
de toi!! Il a *be-soin* de toi!!! She lit another
Gitanes, and blew indignant smoke.

Mauro leaned over to me and said quietly, She
thinks that to need somebody is the worst fault in
the world. She wants to be so arrogant she never has
to speak to anyone. Very French.

Enrico looked up from the menu, The chicken
is good here. Is that alright with everyone? The
chicken?

Everybody agreed. He was buying.

Jacques was having fun ordering bottles of
wine on Enrico's tab. The uniformed waiter bent to
hear him over the noisy crowd.

Jacques raised his voice, En autre… Quelque
chose leger… En Cotes du Rhone.

Enrico didn't seem to mind. He just glanced at Jacques and flashed his baby smile, and Jacques acted nonchalant. Enrico was pretty generous. He bought Mauro a motorcycle so he could get around town faster. It was a two cylinder dirt bike with big knobby tires. Funny those were popular in Paris. But that's how everything worked — personal relationships. Feudal fealty... I asked Jacques what kind of painting he did in school.

Geometric minimalism. He said. Everyone can relate to geometry because geometry is everywhere.

So many Europeans are raised to want to make some kind of sweeping pithy generalization... Like "the wise old German" would say about drinking, "Wein auf Bier das rate ich dir, Bier auf Wein lass das sein!" Or the French about women, "Cieux moutonée et femmes maquillé ne son pas du longue durée."

Mauro winked at me and leaned close again, He thinks he's so smart. Then he said to Jacques, What's the only true geometric shape that's part of the human body?

Jacques thought for a second, then said, The line?

That's not a shape, and there aren't any straight lines in the figure.

Jacques thought a little more, then gave up, What?

Mauro said, You've got two of them right on your face.

Jacques was stumped, and stared intently at Mauro's face, but didn't recognize anything.

What? He asked.

Mauro pointed to the iris of his eye, The circle, genius.

He smiled, leaned over to me, and nudged me, then grinned at Jacques.

Oh, right. Jacques said, and shifted uncomfortably in his chair.

Then Mauro said, By the way, thanks for calling me.

No problem. When he started saying you were fired I got kind of nervous.

He couldn't get me fired. Mauro replied. But I didn't want him to be upset. You know what I mean? We have to stroke their egos. Anyway, I appreciate that. Cheers. He raised his glass and we drank.

* * * * *

One day I walked into the apartment and sat on the edge of the bed and noticed the whole thing had changed. The clothing racks and piles of clothing were gone. An entire wall had been knocked out, leading to a whole new room, with a brand new dark blue Persian carpet. I went into the bathroom, and saw it had been retiled — still mostly white but with randomly placed tiles of red and dark blue. On some of the white tiles were dark blue silhouettes of bull's heads and raven's heads. It looked garish and unattractive. I thought Chloe would have better taste than that. But then I gave her the benefit of the doubt — at least she was trying to improve the place. I went looking for Chloe and walked through the French doors outside onto the stone patio, then into the back yard on lush green grass, and stopped, and thought, Wait a second... this is a house. It's not our apartment... This isn't Paris... Chloe was there in the yard.

I think it'll sell fast with the remodeling. She said.

I walked with her toward the dark brown house next door.

She went on, They're almost all moved out. Maybe they left the door open. We can sneak in and look around.

I realized we were selling the house we left, and we'd bought the dark brown house next door and were going to be moving in soon. Right then the occupants walked out the back door — two beautiful women, tall, slender, elegant, one blond and one brunet, with long flowing hair, wearing small frameless designer glasses, and identical dark brown designer business suits. They walked past me without saying a word, and went toward a corral with an eight-foot-tall wire fence around it, and three muscular chestnut-colored horses inside. One of the women opened the gate and let the horses out. They trotted towards me on the thick grass shaking their manes, ran past me and away... I woke up, and saw Chloe sleeping next to me in the dark, dreaming...

It was early morning. I knew I wouldn't get back to sleep. I thought about the dream. Your first dreams are about the past, middle of the night is the present, and early morning dreams point to the future. It was rare for me to have a lucid dream so real that even though I thought it was weird, I felt like it was really happening. Usually I recognize I'm dreaming. I shuddered. A house in a dream always represents the concept of self, and I was going to move to another one? Big change. Most animals are sexuality, animal nature, especially big muscular horses. I wasn't sure what the two women meant. Maybe duplicitous ideas, or ambivalence? People in dreams are usually aspects of yourself. And Chloe was there. Maybe my feminine side? Weird...

* * * * *

It was a Monday, and cold, and Chloe was walking up the Champs Elysees to the big Virgin Megastore to buy a CD for me, when she stopped dead in her tracks. She thought she saw Candy coming out of a parfumerie where they had 100,000 fragrances, walking down the sidewalk with the Arc de Triomphe in the background, clicking over the wide pavement in high heels and a dark brown designer suit with a small black shopping bag dangling on her arm, going toward a silver Ferrari 456 GT at the curb. She briefly glanced at Chloe standing there with her mouth hanging open in the middle of a river of a thousand pedestrians, and then she froze with her body half-obscured by the car and stared, right as she was about to put the key in the driver's side door...

...Chloe? Oh my God!

She came around the car and threw her arms around Chloe, and kissed her, and then stood back and they looked at each other in the pale winter light, trying to form words. They spoke at the same time.

I thought—

They gazed into each other's eyes, a million thoughts teeming.

What are—

They did it again, and both froze, breath-steam billowing around them in the cold air.

Finally she put a finger on Chloe's lips and said, You first.

Tears welled in her eyes, Terry told me you were dead!

Candy hung her head for a second and then looked up at her guiltily.

I'm really sorry. I told her to say that because I couldn't handle my feelings for you at the time. You remember what happened. My physiological reaction.

Ours...

I'm sorry. Candy said.

...That's your MO, isn't it? Chloe replied. Why do you run away when things get intense?

I was so in love with you, Chloe... I was only twenty-two. There were things I wanted to do. She touched Chloe's shoulder, Can you forgive me?

She stared hard at Candy, I don't know.

Candy reached into her purse, handed her a card, touched her hand and said, Look, I'm sorry, I can't talk now. I have a birthday party to go to and I'm late. But that's my cell. Call me tonight... Okay?

She took the card and stared at it in her hands, then looked up at Candy.

Candy smiled, and kissed her briefly on the mouth, squeezed her hand and said, It's good to see you. Call me.

Then she got in the Ferrari and took off.

Chloe wandered aimlessly down the sidewalk with Candy's card between her fingers; went into a few stores, left both without buying anything, neither of them the Virgin Megastore...

She got home, sat on the edge of the bed, and stared at the card for hours, not registering anything else. She knew what was going to happen. She was going to sleep with Candy, and then she'd have to tell me — because it's impossible for most people to lie about something like that forever, especially if you really love your partner — and I would be crushed. Six months before, she wouldn't have given it a second thought, but she and I had really bonded. Yet the only person in the world she had stronger feelings for was Candy. Chloe called the number, and Candy answered excitedly, and invited her over for cocktails.

It was a hotel particulier, an entire building, six stories tall, in Neuilly, with ornate stonework on the front, and bronze roofing with a green patina. She rang the doorbell, waited, then rang again, and waited some more. She thought, She's probably some rich guy's mistress. And looked up at the baroque details of the stone facade, blue-gray in the evening sky, barely picking up the pink of the streetlights yet — deep horizontal indents in the stone walls, ornate stonework around the windows, chiseled gargoyles with gaping mouths and tongues hanging out under the eaves. Finally, Candy answered the door in a thick white terrycloth bathrobe, with an apologetic smile.

Sorry. I was in the shower. Come in.

Chloe followed her inside, through the foyer down a long hall while she rubbed a towel over wet strands of long dark hair. They passed several rooms with mysterious Asian art pieces — gold-leafed Himalayan Buddhas in vajra posture with wide staring eyes, a full set of Japanese samurai armor with swords on a rack in front of it, a roughly hewn wooden Hindu relief of couples in various sex positions — and went into the huge kitchen.

A brown granite-topped island stood in the middle. Chloe sat at one of the high wooden chairs around it; Candy picked up a remote and pointed it at the stereo in the adjoining den.

Help yourself to anything. She said. I'll be right back.

Now Chloe felt like she slipped into a parallel universe. In the den were plush sand-colored sofas and chairs, bookshelves, a giant flat screen TV, a big sound system, all under low ambient light, with French doors leading out to a patio and a grass yard with an apple tree and flowerbeds. Candy came back in a red silk robe with an elaborate dragon embroidered on the back.

So… How are you? She asked.

I'm alright… Chloe replied.

She opened the big stainless steel refrigerator, What do you drink? I can make you a martini…

A martini would be great.

Vodka with a twist?

My favorite. Chloe said.

Candy pulled a bottle of Chopin out of the freezer, set it on the counter, and took a chrome martini shaker out of one of the teak wood cabinets.

You sound a little shell-shocked.

I thought you were dead, Candy.

…I'll make it up to you.

Candy got two crystal martini glasses out of the cupboard and made them like a pro — chilled the glasses with ice water while she put ice cubes and vodka in the shaker, a tiny splash of vermouth, and shook the vodka and ice eighteen times, raising the shaker over her shoulder as she bruised it. Then she dumped out the glasses, cut two fresh twists of lemon zest, slid them around the lips of the glasses, dropped them in and poured the martinis, filling each glass almost to the rim, and sat down next to her. They sipped and looked at each other.

So, tell me what you've been up to?

The Resurrection of Candy

Chloe arched her eyebrows. Since I last saw you? What haven't I been up to… She said. I got my Master's, worked for a technology distributor in Cambridge; temped all over—

She stopped abruptly.

I don't want to make small talk, Candy. What does it matter what I've been up to?

Candy looked intently into her eyes, and said, I never forgot you, Chloe… Part of me wished you would've kept calling…

Would you have answered?

You were all I could think of for years… Did I make you cynical?

Chloe thought about it, and responded, To be honest, I feel like you did.

I'm so sorry. Candy said again, with tears in her eyes.

After a long pause, Chloe asked, Do you live here alone?

Yes.

How can you afford this place?

She sighed, and said, I had an affair… with the CEO of a big corporation. An American. He embezzled tons of money — tens of millions — and he bought me a lot of things. He set up a Swiss bank account for me — I didn't ask him to… The FBI ended up catching him and was going to throw him in prison, but he committed suicide and left it all to me. …Not a pretty picture, but that's how I got it.

Hmm…

I had to do a lot of work to get through that karma. Candy added. Do you have a boyfriend? She asked.

Xavier. He's the first since college.

You love him. I can tell…

302

Candy held her hand and gazed into her eyes,
Come here...

She leaned toward her and kissed her with
warm wet lips, and Chloe touched her slender body
under her silk red robe for the first time since she
was a teenager...

They parted and Candy took her hand and said,
Let's go upstairs...

She followed her out of the kitchen up the
wooden stairs to her acupuncture studio on the third
floor. The off-white room was full of giant quartz
crystals, some of them three feet tall and ten inches
thick, resting on the floor, and on pedestals. There
were bronze statues of multi-armed Buddhist deities
on custom made stands on the dresser and night
table.

Take off your clothes. She said. I'm going to
work on your back first.

Chloe got naked and laid face down on the
luxurious acupuncture bed, her face cradled in a soft
doughnut shaped support that extended over the
edge.

Candy struck a long-stemmed match and lit
thick white candles all over the room, then lit three
sticks of sandalwood incense from one of the
candles and stuck them in a small ornate bronze
bowl filled with white sand, and turned off the
lights. The white room glowed orange in the flicker
of the flames.

Candy took off her robe stood next to her, and
said, Close your eyes.

She didn't feel anything for a while, and finally
she asked, What are you doing?

She said, It's Reiki. It doesn't involve touch.
You don't have to think anything or believe

anything is happening, just watch your thoughts and feel your body.

She opened her eyes and glanced back and saw Candy naked holding her palms over her back about six inches from the skin.

Keep your eyes closed... She said. And remember what you see...

She settled back down on the bed. She didn't see anything at first. Then she felt the muscles between her shoulder blades suddenly quiver and spasm, and then relax completely. She sighed heavily, and Candy moved away from her as soon as she did, as if her sigh was some kind of signal.

What did you see? Candy asked.

A cloudy night sky lit orange, and a red-breasted finch flying across it.

What does that mean to you?

I don't know. Flying free? Liberation. Isn't that what finches symbolize? Chloe answered.

Candy said, Turn over on your back and close your eyes.

She rolled over.

I'm going to do some acupuncture. Candy took an acupuncture needle out of its white paper wrapper and stuck it in Chloe's abdomen just beneath the sternum. Then she unwrapped another one and inserted it just above her navel; and stuck in third one below her navel. Chloe instantly felt energy flow through her whole body, spreading from the points of the needles like fire burning up paper, and she had the sensation that the bed dropped from under her, and she was floating.

Candy felt her reaction and said, You're going to be like a baby again... Everything new...

She got off of her and kneeled in seiza position on the bed next to her, leaving the needles in.

Chloe's eyes suddenly popped open and it seemed like the walls moved farther away.

I feel like I'm tripping. She said.

Drugs only work because we already have the potential for whatever they do within us. Candy responded.

To Chloe, their voices sounded like they were echoing from somewhere outside the room. Her whole body felt like it was expanding and dissipating into the air around her. Candy pulled out the needles and threw them in the wastebasket and lay on top of her, and breathed slowly, with her mouth an inch from Chloe's. Her in-breath was Chloe's out-breath. Their warm bellies moved slowly together, and she gazed deeply into her eyes. Chloe felt dizzy, losing her sense of here and there, and felt the room dissolving along with their bodies; and the air around them became brighter, and brighter, as they merged in endless space.

She got nervous, and glanced around frightened, but Candy said softly, Relax. Take deep breaths from your abdomen. I'm here... Just breathe...

Chloe took some deep breaths, gazed into Candy's eyes again, and relaxed, and the room continued getting brighter and brighter, and she felt like she was dissolving until they were both gone, and with a hiss there was only white light...

Chloe blasted out of it, and found herself sitting up cross-legged on the bed, Candy screaming in orgasm, riding Chloe's strap-on with her legs crossed behind Chloe's lower back, and her wrists crossed behind her neck with a ritual dagger in each fist. She rolled her eyes crazily in her head, and gritted her fangs screaming and hissing, and there was blood all around her mouth dripping down her breasts as they jiggled. Her red body glowed opalescent and semi-opaque, made of misty light; Chloe's body too.

Blood pooled in places all over the bed, dripping off the sides onto the floor littered with severed human heads, among them, Chloe and Candy's — men and women, white, black, brown, yellow, blue, green, red, scattered over carpet, drying bloody matted dark hair, flesh and muscles, arteries and vertebrae hanging out where the neck was hacked through. Blood stained blond locks draped over bulging staring eyes, pus and mucus running out of noses, tongues hanging out of mouths dripping saliva, necks still bleeding, the carpet soaked with blood.

Other screams filled the room, and it got louder and louder. Blood poured out of the white candles like streams of red melted wax, dripping down the sides in dark streaks, and the candle flames burst into roaring red jets, with sparks popping and flying everywhere. The walls and ceiling became human skin, and undulated like they were breathing. Small cuts opened up all over them, and blood poured out; the cuts grew larger as they split open and naked couples tumbled out, all without facial features, only smooth skin where faces should've been, and bounced on the floors copulating furiously — men with women, women with women, men with men,

306

everyone with everyone else. The walls and ceiling burst into flames. The air around them sparked and popped. Candy's hair burst into red flames, as she tossed her head, screaming, and both of them became made of fire. And their sex became more and more intense as she rose up with her thighs and slammed down in a frenzy on the gleaming dildo, tossing her head, while hundreds of bodies humped furiously all around them. Chloe felt orgasm building like surging hot lava through her whole body, and she saw red flames slowly spreading from her vagina entwining her spine up to her brain, then spreading through her tiniest capillaries, and the air around them began to thicken with red flames and sparks, more and more dense, as the screaming got louder and louder. Their bodies turned glowing ruby red as the orgasmic fire filled them, and they came at the same time, screaming — red lightning bolts streaking to the ends of the universe, and then there was only red light...

Chloe jolted sweaty, hyperventilating, still on her back, Candy on top of her as when they first lay down, their warm bellies touching, now gripping the sheets in her fists, her wet hair dangling against Chloe's face in dark strands. She closed her eyes and touched her hot forehead to Chloe's, rolled off and lay next to her on her back. Chloe tried to catch her breath, and glanced around the room. The candles and artworks were exactly as they were.

That's never happened before... Candy said, panting.

Chloe breathed a short ironic laugh, Ha!

She kept seeing her on the side for a couple of weeks but one time when they stood by the front door kissing goodbye, Candy said, Don't go... I want you to stay with me.

Chloe sighed and weighed the possibilities.

Do you want to? Candy asked.

I need to talk to Xavier...

17

Option Four

*"The Mother Goddess who informs all things opens the way to
the wisdom body. I am yesterday, tomorrow, and today. I am
the light of consciousness disengaged from the field of time. I
am the source and creator of all the gods, and I have the
power to be reborn."*

— Chloe Pentangeli, The Third Cycle

I noticed something was different. I asked her
what was going on and she told me about Candy,
that she was her first and endless love, and of
course I was crushed. We never had the conversation about whether or not we wanted to be monogamous. It never crossed my mind to have it, given
the circumstances of me coming to Paris. My
mistake. Always make an agreement on the terms of
a relationship.

Eventually, I relaxed and I really wanted to
meet Candy. I was curious as to who could have
such a profound affect on Chloe after all these
years. When we met, I found her hauntingly
beautiful, like Salome or some dark Byzantine
princess, with a disarming irresistible eroticism. I
felt small like a mouse under a terminal feline gaze,
and yet wholly fulfilled in some warm mysterious
way. Some say death is our natural completion —
but I wasn't going to give up Chloe without a fight.

The restaurant had a lighted stained glass
ceiling in a colorful Art Nouveau motif, old black
wrought iron pillars, and big tropical plants in pots
surrounding tables with white tablecloths. I started

with an arugula and spinach salad with seared rabbit livers — one of the chef's specialties — followed by truffle ravioli and venison medallions braised in wild cherry and cognac sauce. I drank a Nicolas Potel Pinot Noir throughout and it went well with everything. For dessert I ordered chocolate torte with glazed fresh raspberries and a snifter of Hennessy XO. For some reason Chloe and Candy both had spider crab, slathering the sweet meat in butter, sharing a watercress salad with mandarin orange vinaigrette, and sipped a Corton-Charlemagne Chardonnay, but they joined me in a cognac for dessert, and the two of them shared a large bowl of chocolate mousse.

We ate in awkward silence, the clink of silver cutlery against white china echoing up to the glass ceiling. They seemed to enjoy themselves, communicating nonverbally. I mustered my courage, wondering what to say.

Finally I blurted out, Look, I know you two have a past. But Chloe and I have a future, and I'm not sure you can say the same, Candy.

That took them by surprise, but Candy quickly assimilated it, and responded, If you're talking about having a family, of course it would be different.

We're in love with each other too. I added. At least we were.

I put my hand on Chloe's thigh.

I still love you, Xavier. Chloe responded apologetically. But I've always been in love with Candy, and I don't want to give that up now that we've found each other again.

She put her hand on Candy's thigh under the table and looked me in the eye, then returned her gaze to Candy.

Candy sipped her cognac, and said, The last thing I want is to come between you two. I love Chloe... And I know she loves me. Ultimately I only want her to be happy. And you too, Xavier. That's the present situation, but something has to change.

She looked me in the eye and, surprisingly, put her hand on my thigh under the table. It seemed like she was trying to soften the blow, and I thought I lost Chloe right then, because the only change foreseeable now that everything was out in the open was me leaving. If they'd kept it a secret we could have shared Chloe, but now one of us would have to lose her, and that would most certainly be me. Then it dawned on me like the stained glass ceiling magically opening to the sky above; the sun beaming down through golden clouds.

…Maybe we can all be together? I said. I mean, the past and the future both happen in the present, right?

They stared at me for a moment, glanced at each other, and then briefly laughed, sort of despite themselves.

…I suppose you could both move in with me. Candy said.

She turned to Chloe, sipped her cognac, and looked back to me.

Chloe said, If that's what you want, Xavier...

I took a deep breath. The situation felt good. I raised my glass and said, To the three of us...

* * * * *

We were Peruvian fresh-water dolphins playing at the source of the Amazon, surging in dark currents, backs arching in smooth tender curves, making love in Candy's giant bed with French doors

311

flung wide, letting in breeze and light, long chiffon curtains billowing gently as we took turns coming up for air.

It was spring, and we all felt alive — our hearts aching, and all our senses peaking. The sky was so blue it hurt, dark green city buses drew us in like open fields, dandelions in the park were each like golden towers, and the mirrors all over Paris flashed like portals to other worlds. We were raw, and open, and it was all excruciatingly beautiful, haunted by Erik Satie, The Cocteau Twins, Debussy, Vangelis' soundtrack to "Blade Runner", and Billie Holiday's version of "April in Paris". Chloe woke up singing the lyrics sometimes.

> April in Paris…
> Chestnuts in blossom…
> Holiday tables under the trees.
>
> April in Paris…
> This is a feeling,
> No one can ever reprise.
>
> I never knew the charm of spring,
> Never met it face to face.
> I never knew my heart could sing,
> Never missed a warm embrace,
>
> Till April in Paris.
> Whom can I run to?
> What have you done to my heart?

* * * * *

Max called and said he wanted to have another reunion and Candy agreed to have it at her place. Gaia showed up with him. Hector made a killing on his Apple stock which he bought for $11 a share right before they came out with the iPod when it jumped a thousand percent, so he and Olivia took time off. Lily and Trevor came too. James was there. He finally got out of Alexandria, bought a loft in SoHo, and was painting and showing in galleries downtown, spending a lot of time with Max.

What is it with you and your reunions? Chloe asked Max.

Nostalgia, I guess... He said. But nostalgia ain't what it used to be.

Even Caroline showed up. Candy had room for them all. But Luis was the star of the event, glowing with his newborn daughter, and his new bride Delia — wavy black hair, brown skin, and piercing blue eyes, with dimples in both cheeks.

Caroline asked, How long was the crossing?

Ten days from New York. Luis replied.

How did she handle it? Lily asked.

Delia replied, We're lucky. She's a happy baby.

She's so calm. Candy commented.

How did you two meet? Gaia asked.

Delia glanced at Luis, You tell the story.

I went home to Burlington to visit my parents and at the gas station I went in to get some sunflower seeds and saw Delia behind the register — a lightning bolt went through me and three months later we were married.

They arrived a couple of days after the others because they came by ship, and the women crowded around Delia as she held adorable little Maribel, the natural center of attention, with wide wondering blue eyes under long dark lashes, just like her mom's. All the way around, Candy, Chloe, Gaia, Lily, Olivia, and Caroline each said they wanted one too.

We walked around the city for a couple of days, strolling under the trees in the Bois de

Boulogne, meandering past storefronts spilling out onto the cobblestones of "Boule-Miche", shopping on Rue Cler near the Eiffel Tower, taking the metro from point to point. Candy showed us the boulangerie with the best bread and pastries — most are better at one or the other. At the cheese store the shopkeeper said, This is the smell of the feet of angels. As he handed us stinky samples. We bought fresh fish and crustaceans caught that day at the poissonerie. The butcher had framed awards on the walls behind the counter, and cut veal, lamb, and pork for us. We brought home bouquets from the flower shop, and cases from the wine shop, and then we cooked together, sipping champagne, surrounded by vases of chrysanthemums, roses, babies' breath, daisies, and freesia.

Max suggested we have a party, so Chloe called Enrico, and he invited a few people... Candy invited some of her friends too, and Chloe invited Stephan and Chantal. About twenty-five showed up total. Candy had it catered so she'd have minimum preparation, and she arranged with her house cleaning service to do the extra clean-up the morning after. She hired a DJ and a VJ, and rolled up the carpet in the den next to the kitchen; they set up in there spinning IDM under low lights, with the giant screen playing videos in synch with the music. The buffet was laid out on the granite island in the kitchen. We drank martinis, ate hors d'oeuvres, danced, and talked loudly over the music. One of Candy's friends rolled some joints the European way, hashish mixed with tobacco with a cotton filter on the end, and we all got high.

Then the DJ put on a mix of "Smells Like Teen Spirit" by Nirvana, which surprisingly we found really danceable, and everyone got into it. At the same time the VJ played a video of Nirvana live in a stadium with thousands bobbing their heads, bouncing in unison with their fists in the air. Chloe looked at the ecstatic crowd in the video and thought, They're so excited, like it's the best thing in the world. Even Kurt Cobain said they just wanted to sound like the Pixies. They'd dance like that to any band du jour. All they want is to feel free, to feel like they don't have the constraints of their normal lives for at least one night. And then she thought, Maybe it's time for me to move on; go back to school and get my PhD. Maybe this is the farewell party. I can't imagine it getting better than this. It is starting to seem a bit cozy.

Dénouement...

She could already envision the thousand-mile stares on Candy and my faces when she told us she had to go, but she knew we would understand. She might come back to Paris when we least expected it, or when we needed it most, but she would definitely be back sometime. She thought of packing her bags, saying goodbye to everyone, buying a plane ticket and ghosting. It would be sad. Leaving is always sad, but, C'est la vie. A tear ran down her cheek.

Then she looked at everyone curiously — without thinking — simply aware of everybody and everything around her. Candy's friends talked among themselves. Enrico and his friends did the same. I stood in the kitchen with an arm around Gaia. James, Max, and Candy talked excitedly at the entrance of the den. Lily and Trevor were tripping out on the couch, being antisocial. Hector and Olivia stood in the corner talking with Stephan and Chantal. Luis cradled Maribel in an armchair as Delia stood over him looking down. And then for no apparent reason, Chloe broke out laughing

hysterically. We all looked over at her. I thought it
was odd.

Suddenly her whole built up story about the
situation seemed ridiculous to her. Hilarious. She'd
been leaving people, places, and situations her
entire life because of stories she'd compulsively
made up in her head — or stories her parents made
up when she was a kid — habitually moving like a
cold-blooded sea creature, as if she would die to
simply hold still and be silent. She was laughing so
hard she had to set down her drink.

What's so funny? I asked.

She took a few deep breaths, and said, The
fourth option!

What fourth option?

To be aware! Remember? We always have
three options: to accept, reject, or ignore something.
She said. The fourth option is to be aware. That's
the one thing that never changes; the only thing
that's not temporary. Don't like or dislike. There's
no story to add.

She had her fourth epiphany. She continued
laughing, and Max and Candy came over to find out
what she was cracking up about. Chloe tried to
communicate with hand gestures that she was
alright, that it was nothing, but she kept on
laughing. Pretty soon James started laughing, and
before long Max and Candy joined in; and next
Caroline and Gaia. Luis and Delia came over and he
started laughing too, until Maribel started crying,
and then Luis walked back to the armchair with her.
Trevor and Lily walked in already laughing because
everybody else was laughing. Hector and Olivia
stood behind them and chuckled. We stood there in
the kitchen, with arms around each other laughing
until our bellies ached, as music blasted, trying not

to double over on the floor, trying to catch our breath. The DJ and VJ must have thought we were all insane. At times the laughing died down, then one person would laugh and we'd all start laughing again. We laughed for about half an hour till we were in too much pain to keep on and we could barely breathe. Chloe struggled, gasping for air, and sat on one of the tall wooden chairs.

I touched her shoulder and asked, Are you okay?

Yeah…? Candy chimed in.

Chloe finally caught her breath, took a sip of her martini, set it on the counter, looked at me and Candy with glazed eyes and said, I'm home.

* * * * *

As if that were a cue, everyone except Candy filed quietly out of the room. Chloe looked around, confused.

Candy moved closer, laid a warm hand on Chloe's back, and gazed meaningfully into her eyes. They were alone now. Chloe was secretly terrified.

Do you mean that? Candy asked.

What?

Are you ready to completely let go? She pressed.

…What's going on?

I'm dead, Chloe. So are you.

What d'you mean? No I'm not!

What do gender queers say when a partner dies?

The answer came to Chloe immediately, but she hesitated to say it.

She finally managed, "She went to Paris".

…But I'm bi!

Where did we meet? Candy asked.

Then it dawned on Chloe.

The Elysian Fields...

You tried to help the world, but your efforts were unsustainable, so you brought everyone here to work out your exit. Xavier, Lily, Max, Gaia, Stephan... everybody. They're all aspects of your Self. I came to help you.

You're lying! Chloe insisted.

She shook Candy's hand off her shoulder.

As soon as you're ready to go this will all disappear.

Wh-When? When did I-I die?

She remembered overdosing on all those pills on the plane, and imagined herself on a gurney being rushed by paramedics through Charles De Gaulle. She thought of when she put that red apple pill on her tongue after dancing and sweating for hours with Max at "Off World" in the California redwoods. She recalled taking the spatula from the female police officer, who bore a strange resem-blance to Marcie — Was that her sister? — and that she wore protective surgical gloves. Maybe Marcie had contaminated the spatula with some of her lethal bacteria? Or maybe she'd put some of it in the jar of water she threw in Chloe's face?

Does it really matter when you died? Candy asked. You've resolved all your ties to this life. The question now is, Are you ready to leave it behind? Without regrets...

Chloe became crestfallen. Her life flashed before her eyes in a split-second — all the sadness and the joy. After a little reflection, she straightened up with a look of bittersweet resignation. She took a deep breath.

I'm ready.

Go toward the bright light, even if it hurts to look at it. Candy said. Don't be lulled by the dim soft ones.

Everything disappeared and there was only blackness. After a few moments, an intense pulsating white light appeared, first as a tiny vivid point in the distance surrounded by four soft glows of red, yellow, green, and blue; then it moved closer and closer until it was a roiling blazing sun with intense ravenous tongues of white flames consuming everything.

No!

Chloe, startled by the sound of her own voice, gripped the arm of the high wooden chair and the edge of the granite island in the kitchen, hyperventilating.

There's more I need to do!

* * * * *

She jolted awake from her coma in a hospital bed — everything oddly blue — and agitatedly pulled at the tube stuck down her throat, choking her, as the heart monitor beeped urgent staccato. Out of the blue, she thought, Where am I? What day is it? Whose voice am I hearing?